That Voodoo
That You Do

by

Ann Yost

That Voodoo That You Do

Cover Art by *Kim Mendoza*

The Wild Rose Press, Inc.
PO Box 708
Adams Basin, NY 14410-0708
Visit us at www.thewildrosepress.com

Publishing History
First Crimson Rose Edition, 2009
Second Crimson Rose Edition, 2016
Print ISBN 978-1-5092-1029-9
Digital ISBN 978-1-5092-1030-5

Published in the United States of America

What the hell was she doing here?

Her hysteria was shredding what was left of the undertaker's nerves. There was no telling who he'd shoot. Damn Jessie anyway. How was he supposed to protect her? "Ignore that," Luke muttered.

"If only that were possible," Epps barked. He jerked open the door, and someone catapulted into the room.

It was the Morton Salt Girl.

She ignored Epps as she marched up to Luke and wagged a finger in his face.

"Lucas Tanner," she shouted, "How dare you stand me up?"

Epps's face twisted in fury. "Miss Maynard, this is a mortuary. We try to maintain a sense of decorum here."

She turned toward the mortician as if she'd just noticed him. Would he attack her? More likely she'd attack him. She was a warrior princess. Luke balanced his weight on the balls of his feet, prepared to intervene, but the elf surprised him. She flashed Epps a smile so bright it reflected off the stainless steel surfaces.

"I beg your pardon, Mr. Epps," she said, in a conciliatory voice. "I am so sorry for the interruption. But I'm sure you'll agree that I have a right to be angry. This guy"—she jerked her thumb at Luke without taking her eyes off the mortician—"was supposed to pick me up forty minutes ago. We've got an appointment to get our blood tests."

Epps frowned, apparently as confused as Luke. "Blood tests?"

"For the license," Jessie continued. "We agreed to get married the day after Christmas."

Dedication

To Pete

Chapter One

The rehearsal dinner at the Happy Taco was almost over when the father of the bride asked about his prospective son-in-law.

"Where the hell is Kit?" Howard Maynard growled. "It's time to make the toast, and he's been gone for over half an hour."

Jessie Maynard glanced at the empty chair next to her. She ran her tongue over her lips savoring the salt from the Taco's famous "bottomless margarita." The banquet hall swam as she staggered to her feet.

"I'm on it," she told her dad. Still clutching her red-and-white checked napkin, she tottered out of the private room into a dimly lit corridor, passed doors labeled "Hombres," and "Senoritas," and the kitchen that smelled of refried beans. She finally found her fiancé in a deserted phone booth.

Unfortunately, he wasn't making a call.

He sprawled on the wooden bench, his eyes closed, his handsome features twisted in ecstasy. His fingers, Jessie noted, were fisted in long, silky strands of blonde hair. Jessie watched his head bounce against the phone hard enough to knock the receiver off its cradle. Kit's whimper of relief triggered a burst of fury in Jessie. She'd believed in him, believed in them. They were colleagues and friends, and she'd thought they could build a decent marriage. A faithful marriage.

The jerk had cheated before the vows.

A gagging sound cut through the red haze of betrayal. It drew Jessie's gaze and revealed an additional irony. Not only was Kit cheating on his wedding eve, he was doing it with his ex-wife.

Jessie's eyes met those of her bridesmaid. There really was nothing to say. Following what was left of her instincts, she handed Mary Alice her slightly used napkin.

"Keep it," she said. She nodded at the man who had betrayed both of them.

"You can keep him, too."

****

The following evening, when she and her new husband should have been winging their way to Bora Bora for a brief, pre-Christmas honeymoon, she was tooling down Interstate 81, heading for Small Town, U.S.A. the home of her late great-aunt Blanche, a woman who'd often provided emotional sanctuary for her via phone and letter. But this time Jessie wouldn't get the benefit of Blanche Maynard's no-nonsense philosophy. Great-Aunt Blanche had died several months earlier, and Jessie was going to visit an empty house. Translated, she was just plain running away.

Jessie felt a lightning stab of pain shrouded in disappoint and disbelief. Kit claimed it had been a last, albeit ill-advised, fling. Maybe. They weren't soulmates. Still, she'd thought they'd have their own version of happily ever after. After a night of the long knives listening to Kit's apologies and her mother's rationalizations, after seeing the defeat on her father's face, she needed a place to regroup. Maybe, even without Blanche's bracing presence, the peace and quiet of Podunk would help her forget the humiliation, to heal and help her move on.

She realized, with a shock, it would be easier to let go of her faithless fiancé than her self-assigned role as family troubleshooter. She'd failed to bring her shattered relatives back together as a family.

She turned off the interstate at the exit for Mystic Hollow and Gap. She figured the latter didn't mean the outlet. Half a mile down the two-lane road, she passed a ramshackle string of cabins with a neon rooster and the name "Chick Inn." Kit would get a kick out of that. The thought turned to another stab of pain.

Shit. Chicken shit.

A mile later she passed a weather-beaten city limits sign. *Mystic Hollow, Population: 3,061.*

Make that three thousand sixty. Emotion knifed through her again. This time it was grief. She'd meant to visit Great-Aunt Blanche, but there was always some reason to put it off. Lately, it had been plans for the over-the-top wedding. And maybe because Blanche Maynard, in her wisdom, hadn't approved of Jessie's plan to marry her dad's business partner. Jessie should have listened.

Now Blanche's empty house would provide a lonely cave while Jessie licked her wounds and tried to figure out what in the hell to do with the rest of her life.

She piloted her cherry red Jeep around a corner, and suddenly, she was in Mystic Hollow. The first thing she saw was the lighted Christmas tree on the town green. She squeezed her eyes and refused to think about spending the holiday alone. Instead she focused on the storybook town with its line of storefronts: Ferguson's Market; Bexler's Drugs; The Pink Poodle Hair and Nail

Salon; Bell, Book and Candle. She saw crystals hanging in the window along with pentacle-shaped sun catchers. Ah. New Age had come to the sticks.

A homemade banner stretched along the front of a white gazebo on the green opposite the Christmas tree.

Welcome to the First Annual Mystic Hollow Holiday Starlight Festival Celebration featuring a visit from Santa and other entertainment.

Other entertainment? Probably cow chip bingo.

On the far side of the green, a cobblestone church sprawled like a dragon protecting its adjacent cemetery. The white marble headstones bowed in all directions like Chiclets spilled out of a box. It was odd to see the graves here, in the center of town. In the city, the dead were relegated to smooth lawns miles away from humanity.

She pulled up to the town's lone stoplight just as a tinny version of Purcell's Trumpet Voluntary made her jump. Damn. She needed to substitute a new ringtone. Something like "Your Cheatin' Heart," or that timeless classic, "I Still Miss You Baby, But My Aim Is Getting Better." Jessie punched a button and heard her sister's voice.

"Are you there yet?"

"Yeah."

"What's it like?"

"Brigadoon."

Gillian laughed. "Still got the gazebo on the town green?" The Maynards had spent Christmases with Blanche long ago.

The light changed, and Jessie stepped on the gas.

"That was back in the days when we were all happy," Gillian said. "Before Dad got so rich."

4

Jessie shut her eyes. Happiness had eluded Howard and Monica Maynard for a long time. Jessie had hoped to heal her folks with her own marriage.

An outraged bleat snapped her eyelids up like spring-loaded shades, and she stabbed the brake. A tall, angular figure with a cone-shaped face and a long, narrow nose glared at her through the windshield. The crone shook a bony finger at Jessie as she crossed the street and strode onto the green. A shiver ran down Jessie's spine.

"Hell. I almost hit the Wicked Witch of the West."

"More like Oz than Brigadoon?"

Jessie shook her head, wishing things had been different. "Listen, Gil, I don't think I've apologized to you. I know you had to take care of the, uh, loose ends this morning."

"Don't worry about it." Jessie could almost see her beautiful, blonde sister lifting her narrow shoulders in a shrug. "Nobody was mad. People love scandal even more than orange blossoms. You can probably even keep the gifts."

The gifts. Jessie groaned. Six hundred people had been invited. She'd be returning gravy boats and blenders for a year.

"And anyway, now you don't have to appear in that designer get-up that made you look like mushroom cloud."

"Yeah. Silver lining."

"Kit's still pretty freaked."

"It was his choice to trade ownership of Maynard Properties for a blowjob." Jessie heard Gillian's sigh.

"Life isn't simple."

"I can't take him back. There's just no way."

"I know, but Dad is crushed. He believes you love Kit. It isn't true, is it? This is another one of your heroic plans to 'save the family.'"

"I like Kit," Jessie said, defensively. "Make that past tense. I thought we'd do pretty well together."

"Jessie? Why didn't you tell Mom and Dad the truth about why you called off the wedding?"

Jessie shuddered as she relived the vision of her handsome ex-fiancé in the tete-a-crotch.

"It wouldn't make any difference. It wouldn't change anything."

Gillian sighed. "I can't believe you're trying to protect Kit. What a snake in the grass."

It felt good to feel her sister's sympathy, but it was time to be honest. "He must have known it, too," she said, suddenly.

"Known what?"

"That the marriage was a mistake. That we didn't love each other and we never would. On some level he was just trying to get us both out of a doomed commitment."

"He could've just asked for the ring back."

Jessie turned off Main Street onto Cobblestone Lane where five houses faced the green. They were all substantial, elderly homes that had long learned to be comfortable at their place in society, like a gaggle of matronly chaperones at a cotillion.

"Christmas is gonna suck without you."

Bleakness surrounded Jessie's heart. Last year while they were passing around the creamed onions, the squash, and the sliced turkey, Howard Maynard suffered the heart attack that had triggered their parents' divorce.

This year was supposed to be better.

"Mom hasn't given up, you know. She's got a short list of bachelors for you to consider. I think Donald Culbertson is at the top because, and I quote, 'he's got an MBA, he's between wives, and he's used up his trust fund.'"

"It might work. Donald accepted a bribe to take me to the senior prom."

"You'd be better off with Kit. And to tell you the truth, I think Mom's still barking up that tree.

They've been together all day."

Jessie only half heard her sister as she pulled up to the stone curb in front of number 42 Cobblestone Lane. She sucked in her breath. Blanche had written about her house, but the description hadn't done it justice. It was late Queen Anne, pink and white with gables and roofs at all elevations, a wide porch whose columns were carved into ornate gingerbread, and a triptych Palladium window. At the top, right in front like the horn of a rhinoceros was a black turret. A witch's hat. A generous bay window was dark. Suddenly Jessie caught an image of a brightly lit Christmas tree.

"Oh my god," Jessie breathed.

"What now? Did you hit a munchkin?"

Jessie placed her hand on her chest. Her heart trip-hammered. "The house. It's a surprise."

Gillian made a sound. "Listen, Jess, I'm gonna get some time off. I can't bear to think of you all by yourself in that spooky house."

Jessie's response was immediate and heartfelt. "Don't, Gil. I need some time. I've got some things to figure out."

She climbed out of the Jeep, walked up a short path

under a natural wood arbor covered with winter-dead grapevines and up a flight of three wide, shallow steps.

She inhaled the mingled scents of fresh, cold air, old house, and something she couldn't identify. Something that seemed to affect her breathing.

"You sure you want to stay alone?"

A movement in the gathering twilight made Jessie's heart jump. She gasped as a tall, masculine figure separated itself from the shadows. He moved with consummate ease and a shiver raced up and down her spine as the porch light went on and hit his face revealing sharply defined angles and darkened circles instead of eyes. Mephistopheles. He stepped closer, and Jessie had to tilt her head back to see him. Her eyes narrowed.

She did not care for tall men. At the moment she didn't care for any men. And here she was with a squatter. "Who are you?" She'd hoped to sound intimidating, and she was disgusted at the slight tremor in her voice.

The man stepped closer, and Jessie could make out long, dark lashes, incongruous in that harsh, unsmiling masculine face.

"Aren't you supposed to be smoking a hookah when you ask that?"

She planted her free hand at her waist. Great. A squatter with a sense of humor.

"Jessie? Who're you talking to?" Gillian sounded worried.

Her sister's voice brought her back to earth. This guy must be the caretaker her dad had hired.

"Jessie? Who's there?"

"The hired help," she told her sister. The man's

eyes flashed, and she realized they were the color of kryptonite. "Listen, Gil," she said, swallowing with difficulty, "I'll call you back." She pressed "off."

The guy loomed. Anxiety formed a lump in her stomach. She needed him to leave.

"I won't be needing your services anymore," she said with what she hoped was confidence. "I'm moving in."

A strange look passed over his face. His nose was too hawk-like to be handsome, and his jaw looked like it had broken a fist or two in the past. She tried not to look intimidated even when he failed to reply.

"I imagine you have somewhere to go tonight, right?"

"I'm not moving out."

She felt a faint sweat break out on her forehead and a sudden fierce need to get this guy off her porch. She glared at him. "I'm Jessie Maynard," she informed him, "and this house belongs to my family."

He nodded. "Half of it. The other half belongs to me. I'm Luke Tanner, Blanche's foster son."

The black sheep foster son. Jessie gaped at him.

"The bad seed."

He nodded. For all that he was tall and lean, she could see the strong muscles in his neck. "That's me."

Shame washed over her. She couldn't believe she'd been so rude.

"Not that Aunt Blanche ever called you that." He shrugged as if it didn't matter.

"How come my dad doesn't know about you owning half the house?"

"Maybe because he didn't bother to come to the funeral."

Guilt that had been gathering for weeks overflowed and swept through Jessie's insides. The Maynards had been totally focused on the big wedding. The guilt made her tone sharp. "I suppose you were here."

"Not until after."

She heard the pain in the brief answer even before his eyes darkened. He felt guilty, too. They had something in common. That should have made him seem more human.

Too bad it didn't.

Jessie glanced at the house and then back at Blanche's foster son. He looked about as movable as Mount Everest. Maybe she should get back in the Jeep and head back to the Chick Inn. Just for the night. She knew she couldn't do that. Retreat would send the wrong message. If she wanted to lick her wounds at Great-Aunt Blanche's house, she'd have to suck it up and lay her claim.

"It's a big house. I'll stay out of your way if you stay out of mine," he said. He didn't wait for a response. "I'll get your bags." He strode down the path, opened the hatchback, and extracted her yellow suitcase.

"What've you got in here? Bricks?"

She let out a helpless, hopeless giggle as she remembered. "Lingerie and cruise wear. I'm supposed to be on my honeymoon."

****

Luke had felt restless all day. He hated being back in Mystic Hollow where everything from the gazebo in the town square to Blanche's big Victorian house reminded him of how he'd let everyone down. Blanche. Crystal. Even himself.

He wanted to take a run to let off some steam, but he didn't. The sixth sense he couldn't seem to shake, told him she'd be here soon.

He threw on his battered black leather jacket and paced the length of the wrap-around porch that hugged the house. As usual, when he was in Mystic, he couldn't breathe. He thought longingly of his sparsely furnished apartment in D.C., of the solitude and peace. He didn't know when he'd get back. Days, maybe. More likely a week.

He cursed under his breath. He had no choice. He owed Blanche, and this was his last sorry chance to repay her.

Too bad she'd asked him to babysit.

Luke's eyes narrowed as the red Jeep tooted around the corner. He stifled a groan as he watched the driver park and climb out. Christ, she was short. Just a kid. Her mass of curls barely reached the roof of the car. Like every female he saw these days, she had a cell phone glued to her ear, and despite the chilly weather, she was wearing some kind of loose fitting pajama-like outfit.

What did she think this was? A health spa?

She marched up the short walk, a woman on a mission. He listened to her voice as she spoke into the phone. It was low, a little husky, like pebbles brushing against each other in a shallow steam. Strangely compelling, at least until she spotted him. Then it was more like black ice.

While she glared at him, he found himself staring into a pair of wide, whiskey-colored eyes. She wasn't beautiful like Crystal. Her face was softly rounded without the razor-sharp cheekbones of his ex. Her straight nose was sprinkled with freckles and "short" had been a euphemism. He had her by at least a foot.

Blanche had sent him an elf.

A clueless one.

Luke sucked in a breath.

Blanche had been right about the babysitter. He just wished it didn't have to be him. He let his gaze drop, and it hovered around her sandal-clad feet. He knew she'd come from Chicago. What was wrong with her brain?

"Sinful strawberry," she said, helpfully.

"What're you talking about?"

"You were looking at my toenail polish. I thought you'd like to know the name."

He lifted an eyebrow. "Think it would look good on me?"

She laughed. It was a joyful burst of sound so spontaneous it seemed to surprise even her. It made something move in his chest. He didn't want any complications. He wished, not for the first time, that Blanche had cut him out of her will. Half of this house was not worth the irritation of watching out for the elf from Middle Earth. At least it wasn't forever. At least he hoped. He frowned. Not that it mattered. He owed Blanche Maynard a lot. Everything. It was a debt he'd pay if it killed him.

"I have to tell you," she said, in a confidential tone. "I came down here hoping to be alone."

His eyes narrowed on her. "Well, that's one thing we have in common."

He heard the oohing and aahing behind him as she got a glimpse of Blanche's parlor with its Victorian furniture, lace doilies, and its wide fireplace, but he didn't even slow down. A minute later the two of them and her egg-yolk-colored suitcase reached the tower room.

He dropped the case on the bed and turned to go.

"What's this?" She was looking at the framed certificate.

Shit. He'd forgotten the damn thing.

"Wow." She squinted at him. "A Silver Star. So you're not just a bad seed, you're a war hero, too."

He felt an almost irresistible urge to jump in his truck and just drive. Instead he struck out.

"And you're a runaway bride."

Her yelp surprised him. It sounded more scared than angry.

He glanced down to see Pye twining around her slim ankles.

"Good grief," she gasped. "That cat's as big as Detroit. How'd he get so fat?"

Luke scooped the feline into his arms. "Sex."

"What?"

"Pye's pregnant."

"Pie?"

"Pyewacket."

"Pyewacket. Like in Bell, Book and Candle. Is she yours?"

"No," he said, automatically.

She lifted onto her toes which brought her up to about five-foot-one, and she peered into his eyes. Then she looked at the cat's and back to his. "Your eyes match."

He refused to smile at her. "We're not related."

He finally escaped down the narrow back staircase that emptied into the kitchen. He dumped a can of tuna into the cat bowl and laced it with prenatal vitamins while Pye watched.

She seems nice.

"I'll bet you a catnip mouse she's the kind who minds everybody's business but her own."

Pyewacket didn't respond. She was too busy eating supper.

"I've got to go out," he said. "You all right?"

What he really wanted to know was whether there would be any kittens arriving tonight.

The cat acknowledged the unspoken question with a succinct answer.

All quiet.

Luke believed her.

That was the difference between felines and women.

A guy could trust a cat.

Chapter Two

Giant cabbage roses bloomed on all eight sides of the tower room. The celery colored shade on the bedside lamp made the room seem as restful as a summer day.

The four-poster bed, covered by a well-worn, hand-stitched double wedding ring quilt, stood some four feet off the ground. Jessie made a face. She'd have to hurl herself like a high jumper just to reach it. The bed faced a fireplace smaller than the one in the parlor Luke had hurried her past, but this one had a pink marble surround. Above it was a handmade broom mounted like a trophy head.

Jessie glanced at the books scattered on the padded bench beneath the arched window. The Bible didn't surprise her. And neither did the bloody picture on the front of a suspense novel. The third volume, though, was unexpected. She picked it up and read the title aloud. "A Journey Through Wiccan Rituals: From Imbolc to Yule."

Jessie remembered, again, the sign on the gift shop. It looked like Great-Aunt Blanche had been interested in witchcraft.

It must have been a recent development. It was hard to imagine Aunt Blanche, a staunch Christian, involved in Wicca. But maybe there was another explanation. Jessie felt a wave of sadness. She missed the old lady.

All the Maynards had known Blanche had "adopted" a foster son who'd been in trouble with the law, but that had been years ago. Why hadn't Blanche told her about Luke Tanner? Was there a reason to keep him a secret? Had he killed somebody?

Jessie peeked into a walk-in closet and inhaled the strong scent of cedar. Cotton housedresses hung neatly on hangers along with a few sweaters and a white parka and a bright magenta-colored robe that looked almost shockingly out of place. There were three pairs of black lace-up shoes lined up on the floor. Overhead were hatboxes. Jessie took them down and peeked. One held a small black hat with a half-veil and a white one in the same style. Nothing except the robe looked as though it had been bought in the past twenty years. Maybe thirty.

Waste not, want not. That was her Aunt Blanche, to a tee. But she hadn't been stingy with her heart. She'd always had time to listen to Jessie's ideas and her woes. More time than any of the other Maynards.

The bathroom boasted a claw-footed tub, a pedestal washstand, and a commode set as high as a throne. The walls were sage with cocoa brown colored towels. Colors of the earth. An apothecary jar full of bubble bath looked too good to pass up. Moments later Jessie was soaking in the old-fashioned tub as the scented water washed away the grime, fatigue, and disappointment of the past twenty-four hours. She made a decision to banish all thoughts of the aborted wedding. She was here for R & R, and she wouldn't let anything or anybody interfere with that. Not even the green-eyed interloper downstairs. She thought about him trying to fold his tall form into the tub, and she giggled. She hoped he had a shower stall.

Moments later, cleaner and fresher, she stared at her sartorial choices. A white satin negligee? A polka-dot two-piece bathing suit? She settled on coral colored linen slacks and a turquoise blouse with rhinestone buttons. She ran a brush through oblivious chin-length curls and slipped on her rhinestone sandals. Not exactly country gear. She'd go shopping tomorrow.

When she was dressed, she stepped out into the corridor. Her heart kicked up. She wondered whether she'd run into Luke and which was his bedroom before she remembered she wasn't supposed to be thinking about him at all. They were sharing a house, not a life.

A doorbell produced a three-note chime, and she found herself tripping down the wide center hall staircase in her haste to get to the front door. She didn't know anyone in Mystic Hollow. Maybe Luke had gone out and forgotten his key. Her heart raced as she pulled open the heavy front door. But it wasn't a green-eyed sorcerer.

It was a trio of elderly ladies who reminded Jessie of the eccentric sisters in the old film *Arsenic and Old Lace.*

"Hello, Jessie, dear." The one in the center was both the tallest and the widest. Black hair with a skunk-like stripe down the middle splayed out around her shoulders. Her purple cloak could have hidden half a dozen children, and her smile was merry. "Welcome to Mystic Hollow. I'm Mabel Ruth Doyle."

"And I'm Millicent Underhill," said the tall, thin lady with sharp features and small spectacles to her left. Stiff white lace peeked over the top of her stark black coat. Despite her slender neck, the collar was so tight and high it made her head look separate from the rest of her, like a balloon floating above her body.

"This is Maude," she said. She indicated the third member of the party, who was just Jessie's height and a dead ringer for Mrs. Claus.

"Maude Umphrey," the little lady said. Her blue eyes twinkled. "We're Blanche's friends, and we're so glad you've come, Jessie, dear."

"I'm pleased to meet you," Jessie murmured. "What is that heavenly smell?"

Maude chuckled. "Brownies. My niece, Molly, owns the bakery. She's famous for her brownies."

Jessie realized, belatedly, they were all carrying food. "You brought me supper?"

The old ladies' thoughtfulness nearly brought tears to her eyes. Or maybe it was the smell. She couldn't wait to see what was in the big pot.

"Please, come inside."

The words were not so much ignored as anticipated. Mabel Ruth led, and Jessie brought up the rear as they marched single file through the glass doors to the parlor, into the adjoining dining room, and on through the swinging doors of a tiny butler's pantry, into a big, sunflower yellow kitchen where they began to set a round wicker table with plates and bowls, silverware, and glasses. They chatted easily as if they'd known each other for years.

The unusual stew was so tasty, and Jessie was so much hungrier than she'd thought that she didn't ask the pertinent question until most of the food was gone.

"What a wonderful meal," she said, "but how did you know I would be here?"

"Blanche told us you were coming," Maude said.

"But she's dead."

Millicent cast her friend a quelling look. "We normally bring food for Lucas."

Luke! Jessie's heart jumped. "We didn't save him any."

"Not to worry," Mabel Ruth said, airily. "The pantry's full." If the pantry was full why had they brought more food?

"How are you two getting along? Any sparks yet?"

"Maudie!" It was Millicent again. "That's none of our business."

"Fine," Jessie said, clearing her throat. "I mean, we've barely met, but it is a big house. I don't expect to see much of him."

"Jessie, dear," Mabel Ruth said, "we're going to the festival on the green tonight, and we'd love to have you join us."

"Great," she replied, only afterward remembering she'd come to Mystic Hollow for solitude and reflection.

Later, when Jessie was helping Maude into her cuddly faux fur coat, she remembered an unresolved subject.

"Earlier you said Aunt Blanche told you I was coming here? But she couldn't have known I would call off my wedding."

Maude pulled a bright red scarf around her neck. "Blanche was always anxious for you to come," she said. "She wanted you here. She wanted you both here. In fact," she said, "she summoned you."

"Maudie!" Millicent shook her head. The iron gray hair skinned back from her face didn't move.

Mabel Ruth sighed.

"We'll have to tell her sometime, girls. Now's as good a time as any." Mabel Ruth's kind, dark brown eyes turned to Jessie. "Blanche has an assignment for you."

"An assignment?" That didn't make sense. "But she's dead."

"Exactly," Millicent said. "And we want to know why."

Jessie stared at each of the elderly ladies in turn. Her eyes widened.

"Do you mean you think Aunt Blanche was murdered?"

"Not think," Millicent said, firmly. "Know.

What's more, we know who did it, too."

"We just don't know why," Maude added.

Jessie looked from one to the other of the wrinkled faces. "But if you suspect murder shouldn't you go to the police?"

Mabel Ruth shook her head, her eyes solemn. "The death certificate says natural causes, and Chief Smith said there's not a thing we can do about it. But that's ridiculous. It couldn't have been natural. Blanche was only eighty-six. And sharp as a tack."

Jessie decided to opt for diplomacy and not argue about age. "Whom do you suspect?"

"It was the pastor at St. Michaels," Millicent said, grimly. "The Reverend Dennis Prendergast. Blanche learned his dark secret, and he did her in."

This really was Oz. Jessie tried to absorb the accusation.

"But why would a minister kill her? She was a pillar of the church!"

"Was being the key word," Mabel Ruth said.

"Dennis Prendergast made it impossible for us to continue to attend. We were forced to leave. All of us."

"All of you?"

"The Tuesday Afternoon Canasta Group."

"Including my aunt Blanche."

"Certainly," Millicent said.

Jessie just stared. She expected to see frogs rain down out of the sky.

"We were forced to go in a different direction," Mabel Ruth continued.

Jessie barely heard her. "What was the pastor doing that you didn't approve of?"

"He closed the public library we had started in the Sunday school building," Millicent said, indignantly. "And the preschool, too."

"He disbanded all the committees and eliminated Wednesday potlucks," Maude put in.

"He's locked up the church," Mabel Ruth explained. "Except for Sunday mornings, holidays, and funerals."

"What about weddings?"

"We don't have many of those in Mystic Hollow," Maude said. "More people are getting buried than married."

"His story is that there's a mold problem in the building, and that he is taking bids to have it removed," Millicent said.

"And then there's Mister Epps," Maude said.

"Who's Mister Epps?" Jessie was starting to feel like part of a comedy act.

"The undertaker." Millicent's voice was grim. "Prendergast let him take over the manse to use as a funeral parlor while the reverend and his wife moved into a tiny duplex with Miss Letty."

"Poor Eleanor," Maude crooned before Jessie could ask why having a funeral parlor next to a church was a problem. "I don't believe I've ever seen a woman as squashed as Eleanor Prendergast. She simply hasn't got any life in her."

Jessie's head was spinning.

"Blanche found out something, and she confronted Prendergast?"

"She was fearless," Maude said.

Millicent nodded, sadly. "Blanche was a hero."

Jessie was still at sea. She decided to try another tack. "You said you left the church."

Mabel Ruth nodded. "That's right. We were powerless as insiders, so we took up a new religion."

"We wanted to have some special powers at our disposal," Millicent said.

"Special powers?" Jessie suddenly remembered the homemade broom on the bedroom wall and the book on the window seat.

"Are you telling me you've turned to witchcraft?"

"Wicca," Mabel Ruth said.

"We still call ourselves a canasta club," Maude put in, "but now we use the time to work on our spells."

Jessie looked at each of the ladies. She could see them sitting around a card table. She could see them lined up in a pew at church. She could not see them dancing around a campfire.

"Do you have any idea about the dark secret?"

"Drug smuggling," Maude said. "Maybe white slavery."

"Or terrorism," Millicent put in, darkly.

"We don't know, dear," Mabel Ruth said. "That's

why you're here."

This was getting way too spooky. "That's very flattering and everything, but I'm not qualified to investigate a murder," Jessie pointed out. "I just came to Mystic Hollow for some R&R."

Maude patted her hand. "Don't worry, dear.

That boy wasn't the right one for you."

Jessie nodded. Maude had that right.

"And don't worry about the investigation," Millicent said. "That isn't your job."

Jessie stared at each of them. "I thought you said Aunt Blanche summoned me."

"She did," Mabel Ruth said. "She needed a reason to bring Lucas home."

Jessie still didn't understand. "What does that have to do with me?"

"Everything," Millicent explained. "Lucas thinks he's here to take care of you. Your job is to convince him to investigate the murder."

Anger, frustration, and another old, familiar feeling surged through Jessie. She'd spent her life "helping" everybody else. She'd spent her life marginalized. She made no effort to keep the fury out of her voice.

"I couldn't convince Luke Tanner to walk with me to the mailbox," she said. "Not that I'd want to."

The three elderly ladies exchanged a knowing look.

"Oh, I think you'd be surprised," Mabel Ruth murmured. "Blanche had great faith in you."

Jessie stood very still. This was all too familiar. Déjà voodoo.

She could support Luke while he did all the interesting stuff, just as she'd supported her father and had intended to support Kit, or she could defy

23

expectations and test herself. The problem was she knew next to nothing about investigating an alleged murder. If only she'd spent more evenings watching *Law and Order*.

Still, it might be kind of fun.

"No disrespect to you or Aunt Blanche," Jessie said, "but I believe we can dispense with the middle man. I will sort this out myself." The three old ladies just looked at each other.

"That's fine, dear," Mabel Ruth said.

****

Reverend Dennis Prendergast surveyed himself in the large mirror above the dresser in the bedroom he shared with his wife. His Pepsodent smile reflected back at him as he smoothed the thinning, gel-saturated dark blond hair off his ruddy face. He had a variety of smiles from which to choose. They were all effective, but he liked the toothpaste smile best.

He turned sideways and sucked in his gut. The mirror didn't lie. He might be pushing fifty, but since his recent weight loss, he was as fit and handsome as he'd been at twenty-five.

He'd had to work at it. The women here in the Piedmont cooked exclusively with butter and lard. Hell, Ferguson's didn't even stock olive, vegetable, or peanut oil because of some long ago allergy-related death. During his first months in Mystic, he'd put on some pounds, but recently he'd dropped weight. For one thing, he'd canceled those infernal potlucks. For another, he'd discovered something better than fried chicken, tuna noodle casseroles, and chocolate cake.

Something intoxicating, stimulating, thrilling.

He'd discovered extramarital sex.

His palms itched to cup Lois Epps's titanic breasts. His eyes fluttered shut as the memory of Lois's skillful mouth shot a jolt of pure lust through his loins. He pressed his hand against the front of his fine wool slacks.

The shock of cold steel against the back of his neck caused his hand to jerk. He winced at the sudden pain and swallowed a curse.

"I didn't mean to startle you."

Eleanor's pleasant voice was too close. How much had she seen? He mumbled something incoherent.

"I noticed a stray hair and thought I'd even it up."

Dennis felt the sharp blade of the scissors against the back of his neck. He held his breath, but he couldn't control the trembling that started when she inched the metal against his clammy skin. A crisp "snip" crackled in the air like a gunshot, and his trousers loosened.

"There," she murmured. "Perfect."

That was Eleanor. Precise. Measured. Perfect. He'd never seen her lose her temper. Marrying her was the smartest move he'd ever made. He'd gotten a cook, caretaker, companion, and financial security in exchange for a wedding vow. Not that he took all the credit. God was on his side.

Always had been.

"Thank you, dear." He smiled at his wife.

"You sound a trifle coldish." Eleanor was such a mother hen. "Perhaps you should stay in tonight."

Stay in? When all of Mystic Hollow would be at the holiday festival? When there was a good chance he'd get another sublime encounter with Lois's mouth? And out in public, too. Reverend Prendergast liked to take risks. He found the risk of discovery heightened the sexual excitement.

He gazed at his wife. She wore her pale red hair in a no-nonsense cap. Her skin, the color of skim milk and her pale eyebrows combined to make her features almost disappear in her face. But she was a tireless worker who had secured his place in the community with her willingness to help on every project.

He patted her hand. "People will expect to see me."

He helped her on with the thin brown coat she'd worn for the past five years, then he shrugged into his stylish Burberry.

"I wish you'd replace that with something new, Ellie."

"This one still has some wear in it."

"It doesn't have any lining," he complained.

"How do you stay warm?"

"I never get cold. You know that."

He did know it. He found it a little reptilian. He shook off the image and took her arm. She felt familiar, comfortable. They'd been through a lot together.

They left their modest half of the duplex and walked fifteen yards to the back end of the church's parking lot. From there they crossed Church Street and stepped onto the Green. Dennis spotted Lois immediately. His blood pressure rose, and he issued a playful invitation he knew his wife couldn't accept.

"Come watch the parade with me, Ellie."

"I have to be at the refreshment table with Letty," she reminded him.

He rolled his eyes. Miss Letitica Appleby was a thorn in his paw. His cross to bear. The rotten apple in the barrel. It wasn't enough that the self-righteous old biddy followed him around town, hounding him with tittle tattle about everybody's trespasses. She lived in the other half of his house. She was his next-door neighbor. He was tuned to the all-Letty network all the time.

"How can you stand that woman? She's so danged holier-than-thou."

"Really, Denny!"

"C'mon, Ellie. She's always tattling on someone. She should remember John the Baptist. Someday someone will serve her head on a platter."

"Hush."

The warning was unnecessary. His attention had riveted on the bulbous bosom bouncing toward him. The fisherman's sweater Lois wore couldn't hide their perfectly apple-like shape of her breasts or the way each breath lifted them practically to her chin.

"It's amazing she can even breathe," Eleanor murmured.

The unaccustomed humor startled Dennis, but it didn't cause him to take his eyes off the magnificent glands that loomed before him. He glanced at her husband, tall, rail-thin, with cadaverous eyes and thick, dark-rimmed glasses.

Dennis plastered on a smile. "Evening, Lois, Mort. Looks like we're about to get a storm."

"*Hmph.*" The mortician was a man of few words. He was dressed, as always in a black suit, white shirt, and dark tie, as though he might be called upon at any moment to direct a funeral.

Dennis glanced at Lois's face. Her eyes were too close together for beauty, and her chin receded. She wore too much makeup and dyed her hair the color of a new tire. But when she ran her tongue slowly over her lips, as she was doing now, sweat appeared between his shoulder blades.

Jesus. He had to get her alone.

"Oh, Reverend."

Miss Letty's shrill voice sliced through his building fantasy and twanged his last nerve. He gritted his teeth. Her long, thin face ended in a sharp point that turned up as if it were trying to reach her long, bony nose. She wore a black coat of indeterminate age, and she wore her yellowed gray hair pulled back in a barrette.

"Blanche Maynard would turn in her grave," Miss Letty spat out. "Her great-niece arrived today and already she is living in sin with that scoundrel Lucas Tanner. The bad seed."

"Now, Letty," Eleanor started to say.

"He was always a wrong'un. It was a miracle he never murdered Blanche in her bed. She was just lucky."

"I don't know how lucky she was," Eleanor murmured. "After all, she's dead."

"That boy ruined the Wetherington girl," Letty continued. "Now he's ruined the great-niece."

"I don't imagine she's ruined just yet," Eleanor said. "After all she's only been here a few hours."

"It will happen, mark my words. This town is turning into Sodom and Gomorrah! First Francine Ferris and the Reeves boy. Now this." She stuck out her skinny neck so her hooked nose was only inches from Dennis's face. "I want to know what you intend to do about it!"

"We could build an ark," Eleanor murmured.

Letty whirled to speak to her but was distracted by the sight of the mortician. She grabbed his arm.

"Oh, Mr. Epps. I'm sorry to have to tell you this, but you have a skulker. There's been a man in a cape lurking around your establishment for the past two nights."

"Thank you," he said, his voice stiff. "But you needn't trouble yourself. We have an excellent security system installed."

"What's there to steal?" Lois asked. "There's nothing there but stiffs."

Dennis winced at the crude remark. Then his eyes dropped to her breasts, and his mind clouded. Under the sweater her flesh quivered like Jello. His lower body throbbed, and he prayed for everyone else to disappear.

As always, God answered.

Even as Letty's eyes narrowed and her mouth pursed, Eleanor took the old bat's arm. "Come along, Letty. The parade is about to start. Soon we'll have customers for the brownies and hot chocolate."

Dennis Prendergast sent his wife an appreciative smile.

"I have paperwork to do at the office," the mortician said. "Reverend, could you keep Lois company?"

It was further proof, if any was needed, that God wanted Dennis Prendergast to be happy.

Dennis flashed his patented smile. "Sure thing, Mort. Nothing I'd like more."

Chapter Three

Jessie smiled along with the children thronging the streets that bordered the Green when she saw Santa arrive on the town's volunteer fire truck. It was hard to believe there'd been a murder here in Norman Rockwell country.

She wasn't sure she believed it yet.

But she'd pledged herself to find out.

"Does Mystic Hollow have festivals very often," she asked her companions.

"Too often in my opinion," Mabel Ruth said. "There aren't enough jobs in town to keep young people here. Mayor Foote believes our best hope is tourism. He's always on the lookout for something to lure people. Like the Maple Syrup Roundup."

"I'd think people would flock to that."

Millicent shook her head. For an instant it looked like it might snap off her thin neck. "They might. If this was Vermont. Maple trees don't produce sap this far south."

"Then there was the animal fair," Maude said. "Where there were several, uh, incidents."

"Tommy Anderson's rat snake ate Daniel Erskine's white mouse," Millicent said.

"And we're pretty sure that's when Pyewacket got in the family way," Maude confided.

"Tonight's just for fun," Mabel Ruth said. "Oh, and

uniforms. We're raising money for the Marching Mystics, the high school band." Very Professor Harold Hill.

Maude's fingers dug into her arm causing her to gasp. "Look," Maude hissed. "Over there. That's the reverend."

The alleged murderer looked more like a televangelist than a killer. An overly made up brunette with a bust like a shelf clung to his arm.

"That isn't his wife," Maude whispered. "That's the undertaker's wife, Lois Epps. Eleanor is the redhead." She indicated a tall, thin, woman whose placid countenance matched her pale hair.

Jessie felt a weird disconnect. Lois didn't look like a woman married to a mortician. Eleanor didn't look like a woman married to anybody.

"Oh, there's Francine," Maude said.

They headed to a spot some feet away where two booths had been set up with folding tables and chairs. Francine turned out to be Francine Ferris, a tall, shapely redhead of about thirty with eyes the color of Easter chocolate. She smiled at Jessie.

"I was very fond of your great-aunt," she said. "I miss her."

"Francie owns Bell, Book and Candle," Mabel Ruth said. "We all spend a lot of time there."

Jessie took in the young woman's long black skirt and the giant plastic hoops at her ears.

"Are you a witch, too?"

"No." Francine laughed. "I carry the New Age stuff, but I also display handicrafts made by the locals. It's kind of *Bewitched* meets *The Waltons*." She indicated a crystal ball on a table draped with chiffon scarves. "Tonight I'm a fortuneteller."

"Ah."

"Unfortunately, I'm going to have to shut down the other booth. My partner-in-crime, Thelma Sessions, had to stay home tonight with a sick pig."

The last word came out as a squeal. Francine was suddenly airborne, her long, lush hair and her skirts flying as strong masculine hands swung her around.

"I'm sure my new roomie would love to help you out."

The deep voice sent a shock through Jessie's system. All her senses went on red alert. She glanced from Francie's flushed face to Luke's amused expression. Were the two lovers? Unlikely. The canasta ladies said he'd only been in town for three days.

Butterflies circled in Jessie's stomach. Maybe Francine was an old girlfriend. And maybe, judging by the grin on the redhead's face, the old embers were re-igniting. Jessie didn't want anyone to get the wrong idea.

"We're not really roommates," she babbled. "We just happen to be, temporarily, sharing Blanche's house."

Luke let Francine's feet drop to the ground, but he kept his arm around her. His green eyes glittered at Jessie, and she shivered. The bad seed was definitely dangerous.

"You'd like to help, wouldn't you, Jessie? You've got cruise director written all over you."

Jessie's smile was tight. "Sure."

Francine's smile was a lot more genuine. "It would be great if you could operate the kissing booth."

Kissing. Jessie bit back a groan. If she'd known

how to kiss she'd still be engaged. Hell, she'd be married. And now, everyone in what was supposed to be her sanctuary, would know she sucked at that most basic of romantic interactions. She caught the sly grin on Luke's face.

He already knew.

How? Was he a witch, too?

****

Harlan Foote had been mayor since Luke played tight end on the Mystic Hollow Consolidated football team. The egg-shaped, mustachioed man loved his unpaid position more than he loved his shoe store with its bare wood floorboards and its 1950's ceiling lights, and almost as much as he loved his wife, Hermione, their six daughters, and their hordes of grandchildren. He loved the town, too, just as Blanche Maynard had loved it.

Almost as much as Luke hated it.

Harlan Foote had dreams for Mystic Hollow.

For Luke, this was where dreams came to die.

The mayor toddled up to the chestnut tree where Luke stood with Zachary Reeves, a career marine whose powerful arm had put the football in Luke's hands enough times to take Mystic Hollow Consolidated to the Class D state championship title.

A blast of harsh wind made the egg-shaped man rock on his pins.

"Wind's picked up." Harlan had always been master of the obvious. "Looks like a storm's brewing."

Luke knew exactly what Harlan Foote would say next. He wasn't disappointed.

"How'd you boys like to put up the shelter?"

Luke had already spotted a familiar pile of thin

33

metal rods that looked as sturdy as toothpicks. He didn't bother to point out the thunderheads barreling toward them would almost certainly level the flimsy structure on contact or that most of the festival-goers could sprint home as fast as they could gather under the shelter. It was tradition to have a shelter at a festival and Mayor Foote valued tradition.

"By the way," he continued. "Thanks for bringing out the chairs and tables. Can I count on you boys to haul them back to St. Michael's later on tonight?"

Luke and Zach exchanged a glance. The storm would hit Mystic Hollow in less than two hours, just about the time they'd be loading up his truck.

"No problem," Luke said.

"You boys are real hometown heroes," the mayor continued. "You and Bobby Ray. Back on the gridiron and now on the battlefield. Real hometown heroes," he repeated.

Luke's gut clenched at the undeserved praise. He noticed Zach had frozen like a buck in the headlights.

Harlan Foote looked up into Zach's hard face. "Heard you're heading back," he said, quietly. "You take care now. Come home safe." He left the rest of the thought unsaid.

Not in a wooden box like Bobby Ray.

Luke knew Zach was hurting. He'd been in the convoy when Bobby got picked off.

"Good old Mayor Foote," Luke said, trying to lighten the moment. "He'll never change."

"Why should he? He's happy in this hellhole."

Luke knew Zach was struggling with survivor guilt, but the comment shocked him. The tall marine had always been quiet, solid, dependable. And from as far back as Luke could remember, Zach had wanted to settle down in Mystic Hollow with Francine.

"What's going on with you?"

Zach cupped his hand and bent down to light a cigarette. "I've seen more of the world."

Luke studied his friend. "What part of the world did you find so compelling? Fort Benning? Baghdad?"

"It's a job." Zach crushed the unlit cigarette.

Luke cursed. "Bobby Ray's death wasn't your fault."

Zach drew another cigarette out of his jacket pocket, lit another match, and caught the tobacco on fire. He inhaled in a long, smooth breath. "He was under my protection. Now he's in the ground. I'd say that was my fault."

"C'mon, Z. Even you can't control the war." Zach leaned against the chestnut tree and looked away, but Luke wasn't finished. "You really going back?"

Zach inhaled again. He let the smoke out in a series of fat little circles.

"What about Francie?"

A muscle worked in Zach's strong jaw. He dropped the half-smoked butt and ground it out with his boot heel. "That's over."

For a moment Luke couldn't speak. Betting on Zach and Francine would have been like betting on death or taxes.

"You wanna tell me why?"

"Chicks change their minds. You should know that better'n anyone."

An old familiar pain nearly paralyzed Luke's heart. "We're not talking about me."

"I think we are."

Luke glared at the other man. "What's that supposed to mean?"

Zach's broad shoulders lifted and fell. "Why are you back?"

He didn't want to get into this. "Unfinished business."

"Business with Crystal."

"Drop it, Z."

But Zach wouldn't drop it. "It's Christmastime. Chances are one hundred percent she'll visit her folks sometime in the next couple of weeks. She's like a T-bone to a coon hound, and you're the hound."

All of a sudden Luke was back in high school watching the new girl saunter past the bank of lockers stopping the hearts of every male in the building.

"This is nothing to do with her." He knew the words sounded forced.

"She's poison, Luke. Pure poison."

Zach nodded in Jessie's direction. "Who's the midget?"

It took an effort to return to the present. Luke sucked in the chilly air. A storm was sure as hell coming. "Jessie Maynard. Blanche's great-niece."

Zach's thick eyebrows lifted. "She staying at the house?"

Luke got the implication. He wasn't amused. "She's a kid."

Zach's gaze landed on Jessie, and he squinted.

"You'd better get your glasses checked. She might be a small package, but everything's in the right place."

It was just a comment. Luke knew Zach had never looked at any woman except Francine, regardless of what their problem was at the moment. Nevertheless, he scowled at his friend.

"Hands off, Zach. She's Blanche's kin."

"You said that already."

Despite the wind Luke felt sweat break out on his back. Jesus. Who knew babysitting took so much work?

"Let Crystal go," Zach said, quietly, "the way the rest of us did years ago."

Luke didn't say what he was thinking, that it was easier for everybody else. None of them had married her. Luke picked up a sledgehammer and drove one of Mayor Foote's flimsy spikes halfway to China.

****

Letty Appleby waved her spindly arms like a demented dictator, and her voice spiraled into a pig-like squeal as she spewed out the rules. As chairperson of the now-defunct church social committee, she felt it was her obligation and responsibility to educate the masses even though most of the residents of Mystic Hollow knew exactly how to eat Molly Umphrey's special double-chocolate, chocolate chip brownies.

Eleanor waited for Letty to calm down. Sometimes she felt like she'd spent her whole life waiting for Letty to blow off steam or trying to repair the damage from Letty's words. Between dealing with her neighbor and her husband, Eleanor had learned to compartmentalize, to bide her time, to have extraordinary patience.

Finally, the harridan quieted.

"Have a brownie, Letty?"

The woman took only one bite before she started again.

"Soddom and Gomorrah," Letty muttered. "That's where we're headed. Right, straight toward the Apocalypse."

"I don't know what you're talking about," Eleanor said, mildly.

Letty's back stiffened and her long, witch-like chin lifted high into the air.

"I am talking about morality, Eleanor. And the rising crime rate. Mystic Hollow is sinking into depravity."

The crime rate? In Mystic Hollow? The town's one-man police force consisted of a retired football coach who spent his summers on the golf course over in Gap. Mystic Hollow had no crime rate. Eleanor wisely didn't comment. Instead she seized the moment after Letty's next bite of brownie.

"Letty, dear, you've worked so hard tonight. Why don't you take a little stroll around the green?"

Letty's eyes lit up. Few people shared gossip with the woman, but she was able to pick up tidbits with her inveterate eavesdropping. The crone still managed to be ungracious.

"You will have to supervise the cleanup."

"Of course." It was a small price to pay for peace. Besides, Letty seldom did any real work. She was too busy cataloguing everybody else's sins.

****

The twinkle lights on the gazebo danced like marionettes as the wind picked up and the temperature dropped. As the fire truck headed back for the station, Santa flung handfuls of candy to the children lining the street.

Jessie had been pleasantly surprised at the success of her kissing booth. Most of the young males in town, including teenagers, had flocked around egging one another to "kiss her again." Turned out she was just fine with the art of kissing as long as no passion was involved.

As the wind kicked up, whipping up the corners of the paper tablecloth on the fortune teller's table and producing a dull roar, festival goers helped themselves to lemonade and brownies.

Jessie turned to Francine. "Shouldn't we close down before the skies open up?"

The redhead laughed. "Mayor Foote's the eternal optimist. He always thinks a storm will hold off. I can't tell you how many town events have ended with everybody dashing for home in between raindrops."

Jessie smiled. She liked her new friend and she decided to trust her. "Can I ask you a question?"

Francie nodded.

"Do you think my aunt Blanche was murdered?"

Francine looked thoughtful. "The truth? I don't think so. She died in bed, and there was no apparent sign of foul play."

So the murder theory was only in the minds of the imaginative would-be witches. Jessie knew she should be relieved.

"It's possible, though," Francine continued. "There's definitely something shady going on at St. Michael's. Blanche, as you know, wasn't one to ignore a problem. If she discovered something, she probably confronted the reverend."

"But why would she do it alone?"

Francine smiled. "I know you and your aunt stayed in touch, but you couldn't have known her very well if you could ask that question. She wouldn't have wanted to humiliate the 'sinner,' and she wouldn't have wanted to endanger anyone else."

Jessie's heart twisted. She'd lost a very special woman. She wished she'd made more of an effort to visit Blanche Maynard.

"Do you believe the reverend could have murdered her? I mean, he took vows."

Francine's eyes flashed with cynicism. "Everyone who gets married takes vows, too, and look where that's led—to a fifty percent divorce rate."

She had a point.

"So what's going on with the locked church?"

Francine shrugged. "There probably is a mold issue. Besides, it isn't locked all the time. I'm sure it's open tonight so the volunteers can return the tables and chairs."

The church was open tonight. Oh my god. Here was an opportunity just staring her in the face. Her heart thumped hard against her ribs. She glanced at the darkened building across the green. Francine noticed. She put her hand on Jessie's forearm.

"Don't get involved with this. Blanche never would have wanted anything to happen to you."

Maybe not, but according to the three canasta witches, Blanche had summoned her to deal with the problem at St. Michael's. At least indirectly.

"I'm just here for rest and recuperation," she assured Francine. "Nothing will happen to me."

****

"I've found the perfect spot, sugar."

Dennis Prendergast leaned his head against the rough brick wall. Lois had cut him out of the crowd like a prize heifer and brought him to the alley behind Bexler's Drugs. He squeezed his eyes. The distant shouts from the festival added to his anticipation as did the contrast between the chilly wind and the fire in his blood. He moaned with pleasure as she touched him.

"Baby," he rasped, "you always find the perfect spot." He moved against the wall. The bricks would snag his coat, but he couldn't bring himself to care. Lois's talented fingers massaged him. Any minute now he'd be in her mouth. He felt the first flicks of her tongue, and his head bounced against the brick.

"Jesus," he whispered. "Mary and Joseph."

"Saints alive!"

The unholy shriek caused Lois to pulverize his balls, and he yelped. Suddenly he was free, his erection bobbing like an overloaded grapevine.

"Reverend Prendergast."

His eyes snapped open, and he cursed again. Miss Letty. The old witch was staring at his genitals as though she'd never seen an aroused man.

Probably she hadn't.

The haze of sexual desperation couldn't disguise the imminent disaster. Miss Letty Appleby was the town crier. He was ruined. He closed his eyes, briefly, hoping it was just a nightmare and he'd wake up. For a moment it seemed his prayers had been answered. Neither Letty nor Lois was still in the alley with him.

His hands shaking, he jammed the still-hard flesh back into his trousers.

"Hey, Reverend, you all right."

It was a new voice, high, sweet and incredibly irritating. What was this? Disneyworld? He should be charging admission. Dennis grabbed the edge of his coat and covered his open fly.

"I'm fine." He forced himself to smile at the boy. "Timmy."

"I'm Tommy. Tommy Thompson. Timmy's my brother."

Timmy. Tommy. Satan. Whatever.

"What're you doing back here?"

There was no good answer. Dennis stared at the boy and prayed for a miracle.

An instant later hailstones cracked against the bricks behind him.

"Gotta go," the boy yelled as he raced out of the alley.

Dennis smiled grimly. As usual, God had saved him. Now, if the Man would just strike Letty dumb.

****

A few of the teenage boys reappeared but it became clear the festival was winding down and Jessie called a halt to the kissing. She glanced with satisfaction at the fishbowl of cash. She was proud to contribute to the uniform fund for the Marching Mystics. She dipped her hand in the bowl to remove the bills, but froze when warm masculine fingers circled her wrist.

"I haven't had my turn."

The voice was deep, pleasant, and unfamiliar. Jessie looked up into a pair of electric blue eyes.

The man held her gaze as he deposited a twenty-dollar bill, then with one coordinated move, he gathered Jessie into his massive arms. She felt like the bride of King Kong.

"Amateur hour is over," he continued, his voice low and intimate. Firm lips feathered over hers. He'd spoken the truth. The kiss bore no resemblance to the ones she'd shared with the boys. It was crisp, clean, expert. Designed to tantalize. When he pulled back a moment later, she grinned at him.

"Is this how you greet all visitors in Mystic Hollow?"

"Just call me the Welcome Wagon."

His head lowered and bestowed another delicious kiss. It was fine. Better than any kiss she'd ever shared with Kit. His big body shielded her from the first plump drops of rain.

And then she was spun free.

"I told you," another masculine voice growled, "hands off." Luke. Jessie's heart flew into her mouth. Her eyes darted to her housemate's hard features. The green eyes were dark with annoyance, but they weren't aimed at her.

Luke was looking at Francine. Jessie tried to swallow and couldn't. Zach had let go of her, but he didn't sound intimidated.

"She still owes me nineteen kisses."

"Eighteen," Jessie corrected, in a hoarse voice.

Luke's gaze narrowed on the other man. "Get change."

"I've got a better idea. You take 'em. I dare you."

Raindrops began to slide down Jessie's face like uncontrolled tears. She opened her mouth to protest.

"Not interested."

For some reason his rejection infuriated her. The kissing booth was for a good cause, and what was she? Chopped liver? Everyone else seemed to enjoy kissing her.

"Coward." The taunt was out of her mouth before she could stop it.

The green eyes narrowed, and she felt strong fingers dig into the soft flesh of her upper arms. It hurt.

Ann Yost

She wanted to push him away, but he was a man on a mission. His hard mouth covered hers, and he bent her back into a pretzel. She wondered, briefly, if her spine would snap. There was no time for anger or humiliation. The masculine lips softened, and she felt a warm, irresistible tongue slip into her mouth.

Holy shit.

Desire rocketed through her. Her blood rushed, her heart drummed, and moisture pooled between her legs. Shocked and aroused, she recklessly thrust her own tongue behind his strong teeth. Her arms lifted of their own volition, and she realized she was sliding her fingers into his thick, damp hair.

The urgency was stunning. And unique. And, of course, disastrous. She couldn't afford a complication like this. She needed to pull away, but she knew, in her soul, she'd stay like this forever if she could.

The choice was taken out of her hands. A harsh groan worked its way up Luke's hard body and seemed to set off an alarm bell. He pushed her away. And then he disappeared into the dark.

****

He should never have kissed the elf. It was a mid-air collision; a spinout on the Indy 500; a tsunami.

He'd been a fool. He should've recognized those protective feelings. Hadn't felt them since Crystal. He swore silently as he heaved tables and chairs into the pickup. He knew what it was. Chemistry. God damn chemistry. Had Blanche known? Had she planned this?

He rejected that idea. This was just one of the universe's nasty little tricks. He sucked in a breath of rain soaked wind and tried to slow his heart rate. He could deal with it. All he had to do was keep the

44

chemistry from turning into biology. A piece of cake. He could babysit the damn woman without touching her.

God, she'd felt good. Soft and warm, surprised but responsive. He felt the blood rush to his groin. His zipper tightened. Shit.

Lightning seared the sky, thunder cracked, and rain slashed across his face. He didn't mind. Nature's holocaust matched the shrapnel in his gut.

Chapter Four

Thunder bellowed, and rain pasted Eleanor's polyester slacks against her legs. Even her waterproof rain jacket was no help against the driving storm. There was chaos on the green as parents grabbed their children in a hopeless attempt to get home without getting soaked. Mayor Foote's shelter blew away.

Eleanor continued to pick up soggy paper products and stuff them into a green plastic bag, blinking her eyes against the onslaught. With the storm in her ears and her eyes on the ground, she didn't hear anyone approach, so when claws clamped onto her wrist she jumped in pain. "Letty! For heaven's sake!"

"I have to speak to you at once, Eleanor. There isn't a moment to lose."

The woman was as reliable as the post office. Neither rain, nor sleet, nor dark of night could keep her from spreading gossip. Eleanor wondered whose head was on the block now.

"You should get on home," she told Letty. "You'll catch pneumonia."

Letty's grip tightened. Her long sallow face was flushed with fury; her pale eyes were crystals of anticipation. She already looked ill. Eleanor softened her voice. "Seriously, Letty. You need to get out of the rain."

"This will not wait." God, the woman was

stubborn.

"All right." Eleanor decided to abandon the rest of the un-biodegradable trash. "Let's go back to the duplex and have a cup of tea."

Moments later, Letty had shed her voluminous black raincoat. Her feet, still clad with galoshes, rested under Eleanor's Formica topped kitchen table. The old woman's soaked yellow-gray hair looked like seaweed plastered against a rock.

"Green tea or Oolong?"

"This is more important than tea, Eleanor. You'd better sit down."

"I will. Just let me boil the water."

Letty apparently gave up the effort to control the pastor's wife. She let out an exasperated puff of breath. "Sin, Eleanor. I'm talking about the devil's work. I am sorry to have to tell you, but this is not something a God-fearing Christian can ignore. Evil waits for no man."

Eleanor stifled a sigh. Someone was about to get skewered. She left the kettle to boil on the pristine avocado stove top and she took a seat.

May the bloodletting begin.

"I saw them behind Bexler's."

Eleanor strove for patience. "Saw who, Letty?"

"Him. He was having carnal relations with that hussy!"

Eleanor's jaw dropped. "How upsetting."

It obviously wasn't the response Letty wanted. She blinked several times.

"Very upsetting," she clarified. "Especially since he is a man of the cloth."

A stillness came over Eleanor Prendergast. Years

of practice gave her the control she knew she needed at that moment. She refused to make this easier for the Gossip.

"Not just carnal relations, either, Eleanor. It was, it was…" Letty searched for the right word. "It was bestiality!"

Oh Lord. She stared at the over bright eyes of the woman across the table.

"Don't you understand? It was the reverend!

Thou shalt not covet thy neighbor's wife!"

Eleanor put up a token resistance.

"You mean Denny? You must be mistaken, Letty."

Letty's thin gray eyebrows arrowed toward her long nose.

"My eyesight is perfect. I know what I saw."

Eleanor tried again. "Why would someone carry on in that dank alley behind the pharmacy? There's no place even to sit down."

"She was kneeling," Letty blurted. "In front of him."

Eleanor knew exactly how to compartmentalize. She decided to focus on irritating the old bat.

"Maybe she was praying."

Letty turned chartreuse. "What is the matter with you, Eleanor? She was most certainly not praying. She had her mouth open and, oh botheration!"

Eleanor waited while Letty sucked in a fortifying breath and delivered the *coup de grace*.

"He was putting it in there."

"Putting what? In where?"

"Oh, great heavens! How can you be so obtuse? She was giving him a blow job!"

Eleanor was speechless. It was almost worth the destruction of Denny's career, and her life, to hear the wicked old spinster use those words. Almost. She still refused to give Letty any satisfaction.

"Eleanor, let me spell it out for you. Your husband, the reverend of St. Michael's parish is a sinner!"

"That's enough."

Eleanor's tone was stern, and Miss Letty paused. She soon took up the cudgel again.

"A sinner cannot preach the gospel."

"We're all sinners, Letty. I challenge you to find anyone, preacher or no, who hasn't sinned."

Letty's nose lifted. "I'm sorry for you, Eleanor. You will, necessarily, be tainted by association."

"It isn't necessary, Letty. Not if you don't speak of this to anyone else."

"Impossible."

Eleanor was not above begging. "Wait, then. Until after the pageant. Surely you don't want to ruin Christmas for the rest of the town."

Unfortunately, that was just what Letty Appleby wanted.

"It can't be helped. The man must not be allowed back in the pulpit."

Eleanor felt her control begin to crack. Fury at Denny seeped through the fortress she kept around her heart. She needed to get away from Letty's self-righteous vitriol. She had to figure out damage control. She must have looked upset because finally Letty's face reflected her satisfaction.

"I know this is painful, Eleanor, but consider John 8:32. 'The truth shall set you free.'"

Eleanor stared at the smug smile. "Matthew 7:1,"

she said, softly, "judge not lest ye be judged."

Letty looked startled but only for an instant. The kettle whistled, and she nodded at it. "I believe I'll take green tea. It's good for the digestion."

It was a ridiculous thing, a tiny, insignificant detail, but Eleanor couldn't resist. "I'm out of tea,

Letty. How about some hot cocoa?"

****

So far the sleuthing expedition was going very well. Jessie had managed to slip in the side door and up the stairs to the second floor. There was just one small problem she hadn't anticipated. Storm clouds shrouded the moon, blackening the windows.

She couldn't see a thing.

She stood in the second floor stairwell waiting for her eyes to adjust. If only she'd brought a flashlight! In her own defense, she hadn't expected this opportunity to arise. If she were going to solve this alleged crime, she'd better get prepared. Blanche's white parka was soaked. It was also holding the moisture in, and she was getting cold. She stripped off the heavy garment as she tried to remember what Miss Marple wore on her investigations. Since there was little else she could do, she pressed a tiny knob on her gold watch. The face lit up, a tiny circle of light in the pervasive dark. She was surprised to find it was only eight forty-five.

It felt later. But then it had been a full day.

Her wedding day. And this was supposed to be her wedding night. She pictured a king-sized bed in a breeze-swept island room, and heat flashed through her followed by a stab of horror. The imaginary groom holding her body against his wasn't tall and blond. Green eyes glittered at her in an unsmiling face. Good grief.

She had to stop thinking about that kiss. She was here in Mystic Hollow to recover, regroup, to find the Jessie that had somehow been lost in the chaos of the Maynard family's struggles.

Finally, the darkness started to thin. She put her hand on the cement-block wall and started, cautiously, down the darkened corridor toward what she hoped was Prendergast's office. She wondered if the door would be locked. Would he really be so careless as to leave clues sitting around? She wasn't sure what she hoped to find.

A pouch of marijuana? A briefcase full of small, unmarked bills?

A sudden loud crash cut off her thoughts and her breath.

"You okay?" A gravelly masculine voice drifted up the stairwell. It did something to her insides.

"Fine," another male voice responded.

She sucked in a little air. It was Luke and Zach returning the furniture. There was no way they'd know she was there. She just had to hold still until they finished their business and took off.

****

"I'm gonna take off."

Luke looked up from the table he was drying off with a paper towel from the kitchen.

"Give me thirty seconds. We'll get a beer."

Zach didn't bother to answer. He threw up a hand, strode across the social hall, and out the side door. Luke realized he was disappointed. And worried. He didn't want to be alone in Blanche's house with the elf. And he wondered what the hell had happened between his buddy and Francine. He'd bet his new start-up it involved Bobby Ray. Mystic Hollow's golden boy had always been full of the devil.

Luke shook his head. It wasn't his problem. He was done with this town and everyone in it. He slid the table into a storage closet and slammed the door then he crumpled the paper towel and lofted it toward a trash can.

"Two points," he murmured.

He killed the lights, dug his keys out of his pocket, and headed for the side door. A small, unmistakable sound made him freeze with his hand on the knob.

It was a faint, ladylike sneeze.

Damn it all to hell. Someone, and he was pretty sure he knew who, was upstairs snooping around. Blanche's posse must have floated their murder theory. It didn't take a sixth sense to know Jessie Maynard would jump at the chance to get involved. She was a born meddler.

He expelled a long breath. It didn't concern him. It wasn't his problem. She wasn't in danger here in the empty church. He felt the knob turn under his hand.

Someone was on the other side of the door.

With the sure coordination that had aided him in football and saved him in the war, he vaulted up the stairs.

****

The private security alarm hidden in his office let off its disturbing beep. Dennis's hand stilled, and his heart lurched. He wasn't expecting anybody tonight, but it wasn't like he controlled his schedule. His gut twisted, and heat surged into his lower body. Shit. Double shit. The sense of uneasiness that had become his constant companion nearly overwhelmed him. It was getting harder and harder to pretend everything was all right. He wished for the thousandth time he hadn't made a pact with the devil.

He released his erect shaft, removed his hand from his soft, warm sweatpants, and snapped off the tantalizing image on his computer screen. With an irritated grunt, he bent to unlock his bottom desk drawer and grabbed his pistol. He didn't bother to check for bullets.

The gun was cocked and ready.

Like him.

****

Jessie inhaled the scent she'd noticed earlier at the witch hat house. Pine, maybe, and leather? Definitely testosterone. She heard the downstairs door open and then the clack of stilettos.

Stilettos? Before she could move, a warm hand clapped across her mouth, and an arm came around her waist and tightened. Like a boa constrictor.

She made a little sound.

"Quiet." The low growl released the rest of the butterflies in her stomach. The ones that hadn't escaped with Luke's scent and touch. She suppressed a nervous giggle as she wondered if they were squashed by his powerful arm. Between the overpowering sensation and her collapsed lungs, she was having trouble breathing.

Suddenly her mouth was free, but she felt herself slung up into the air. One arm flew out to her side in an instinctive effort to catch her balance. Her hand grazed fur and she yipped.

"What?" His voice was a hiss.

"Dead animal," she whispered.

She felt his washboard stomach ripple against her. The jerk was laughing at her! His voice was so quiet she had to strain to hear it.

"It's a sheep. This is where they keep the costumes for the Christmas pageant."

The explanation softened Jessie's heart. Not only because he'd bothered to make it but because of what it told her about him. He'd been involved enough in this church to know where the camels were kept. He'd come here with Blanche.

In that instant she understood the extent of his loss.

The clack of high heels came closer. Who on earth was it? Not the murderer. Not Prendergast. Unless he was a cross dresser. Jessie had no time to contemplate that concept. A husky voice sliced through the dark.

"Hey, sugar. Is that a gun in your hand, or are you just happy to see me?"

At the sound of a masculine curse, Luke's muscled arm crushed Jessie's diaphragm.

"Christ almighty. I almost shot you."

Jessie's heart jerked. That had to be Prendergast. And he had a gun! She refused to think about the strong probability that he'd been here the whole time she'd been making her way down the corridor.

"Don't pretend you're not happy to see me, baby," the woman purred. "You're already hard as a rock."

"Lois." There was a low, masculine groan of need. "Yeah, okay," the preacher gasped. "Harder. Yeah. Like that."

Lois. Prendergast's wife's name was Eleanor. Was the good reverend conducting an affair? Jessie felt a surge of sympathy for the pastor's plain wife.

"Let's go to your office, sugar."

54

Jessie wilted in relief, but thanks to Luke's arm she didn't fall. Thank God for small mercies. At least the dynamic duo weren't going to carry on in front of them.

"No," Prendergast puffed. "In here."

The breathing got louder, harsher, and she heard the rattle of hangers nearby. The fumbling lovers had stumbled into the closet! She couldn't see anything and surmised they were hidden by some kind of a board or a wall. Maybe part of the stable.

The breathing got heavier, quicker. Jessie prayed they'd talk.

Naturally that prayer went unanswered. Prendergast moaned, and she heard the faint sound of a zipper.

"Pull me out," Prendergast growled. "Suck me."

Heat exploded in Jessie. She prayed for a swarm of locusts, an earthquake, one of those rare Virginia monsoons.

Naturally that prayer went unanswered, too.

"You taste good, baby," the woman said. "Big and warm and hard."

Another hot flash. This time the embarrassment was mixed with something else as she felt Luke's muscles clench against her body, and she felt his hot breath on her neck.

"Oh god, oh god, oh god," the preacher crooned.

Jessie felt her breasts graze the top of Luke's arm. She smelled his excitement, felt the involuntary response of Luke's body against hers, and she shuddered as she heard a moan rumble through his chest.

For the first time in her life she felt sympathy for a murderer. This was more than wanting. It was needing.

She arched back against him and felt his free hand unfasten her slacks. Then it was on her skin, warm and soothing at first then ticklish and rhythmic. She sucked in her breath as those fingers sought and found the sensitive spot between her legs. She sucked in some more. She wondered at what point she'd black out. And then the rubbing got faster and harder, and she didn't care.

Jessie couldn't hold still. She was still imprisoned in his arms, but she twisted against them, against him. Tension piled upon tension until she felt like a rubber band stretched beyond its capacity. She was a rocket about to launch.

"Now," she whispered.

"Shh," he said.

He stroked once more. Fireworks. Bursts of sensation pummeled one another until she lay limp in his arms. When it was over, she discovered she still couldn't breathe.

Once again Luke had his hand over her mouth.

She edged backward and discovered he had a full-scale erection behind his zipper.

Chapter Five

Dennis crumpled on the mauve-and-blue striped sofa like a used condom. He groaned as he felt the cushion depress. Lois. Why didn't she go home?

"Denny."

"Hmm?"

"What're we gonna do about Miss Letty Appleby? She'll have it all over town tomorrow. Mort'll kill me."

Damn. Damn. Damn. "I'll take care of it." He said it to shut her up. He just wanted her to leave.

"There's something else I want to talk to you about."

"Can it wait? I'm beat."

She slipped a finger into the waistband of his slacks. He wanted to bat it away. She'd stroked and sucked his flesh until he was sore.

"Do you love me?"

Ah. An easy question. One he'd fielded dozens of times. "'Course I do, sweetheart."

"Have you thought about the future?"

He couldn't think about anything but the future. At least the next eight hours of it. He longed for the oblivion of his bed.

"Because I think we're good together."

"Uh-huh." Where the hell was this going?

"I, well, I'm thinking of leaving Mort." Her laugh was brittle. "Not that he'd notice. He's only interested in women if they're dead."

"Mmm." Dennis didn't want to hear about Mort.

"He doesn't care what I do," she whined. "In fact, to be truthful, he kind of scares me."

Dennis could relate.

"He's unisexual, ya know?"

"Asexual," he corrected. Like Ellie. He stared at his lover's heavily made up face. Foundation caked around the crow's feet around her eyes. Her lipstick was gone, used up on his cock. She looked like what she was: a woman trying to look twenty years younger. The illusion worked pretty well in a bad light.

"You're just imagining things, honey."

"Let's go away together. You've got plenty of money."

He didn't now, but he would soon. Thanks to his deal with her husband.

"Denny." Her face was only inches away. He could smell onions. He struggled to push himself off the sofa. He held out a manicured hand and helped her to her feet.

"Come on, honey. It's late. We'll sort this out tomorrow, okay?"

"I'll be working."

He hid his distaste. Even though the funeral home was housed in the old manse and connected to the church, Dennis gave it a wide berth. Not that it mattered. He'd have his hands full tomorrow morning trying to deal with the Miss Letty crisis.

"Sure," he lied. "Yeah."

He'd gotten awfully damn comfortable breaking the commandments. Of course, he'd been doing it for a long, long time.

****

Eleanor Prendergast stretched out in the king-sized bed she shared with her husband. The giant mattress allowed them to pretend they still shared the physical relationship that had been over for years. She'd managed to overlook the affairs, but when she'd discovered her late father had "bought" her a husband, she'd discontinued the sex.

Denny's greed had merely annoyed her.

Her father's betrayal had nearly killed her.

During her childhood it had been Eleanor and her father, Felix Mooney, living on the top floor of the Mooney Funeral Parlor. Eleanor helped with everything from bookings to embalmings, from playing the small organ to serving punch at the wakes. She'd been enough for Felix until Gloria Fineman showed up to bury her husband, and the longtime widower fell hard. After that, nothing was the same, and when Denny had asked for her hand, she'd agreed. It was only later she found out the nuptials had been arranged, and paid for, by Felix himself.

Eleanor's guts writhed as if it had been yesterday instead of a quarter of a century earlier. She cut off the familiar pain the way she'd turn off a faucet. There was more to concern herself with than ancient history, like Miss Letty's eyewitness account of Denny's most recent indiscretion.

Just for a second, for a fragment of a second, she wanted to erase her husband, his lover, and her tale-carrying neighbor from the face of the earth. But only for an instant.

She heard the door open and close. She heard Denny's quiet footsteps on the uncarpeted stairs. She turned on her side, closed her eyes, and retreated to a happy place: the embalming room in the basement of the Mooney Funeral Parlor some forty years ago.

****

Silence filled the truck cab as Luke drove the half block between St. Michael's and Blanche's house. He wished he were any place else. He wished she were any place else. There was no way to open a discussion of the incident without bringing sex into their odd situation.

Hell. Sex was already between them like the proverbial elephant in the room. An elephant with a still hard cock. He shifted in the seat. He'd never been out of his mind like that from just touching a woman. If he didn't know how inept they were, he'd think Mabel Ruth and the girls had cast a spell on him.

It was abstinence. Had to be. Abstinence with a little chemistry thrown in.

He turned down the alley that ran behind the houses on Cobblestone Lane, and then he pulled into the double driveway behind the house. He thrust the truck into gear, and Jessie yanked on her door handle. It was too high. She'd lose her footing.

"Hang on. I'll come around."

"No thanks," she said, as she pushed open the door. "I'm tired of being treated like a backpack."

He clamped fingers around her wrist and stared at her. The sun-streaked curls had begun to dry. They formed little "c's" all over her head.

She looked like a poodle.

"What're you talking about?"

Her eyes flashed. In the cab's interior light, they looked like peat water.

"I'm talking about the way you keep slinging me around. Like I was a sack of potatoes. I have perfectly good legs."

"They're good," he admitted. "But they're too short."

She gaped at him.

He thrust his long fingers through his damp hair. "It wasn't a criticism. I don't find you unattractive." Obviously.

"That was just circumstances," she assured him. "Anybody'd be turned on in the middle of a live porn show."

He gazed at her small, straight nose. He wondered how many soldiers there were in the small brigade of freckles. She wasn't beautiful, but there was an animation in her manner and her eyes.

"I see you've got it all worked out."

A look of relief appeared on her face. She didn't want involvement any more than he did.

Thank God.

"Do you think they knew we were there?"

He recalled hearing Prendergast's groans while Jessie's sweet butt ground into his groin. His zipper tightened. Again.

"No," he said, shortly. "What were you doing there, anyway? Snooping?"

She hesitated as if she didn't want to tell him.

"C'mon, Elf. What's going on under that mop of curls?"

She looked undecided as if trying to weigh the consequences of the truth.

"Mabel Ruth, Millicent, and Maude told me about the murder."

His lips thinned. "Imagined murder."

For some reason his response didn't seem to irritate her.

"Let's call it 'alleged.' I figured last night was my chance to take a look around the church."

"Find anything?"

Her soft lips twisted into a half smile. "You know exactly what I found."

His jaw loosened. "Yeah. And I know what you learned, too."

Her face flushed. The color created an attractive pink background for the freckles, then her eyes widened.

"I discovered the secret. The secret that killed Blanche."

"What?"

"You know. The reverend. He's having an extra marital affair with someone named Lois."

"Lois Epps. The mortician's wife. For the record, I don't think Blanche was killed, but if she was, it wasn't over a moral indiscretion. Blanche didn't care about anybody else's morals." Except for his. He looked at her great-niece and felt a stab of guilt.

Oblivious to his moral dilemma, Jessie's head cocked to one side like an inquisitive bird. Her whiskey-colored eyes glowed.

"So what're you saying? What did I learn?" I? Had she forgotten he'd been there, too?

"Think, Jessie. Prendergast said he almost shot Lois. That meant he was packing a gun."

She looked at him a long minute, and then her expressive lips curved into a half smile. "Or maybe he really was just happy to see her."

****

Two hours later Luke crushed his sixth can of beer and dropped his head against the high back of Blanche's Victorian sofa. He stared into the blackened fireplace. He'd had a choice of Mountain Top, the local brew or something called Pappy's Wine. Christ.

Mystic Hollow was still in the Stone Age.

He glanced at the rosewood rocker on the opposite side of the hearth. He could so easily picture Blanche sitting there, working away at the blankets and booties she'd send to children's hospitals all over the world. She never quit. Even when arthritis made the work move at a snail's pace. Even though she knew her efforts had next to no impact on the problems in the world.

Blanche had been a sucker for a lost cause.

That's why she'd taken on Luke.

That's why she hadn't given up despite the gossip, despite the delinquent behavior, despite the heartache he'd handed her.

His gaze moved to the photo on the knickknack shelf.

He hadn't deserved the medal. The incident happened outside of Baghdad in the Triangle of Death. A sniper got three of the five guys in the Jeep. Luke managed to pull a wounded buddy to safety and hid them both until another vehicle picked them up. He was no hero. He was lucky. The sniper had poor aim.

Blanche insisted on displaying the award because, she said, it paid tribute not to his heroism but to his conscience.

A sense of loss twisted through him. He'd let her down so often. His teenage arrests, his refusal to come home from college, his minimal phone calls, his enlistment without consulting her, and most of all, his marriage. She'd stuck by him through it all.

The very least he could do was keep his hands off her great-niece.

He stared at the empty bay window. His last good memory of Crystal had been the night they'd trimmed the tree. He pictured her, ethereal as always in her signature white, the scent of Chanel Number Five drifting in the air, her long, slim fingers attaching the lights to the blue spruce. He hadn't known there was a problem. It was his fault. He'd let her beauty get in the way of communication.

He propped his feet on the oval coffee table and slouched so he was nearly horizontal while he sucked down one beer and then another. He balanced a third on his washboard stomach and tried to ignore the questions that slammed into him with the repeating precision of machine gun fire.

Would she come back to Mystic Hollow for Christmas?

Would he see her?

Did he want to?

He'd told Zach it was over but, hell, he'd lived in denial so long he didn't even know.

The footsteps overhead pulled him out of the painful memories. She made a lot of noise for an elf. When the clumping finally stopped, he envisioned her climbing into the big four-poster bed wearing some sort of honeymoon negligee. She was shorter than Crystal but rounder. Not fat. Curved. The filmy nightie would cling to her plump breasts. Desire jolted through him like a sudden lightning strike, and his instant erection toppled the nearly empty beer can.

He cursed. Time to do something about this mess.

He grunted as he stretched to pull his cell phone out of his pants pocket and hit a button.

"Reeves."

"What're you doin', sitting on the phone?"

"You sound shit-faced."

Luke grunted. "Wanna take a drive?"

Zach paused. "Yeah," he said, finally. "Okay."

****

Zach's forearms rested on the bar. Smoke drifted skyward from a lit but unsmoked cigarette in his right hand. It was late now, most of the patrons gone. The bartender was sitting at a table, chatting with a couple of regulars. For all intents and purposes, Luke and Zach were alone.

In spite of the buzz in his ears and the throbbing in his temples, in spite of his own unsettled evening, Luke was aware of the tension in his friend. Luke was a big believer in not prying into another guy's business but the pain emanating from the ex-marine was tangible. It was time to find out what was going on.

"I've known you and Francie since high school," Luke said, finally. "I've never seen you like this. And Francine's lost weight." He kept his voice low and gentle. "Maybe it'll help to talk."

Zach stared at the ashtray between his muscular forearms.

"She's in the hospital."

"What? What're you talking about?"

"Francine. She's all right. Or she will be by morning."

"What the hell happened?"

65

"I stopped at her house after we dropped off the tables. Thought she might be locked out." He glanced at Luke as if he knew what the other man was thinking. "There's precedent. She locked herself out the night of Bobby Ray's funeral."

"So you broke into her house. Twice. That doesn't explain how she got hurt."

"Her bedroom's in the back of the house. I detached the screen then boosted her over the sill. Both times. Tonight I shoved too hard. She was wearing that long skirt for the gypsy thing. It tangled around her legs and she lost her balance, hit her head on the wooden floor."

"Jesus. Was she unconscious?"

The long, lean fingers holding the cigarette trembled.

"Yeah. Doc says it's a slight concussion. She'll be okay."

Luke wasn't sure who Zach was trying to convince. He knew the mishap was only the tip of the iceberg.

"Something happened that first night. After the wake for Bobby Ray."

Zach was quiet a long time. Finally, he straightened on the barstool. The normally clear blue eyes were flecked with ice.

"I was suicidal," he said, emotionlessly. "Bobby Ray—he was my responsibility. I'd let him die."

"It wasn't your fault."

Zach held up a protesting hand. "I let him die, Tanner, and I was glad he was dead."

The words nearly shocked Luke sober. Zach Reeves was the most honorable guy he knew. What the hell was he saying?

"He'd been with her. Francine." The words were spoken in a deep, husky voice. "All the time I was overseas. They were in love. Gonna get married."

"You believed him?"

The response was automatic. Luke knew about betrayal, but he'd have bet his last dime on Francine and Zach.

"He showed me proof. Letters and stuff."

"What'd Francine say?"

The icy eyes narrowed. "What the hell could she say. I saw proof."

"She didn't admit an affair with Bobby, right? It was all circumstantial."

Zach's jaw tightened. Anger replaced the pain radiating from him.

"She was in love with him in high school. He dumped her for Crystal."

Crystal Wetherington Tanner. Ruining lives for more than ten years.

"Francie got over him years ago. Besides, she'd never have cheated on you. If she wanted Bobby Ray, she'd have told you. Don't you know the woman at all?"

"Bobby made her his beneficiary."

Luke shrugged. "Looks like she's gonna need it. She's alone in the world. All she has is you and your family."

Zach didn't say a word, but his rugged features hardened into Mount Rushmore.

Luke couldn't believe the conversation. Was this really happening? Zach and Francie broken up by Bobby Ray? Maybe he was asleep in the soft, creaky bed at Blanche's house. Maybe this was a nightmare.

He gripped the can of beer more tightly. It felt cold, moist, real.

A tense silence hung in the air like the last drifts of smoke from Zach's cigarette. The ash had burned nearly to his fingers, but he didn't seem to notice. There was still something unexplained in the story. Luke struggled to figure out what it was.

"The other night, the first night you broke in to Francie's house, something happened, right?"

Zach's face twisted, briefly. "She wouldn't let me leave. I'd already told her it was over, but she knew the kind of shape I was in."

Luke's heart squeezed. Francie must have been in despair over the death of her childhood friend and the defection of her longtime love, but she'd protected Zach from himself. It was like her. "So I'm guessing the inevitable happened."

Zach was staring back at the ashtray. "Three times." He tried to take a drag on the cigarette that was ash. "I haven't been alone with her since."

"Until tonight."

He nodded. "And I put her in the hospital."

Booze had fogged his brain, but Luke knew there was something else. He struggled to think back through the conversation. There was an element missing. What? And then he knew.

"You didn't tell Francie why. You just told her it was over. After ten damned years, you broke up with no explanation."

Zach shrugged his big shoulders. "I didn't need to hear any lies."

"Was it lies you were afraid of? Or the truth?"

Luke thought his friend would get angry but his

voice was low, controlled.

"I saw proof. Case closed."

"You're making a mistake, Z. Talk to her. Give her a chance to explain."

Zach straightened on the chair. He glanced around the roadhouse. Luke saw him make eye contact with a woman at a nearby table.

"I'm goin' back to my unit," he said, with finality. "But first I'm goin' upstairs with that redhead."

Chapter Six

Luke awoke in a rose-colored haze. It took him a minute to realize the glow was caused by the sun's penetration of a red curtain. He patted the blanket-covered butt next to him, hoisted himself to his feet, and scouted the room for his clothes. His teeth felt mossy. Shoulda packed a toothbrush with his condoms. He sucked in a breath. He had used condoms, hadn't he? He could barely remember last night.

He got on his hands and knees. The foil wrapper had blown into a dust bunny. The thing looked lonely down here. Pathetic. He was pathetic. He had a willing woman, a bed, a whole night, and he'd only used one condom. He got to his feet and checked his wallet.

Hell. He'd only had one condom.

Since his divorce he'd used sex to scratch an infrequent itch. He hadn't wanted anybody in particular. 'Til now.

He shouldered into his shirt, dragged on his jeans, whispered something to the still-sleeping woman—Tracy? Stacy?—and clattered down the creaky wooden steps. He figured Zach would be gone, and he was right. Luke reviewed his options for getting down off the mountain. He could run. He could hitchhike. He could call Z for a ride. He did none of those things. Instead, he dug his cell out of his pocket and punched in Blanche's number. Jessie Maynard would come get him.

His sixth sense told him the elf was a born rescuer.

****

The Jeep attacked the mountain road like an ornery bull with an unwanted rider on his back. Jessie ground her teeth together. What in the world was wrong with her? She'd driven this stick shift all the way from Chicago. Now she was stripping gears and sweating like a Sumo wrestler. It had to be the serpentine roads, or the early hour. It couldn't have anything to do with the hunk of masculinity slumped in the seat next to her, his emerald eyes glittering under half-closed lids.

"Anything wrong?" The morning voice was full of gravel, as if he'd just rolled out of bed. Undoubtedly he had.

Her eyes narrowed. "I can't see anything in this pea soup. These roads are too narrow and too winding."

"Enjoy your lower gears a little longer," he advised. "You're doing fine." He yawned.

"How come you're so calm?"

She glanced at him and watched a lazy, satisfied smile appeared. The Jeep bumped as it hit the shoulder, and the answer smacked her in the face.

Of course he was relaxed. He'd just gotten laid. Her fingers clenched the steering wheel, and the Jeep jerked again. She didn't know why the revelation should bother her. Luke Tanner's sex life was none of her business. A growled snore interrupted her thoughts, and she laughed in spite of her irritation. The snore matched the man, all right. Cagey, wild and dangerous. She should be grateful he was keeping his distance.

Jessie blinked against the morning sun. The stress of the ruptured wedding and the second sleepless night in a row were taking its toll. She'd paced the second floor corridor until the early hours, and then she'd lain on the four-poster and stared at the ceiling waiting for him to come home. She shook her head. No more playing nursemaid. She'd come to Mystic Hollow to find peace, but it had become increasingly important to her to answer the questions about Blanche's death.

Luke's head flopped against her arm. The movement triggered a tremor that went through her whole body, and she fought with the gearshift again. Nuts. It was time to concentrate on something real, like how to drive her car safely down the mountain.

****

The alarm splintered the silence of the dark room.

"Turn that thing off, Ellie," Dennis Prendergast growled. "It's too early to get up."

"I've got a meeting with Edna Smith to finalize arrangements for the Christmas pageant."

The pageant. Dennis lurched up to a sitting position. He'd left the closet floor strewn with costumes, some of which were probably stained with semen.

"You're meeting where?"

"Molly's Bakery."

"Oh." He fought to get his pounding heart under control. It would be all right.

"I'm stopping by to get Letty."

Letty! Dennis twisted upwards, his heart flapping wildly. He'd forgotten about the old bat. Damn meddling old crone. He had to find a way to shut her up.

Eleanor stepped into the bathroom. A minute later he heard the shower running. His wife lived by a schedule. He knew it would take her precisely twenty-five minutes to get ready to leave the house. That gave him half an hour minus five minutes to find a solution to the Letty problem.

It wasn't much time, but it would have to be enough.

****

By the time Jessie turned the Jeep off the county road onto Peach Street, the sun was up. She cracked a window and breathed in the fresh, cold air.

"That wasn't so hard, was it?"

Startled, she jerked the stick, and the car stuttered a few yards.

"How do you go from stone dead to fully aroused in a heartbeat?"

Ah Jeez. Nice choice of words. She shut her eyes.

"Look out," he said, calmly, "we're heading for a gnome."

Her eyes snapped open, and she gasped. She missed the figurine by inches but clipped a rooster-shaped mailbox.

"Pull over," he said.

She should have known he'd be a stickler for honesty. He might be a playboy, but she'd seen the silver medal in the parlor. Still, she protested.

"I barely touched the bird."

"This isn't about the mailbox. There's an ambulance in front of the rectory."

Jessie's mouth dropped open as she connected the dots. "Oh no! Eleanor Prendergast found out about the affair. The reverend must have murdered her, too!"

"Guess again, Sherlock. The action's next door. At Miss Letty's."

"Oh. Thank God. It's probably just indigestion. Francie told me all about her. She said she's prone to allergies and digestive attacks."

Luke indicated a black van pulling up behind the ambulance. "Guess that's why the medical examiner's here. He must've brought her Tums."

The first thing Jessie saw upon entering Miss Letty's parlor was Miss Letty's body draped over a short, grape-velvet sofa. From a distance she looked a little like a starlet lounging on a casting couch. Up close she looked more than ever like the Wicked Witch of the West. Death had turned her face the color of guacamole.

Jessie glanced away from the corpse and focused on the room. Miss Letty's long, narrow parlor resembled a crowded antique shop more than a home. Chairs, tables, lamps, and desks littered the floor like trees in a forest. The place was barely navigable. Floor-to-ceiling bookshelves filled each wall. There was a newspaper on the coffee table. It had turned the color of saffron the way newspapers do after only a few weeks. Curious, Jessie picked it up. It was an edition of the *New York Times* dated September Fifteenth. Three months ago.

Why on earth would the spinster keep an old paper like this?

Jessie scanned the headlines on the front page. The headliner was an anniversary story about 9/11. Further down was a piece on the city's s garbage strike. It was the one-column headline in the lower left-hand corner that caught her notice.

"Local Man Named in Macabre Celebrity Scandal."

She didn't get a chance to read the story. A middle-aged man built like a cube, his gray hair buzzed into a conservative cut, entered the parlor from a back hallway. He strode over to where she stood with Luke.

The newcomer slapped Luke on the shoulder and pumped his hand. Luke's rare smile twisted Jessie's heart.

"Coach," he said.

"It's Chief, now. I turned in my whistle for a badge. But, hell, Magic, you're grown up now."

"Call me Ezra."

Magic?

The older man read her confusion. He smiled. "Luke here had magic hands on the football field. By gosh, he coulda caught the sun if Zach threw it to him." His smile faded. "And Bobby, Bobby could run like the wind."

Luke's smile faded, too. He introduced Jessie.

The chief's gray eyes met hers. "I thought a lot of Blanche. Everybody did."

The words were kind. Jessie's instinct was to like the chief. She remembered he didn't believe Blanche had been murdered.

Ezra Smith turned back to Luke. "It's good to see you back here, boy. It's time you came home." Luke's lips tightened. He nodded at the body. "What happened here?"

Smith's shrug brought his chest up to his chin. "Natural causes. Preacher's wife found her half an hour ago. They were supposed to meet Edna at the bakery for a pageant meeting." He glanced at Jessie. "Edna's my better half."

Luke nodded. "You going to call for an autopsy?"

The chief rubbed his hand across the stubble on his triple chin. "County don't like to spend the money unless there's some sign of foul play."

"That's two deaths in six weeks."

Luke's words reverberated in Jessie's head. Two deaths in six weeks. Did that mean he believed the canasta witches' theory?

"They were old ladies, son."

Jessie could tell Luke wasn't buying it. She hoped that didn't mean he'd interfere with her investigation.

A wrenching sob grabbed Jessie's attention, and she recognized Eleanor Prendergast sitting on another flowered sofa, a lacy handkerchief in her hand. The preacher's wife wore the same serviceable coat she'd had on last night, but her thin red hair was disheveled and her face was the color of rice paper.

Poor soul.

Jessie started toward her, but Dennis Prendergast appeared in the door and neatly shoved Jessie aside. He sat on the sofa next to his wife. He picked up her hand, but he didn't put his arm around her shoulder or hold her close to him. Jessie's stomach churned. She hoped the poor woman never found out about her husband's infidelity.

"There, there, Ellie. It was just Letty's time. God called her home."

He pronounced the creator's name like a televangelist—Gawd.

Prendergast looked at Chief Smith. "I'll take Ellie on home now. She needs to lie down."

"In a minute." The chief knelt in front of Eleanor Prendergast, and his voice softened. "Is there anything else you can tell us? Anything you noticed?"

Eleanor let out another graceless sob, and just for a second, she buried her face in her hands. Her voice shook. "I blame myself, Chief. I was the last one to see her last night, too. We came home from the festival together, and I made her a hot drink."

"Coffee?"

"Tea, I think. Or maybe hot chocolate. I don't really remember. She'd gotten soaked, and we were trying to ward off a chill." Eleanor's pale eyes filled. "She'd been having some problems lately, shortness of breath. She'd promised me she'd see a doctor, but I don't think she ever did." Eleanor's homely face crumpled. "I should have at least walked her home."

"Edna said she looked upset last night. She was jumping around just about the time the storm hit."

Eleanor's face twisted as if she were trying to remember. "The Christmas pageant, I think. We haven't had enough rehearsals." The woman glanced at Jessie. "And, of course, she was beating the drum about morality."

Jessie's cheeks felt hot. She wanted to point out that she and Luke were keeping their distance in the big house, but there was no graceful way to say it. Ironically, it was Prendergast who changed the subject.

"Chief, can't this wait?"

"Certainly." Smith's voice was gentle when he addressed Eleanor. "Thank you, Mrs.

Prendergast." Then he stood and eyed the pastor. "Where were you last night?"

The question clearly caught the reverend off guard. He swallowed, convulsively. Jessie wondered why. Surely he'd expected the question. "I was at the festival," he said, finally.

77

"Did you return home immediately afterwards?"

"Of course."

"Then you must have been in the house when Mrs. Prendergast gave Miss Letty a cup of tea."

Two bright spots stood out on Prendergast's florid cheeks. "Oh, no, I wasn't there then. I'd forgotten. I stopped by the church to work on my Christmas Eve sermon."

Jessie flashed back to the moments in the closet. She avoided looking at Luke, but she felt his emerald eyes on her.

"You must have gotten soaked in the storm," Smith murmured.

"I keep a change of clothing in my office. You know. For emergencies. I got home shortly after Letty had left." He flashed a grin at his wife. "Both Eleanor and I were exhausted. We went straight to bed."

"What time was that?"

"Eight thirty," Eleanor said, with a sniff. She patted her eyes with a lace-edged handkerchief. "I remember hearing the clock in the hallway."

Jessie avoided Luke's eyes. At eight-thirty last night the reverend Prendergast had been up to his gonads in Lois Epps's mouth. Did Eleanor know? Was she trying to protect her philandering husband? Or was she just mistaken? Whatever it was, she hoped Luke wouldn't figure it out. The last thing she needed was his interference in her case, and she knew he was starting to get interested. Letty Appleby's unexplained death raised a red flag.

"Letty has no family," Prendergast told the chief. "I'll call Mort to come pick up the body, and I'll make the arrangements."

"What about an autopsy, Chief?" Luke's voice was quiet but authoritative.

"There's no indication of foul play," Ezra started to say. He stopped and let out a sigh. "All right. Hold off on those arrangements for a day or two, Reverend."

The minister looked even more irritated. Had he hoped for a quick, no-questions-asked cremation like the one they'd done with Blanche?

Ezra scratched his head. He flipped the pages in his spiral notepad. "You know, speaking of Mister Epps, Miss Letty spoke with me last night at the festival. Said she'd seen someone skulking outside the mortuary the previous night. You heard anything about that?"

Prendergast shrugged. "You know Letty. She saw a bogeyman behind every tree."

"In this case she was right," Jessie said, without thinking. "I saw a skulker, too. He was in the church parking lot. Last night. Around midnight."

She felt Luke's gaze on her, and blood surged into her cheeks. Too late she realized she'd given herself away. He had to know the best vantage point, the only vantage point for watching the church and mortuary from the witch hat house was from the window at the top of the back staircase; the window that looked out onto the driveway.

He had to know she'd waited up for him.

She spent the short drive home trying to figure out a plausible excuse for her midnight watch, but for some reason he didn't bring it up. Not even when they shared toast and eggs and their theories about Letty's death.

His question, when it came, was the last thing she expected. He leaned back in his chair, his arm outstretched on the table with a coffee cup in his hand.

"Why'd you run out on your wedding?"

No way was she going to tell him about the humiliating scene at the Happy Taco. "Cold feet. We were really more friends than anything else.

In the end, it seemed kind of silly to involve tulle."

"But you'd accepted his proposal."

She should tell him it was none of his business, but the words seemed to fall out of her mouth. Maybe she needed to confide in somebody.

"My dad owns a business—Maynard Properties, Inc. He needs to retire for health reasons and well, because my mom won't speak to him until he does. Kit is Dad's first lieutenant, and married to me, he could take over the whole shebang."

Luke leaned back in his chair and squinted at her. "So this wasn't about friendship. It was about business."

She shrugged, on the defensive. "Being in love is no guarantee of a successful marriage."

"You got me there."

A charged silence filled the room until Luke spoke again.

"Okay, Jessie. So what really made you run?"

The man saw way too much, but Jessie had confessed enough. "Turned out I hadn't read the fine print on the marriage contract."

Chapter Seven

The low-flow pressure of the shower spray didn't do much to wash away Luke's fatigue. It didn't relax him, either. He was on edge. He tried to convince himself it was being back in Mystic Hollow, back where he could run into Crystal, where all the old pain of the failed marriage would pile on top of the new pain of losing Blanche. But it was more than that.

He was way too intrigued by Blanche's great-niece. And that way, he knew, lay madness.

He wished it were only physical, but he couldn't fool himself. She was only a couple of years shy of thirty, but she carried a curious innocence, as though she'd missed the most important life experiences. And she had that warm heart. He knew he made her nervous, yet she'd waited up for him last night.

Then there were the sparks between them. But Luke was never getting serious about a woman again. No way. He'd never want to hurt anyone the way Crystal had hurt him. Especially not Blanche's great-niece. He needed to focus on his mission.

Unfortunately, his mission was watching out for Jessie Maynard.

He turned off the water and grabbed a towel. The rough terrycloth rubbed against him, reminding him of the way she'd ground herself against him last night. His body shot into launch mode. Well, damn. He thought he'd bought a little relief with his visit to the roadhouse.

Guess he was wrong.

He stared into the mirror, but he couldn't focus on his face. It was definitely time for a run.

Last night's storm had swept away the clouds, but the temperature had dropped. He wondered if there'd be snow for Christmas. He hit the pavement on Cobblestone Lane, circled St. Michael's, and turned left on Peach Street. Minutes later he pushed out gusts of visible air as he pounded out a run in the fields outside of town.

He'd run daily in Germany but since Blanche's death and his return to the U.S., he'd fallen behind. It felt good, invigorating. He picked up the pace hoping to clear his mind, but his thoughts kept returning to the same thing. If Letty had been murdered then maybe Blanche had been murdered, too. Her phone call had sounded deadly serious but not urgent. She'd asked him to come home. She'd asked him to keep an eye on Jessie. He'd understood on some instinctive level there was more to it, but what? Had Blanche known she was in danger? How the hell had she figured Jessie would show up?

Luke pounded out a few more steps. He was used to unanswered questions. He was used to waiting for the answers to appear. He just wasn't sure he could handle sleeping in the same house as Blanche's elfin great-niece.

Not that he'd slept there yet.

He jerked his thoughts back to his foster mother's death. If, as the old ladies claimed, Prendergast had killed Blanche, the question was why? To shut her up? And what about Letty? The woman never let grass grow under her feet. If she'd unearthed a secret about Prendergast, it had to have been last night. Now she was dead.

Coincidence? He didn't think so.

Something niggled at the back of his tired brain. He concentrated on his breathing and let it come to the surface. Finally, he had it. It was the lie. Eleanor Prendergast had lied about the time her husband got home last night. Why? Spousal loyalty? Had she long since reconciled herself to his philandering? Did she have any sense at all that she might be married to a murderer?

Except he didn't think Dennis Prendergast was a murderer. He was too shallow, too visible. He didn't blend. But if he hadn't killed Blanche and Miss Letty, who had? What about Prendergast's buddy, the cuckolded undertaker? Luke had only met him once, but he'd seen no humanity in Epps's eyes. Had he killed the old women to keep them quiet about his wife's affair? Or was there something else going on at St. Michael's?

Despite the plummeting temperatures, sweat trickled down his face and slid under the gray cotton jersey. He was panting now, heaving and blowing like an overworked horse. Maybe he should have tried harder to get some sleep. He pictured Jessie asleep up in the tower room. She'd be soft, flushed, warm under the quilt on Blanche's four-poster. Was she wearing a skimpy nightie bought for her honeymoon? The image sent a bolt of longing through Luke's tired body. He stumbled, his rhythmic stride interrupted. He kept on, refusing to give in to the discomfort.

Drenched with sweat, his breathing hoarse and

labored, he re-entered town from a different direction. Gradually he realized he was in a familiar neighborhood. This was Third Street.

Luke stopped dead in front of a two-story brick colonial. He knew he should keep walking to cool down, but he couldn't seem to make himself move. The same ruff of yew bushes separated the porch from the lawn. The wooden swing still hung from the beams on the front porch. The porch itself looked weathered, probably from the endless train of would-be suitors who never gave up trying to woo Crystal. That should have been a clue. If she'd loved Luke, she'd have turned everyone else away.

There was a lighted evergreen wreath on the door and a late model van in the driveway. The garage door started to move. Luke's heart shot up into his throat. He didn't want to see Crystal's folks. He told his feet to move but nothing happened. He was rooted in the street; rooted in the past.

A young woman with glasses and a snow suited baby on her hip stepped out of the garage. An unfamiliar young woman. She waved at him and called out. "Merry Christmas!"

Luke couldn't get enough air in his lungs to answer her.

The Wetheringtons had moved. He wouldn't see Crystal after all.

He finally started to jog but without any destination. It really was over. The dreaded confrontation wouldn't take place. He was free of his ex.

He didn't feel free.

He looked up to see Zach's old truck parked in

Francie's driveway. Jesus. He'd forgotten all about Francie's accident. He mounted the front steps and pounded on the door.

Zach appeared at the door. He looked like he'd aged ten years overnight.

Luke stared at his friend. "Is she all right?"

Francine must have heard him. She called out from the back of the house.

"Luke? Is that you? Come back here and see me."

He sprinted past Zach and down the short hallway to find Francie's bedroom. She was sitting up in bed dressed in puke green scrubs with an afghan pulled over her legs. Luxuriant red hair lay limp on her shoulders, and her face was Kabuki white except near the left temple where there was a bruise the size of a silver dollar. He sat down next to her.

"What happened, honey?"

"Don't jostle her. She's got a concussion." Luke ignored the man who filled the doorway.

"I'm okay," Francie said. She described what had happened blaming her own clumsiness. She was clearly trying to keep Zach out of it.

Luke nodded. "So he threw you on the floor."

"Pretty much." Francie's chuckle turned into a groan.

"Don't make her laugh, Tanner."

Christ. Luke shook his head at the other man's possessiveness. Maybe there was hope for this relationship, but at the moment Francie needed a break from her guard.

"The big guy here seems a little tense," he said, putting his arm around Francine. "How about we give him a break. Jessie can come and sit with you."

It was the perfect plan. It would give Luke a breather, too. If Jessie was with Francine, she couldn't get herself into trouble.

"I barely know her. I can't ask her to do that."

Luke waved away the objection. "She likes to be needed."

****

The Trumpet Voluntary jerked Jessie awake. The morning light slanted into the tower room at the same angle it had when she'd gone to sleep. She glanced at her watch and groaned. She'd tossed and turned and she'd only been asleep about twenty minutes, just long enough to relive the costume closet scene in a highly erotic dream.

She punched "speak."

"Whoever you are, I hate you."

"Hey baby. You sound soft and sexy. Forgiven me yet?"

Kit.

She couldn't keep the irritation out of her voice. "What do you want?"

"To apologize. I'd been drinking, and Mary Alice cornered me. I never meant to hurt you."

"You didn't hurt me." She pinched the bridge of her nose between her thumb and forefinger.

"You cheated on me."

"It didn't mean anything."

It certainly didn't mean anything to Jessie now. She sighed.

"Why are you calling?"

"It's the season of forgiveness, remember? The season of second chances. I want one. A second chance, I mean. We can still go to the islands. The tickets are good for a week, I checked. We can get married down there."

"You must really want a tan."

"I really want you. I screwed up, Jessie. Bad. Come to the islands with me."

The wave of disgust that rolled through her was aimed at herself. She couldn't believe she'd bought into his slick lines. "Take Mary Alice."

"No way. She ruined my first honeymoon."

"I thought you were all about second chances."

"C'mon, Jess. We can make this work. I know we can."

Jessie couldn't blame him for thinking that way. She'd thought the same thing until forty-eight hours ago. She tried to think of a way to short circuit the appeal. "It's too late, Kit. I've met someone else."

The stunned silence told her how completely he hadn't expected to hear that. Well, to be fair, it was a lie.

"Who?"

She only hesitated a second. "Aunt Blanche's foster son, Luke Tanner."

Kit took a moment to absorb that. "You've known him, how long? Two days?"

"When something's right, it's right," she said.

"Honey, he just wants Blanche's property. He's using you, Jessie."

She didn't bother to point out that Kit had used her, too.

"Listen, I'll make this right," he said, confidently. Kit always sounded confident. "I'm coming down there, darlin', and we're gonna get married."

She was starting to get bored with the conversation.

How on earth had she thought she could marry this man? "I'm not interested."

"I know what you're doing, babe. You're not serious about this guy, if he even exists. You're scared to death of commitment. That's why you're still single. It's why you agreed to marry me to solve your father's problems. As long as you can stay on the sidelines, keep your heart out of the mix, you're okay."

The words stung, probably because there was truth in them. "I didn't marry you, Kit. I came to my senses. I want you to leave me alone."

"You gotta get off the bench, babe," he continued as if he hadn't heard her. "You gotta get into the game."

"Maybe," she said, after a long pause. "But not with you."

She clicked off the phonem but she was still holding it when it rang again.

"The answer's still 'no.'"

"Elf?" The low voice rumbled through her like a powerful minor chord and her blood rushed.

"Can you come over to Francine's?"

****

He was bulletproof. God dammed bulletproof.

Adrenalin bubbled up Dennis Prendergast's chest like the fizz in ginger ale. No one but Letty knew about the affair. And Letty was no longer in a position to tell anything to anybody.

Ding dong the witch was dead.

He didn't dare get too cocky though. The Letty incident had been a warning. He needed to cut his losses and get out. He'd collect the big payoff on Christmas Eve, take Ellie and split.

In the meantime, he needed to get Lois under

control. She was turning into a loose cannon. He'd get her to agree to a little time apart.

He helped Eleanor up to their room, removed her shoes, and rubbed her feet. Then he covered her in an afghan.

"I'm all right," she protested. "I really don't need a nap."

"Doctor's orders," he said. He winked at her. "Doctor of Divinity. You close your eyes for a bit, and I'll be home in no time. I'll make you some lunch. Maybe a couple of Monte Cristo's."

"We're out of lunchmeat."

"I'll stop by Ferguson's. Will they know what I want if I tell them the name of the sandwich?"

Her thin pale cheeks creased in an approximation of a smile. "Never mind the market, Denny. I'll get up in a bit and take care of it."

He planted a chaste kiss on her cold cheek. "You, my dear, are the perfect wife."

A moment later a lighthearted Dennis Prendergast stepped out into the morning sun.

Although the church and mortuary were connected by an interior door, it was seldom used. Dennis had to hike around the church to the mortuary entrance on Potter Street. He didn't mind. The day was fine.

He mounted the steep steps to the door etched in gilt letters that read: J. Mortimer Epps Mortuary, Embalming A Specialty.

Daylight disappeared as he entered the shadowed foyer. The only illumination came from a small lamp on the reception desk. The bulb was strong enough to illuminate two familiar, bubble gum pink mounds. Lois's breasts. Gone was the distaste of last night.

Dennis's penis began to quiver.

"Mornin', sugar."

Her voice reminded him of her skillful, collagen-enhanced lips, her talented tongue. He watched, speechless, as she stepped out from behind the reception desk dressed in some kind of Spandex. The material hugged her body and created cleavage as deep as the Grand Canyon.

Dennis's body reacted immediately. He watched helplessly while Lois teased him by stretching her arms behind her. Her breasts jutted and jiggled.

Christ.

"Morning, Reverend," Mort said.

He seemed to appear out of nowhere, and Dennis quickly stepped forward to shake his hand, hoping Mort couldn't read his mind. Or his trousers.

"I stopped by to select a coffin for Letty." He was relieved his voice sounded normal. He gave Lois's chest a last glance before he followed Epps down the hall.

****

Jessie inhaled the fragrant smells of casseroles, cakes, cookies, and the warmth of camaraderie that mingled in Francine's small house. The women of Mystic Hollow pulled chairs from the kitchen and bedroom and formed a circle around the sofa where Francine rested next to Judy Reeves.

Jessie passed out cups of coffee and tea and kept an eye on the plate of doughnuts fresh from Molly's Bakery. Everyone expressed concern about Francine, but very soon the topic changed to Miss Letty's death.

"Poor Eleanor," Hermione Foote said. "I heard she was the one who found the body." Hermione, Jessie thought, was Olive Oyl to the mayor's Popeye.

Clara Ferguson nodded. She reminded Jessie of a stack of Firestones. Clara owned the market with her husband Frank and their son, Frank, Jr. She liked to share news, but unlike Letty who snooped and pried, she waited for it to come from the normal channels. "I know exactly what happened. Letty was shot clean through the heart."

"Where did you get that, dear?" It was Hattie Bexler, who, with her son and daughter-in-law, owned and operated Bexler's Drugs and the Emporium, Mystic Hollow's only general department store. Jessie suspected that Hattie and Clara were the kingpins of the Mystic Hollow Grapevine. "I heard from Horace that she was stabbed."

"Horace." Clara sniffed. "He can't even get the mail delivered to the right address."

Thelma Barstow lived on a pig farm several miles from town, and she apparently pulled no punches.

"I say she died of plum cussedness."

"Jessie was at Letty's house this morning," Mabel Ruth said, in what appeared to Jessie as a clear attempt to help straighten out the facts. "She actually saw the body."

All eyes focused on Jessie and a barrage of questions followed.

"You were there? Where did it happen? Were her eyes open? What was she wearing?

Jessie did her best to fill them in.

"She was on a sofa. Hadn't had a chance to go to bed, so she had on the clothes from the festival. She looked very peaceful."

"Peaceful." Clara shook her head. "That's a new

look for Letty."

"Well, I certainly hope Ezra calls for an autopsy," Judy Reeves said. "After that hushed up business with Blanche."

Jessie's ears perked up. So it wasn't just the witches who were suspicious about Blanche's death.

A motherly looking woman sat on Francie's other side. She'd been introduced as Charlotte Russell. Her voice was pleasant and kind.

"I've got to get to the hospital," she said, patting Francine's hand. "I'll see if I can't hurry those test results." She kissed Francie on the cheek before she left.

"Lottie's holding up well," said Judy Reeves. "I don't know how she does it. I'd have to be institutionalized if anything happened to either of my boys."

Jessie saw Francine flinch.

"Lottie's son, Bobby Ray, died in Iraq," Mabel Ruth explained to Jessie. "She works up at the hospital." The heavyset woman turned to Francine. "I imagine it was nice to see a friendly face last night."

The redhead's smile was wan. Was the lack of color just because of the head injury, or was Francie upset about Zach?

"I wonder," Maude said, thoughtfully, "if there was any connection between Letty's death and Blanche's."

Jessie was surprised at the smallest witch's insight. She realized this might be a good chance to hear more details about her aunt.

"What exactly happened with Great-Aunt Blanche?" she asked.

Clara Ferguson's brown eyes were bright with

indignation. "She was cremated the same day, poor old thing. Mort Epps claimed it was her wish, that she'd asked him to do it that way. But,

of course there's no proof."

That sounded pretty suspicious.

Thelma spoke up. "Did Letty look as if she'd been murdered?"

"There wasn't any sign of foul play," Jessie admitted. "It was just odd that she came home from the festival, sat down on the sofa, and died."

"I guess it could happen like that," Thelma said.

"It could," Millicent put in, "if it were anyone but Letty."

Judy Reeves nodded. "That woman knew too much for her own good."

"The chief mentioned that her throat was a little swollen," Jessie said, suddenly remembering.

"Oh. My. God." Mabel Ruth stuttered. Her kind eyes had rounded into dark plates giving her a stricken appearance. "She was allergic."

Jessie felt a prickling sensation on the back of her neck. "Allergic to what?"

"Strawberries," Millicent said promptly.

"Peanuts."

"And peanut products," Maude added.

"I'd forgotten all about that," Clara murmured. "We haven't stocked peanut butter for years, and I'd forgotten why."

"Just the scent of peanuts could put her into a coma," Millicent said. "She didn't like people to know."

Jessie felt a small shock of excitement. "We need to find out what she ate last night."

"I saw her at the festival," Clara said. "She was eating one of Molly's brownies."

Food continued as the topic of discussion until most of the visitors left. Mabel Ruth, Millicent, and Maude cleaned up the kitchen while Jessie tucked Francine back into bed.

"You've got enough casseroles and cakes for a month."

"That's Mystic Hollow. Folks believe everything from a broken leg to a broken heart can be cured with a homemade coconut cake.

Most of the time they're right."

"Zach's mother seems nice."

"The whole family's great. There's a younger brother and their dad. Carl owns a garage. I always thought Zach would work there after he mustered out and we got married. Instead, when he brought Bobby Ray's body back, he broke up with me."

Jessie felt a wave of sympathy for her new friend. How horrible to have your dreams snatched away with no reason given. Jessie's dreams had been snatched away, too, but Kit hadn't broken her heart. She sat in a rocker near the bed. She sensed Francie needed to talk.

"He thinks I cheated on him with Bobby Ray," Francine said, in a low voice. "He found letters and things."

"Forged, of course."

Francie smiled, faintly. "Thanks for the vote of confidence." She sighed. "I don't know. I don't understand what happened. It's like an atomic bomb went off in my life and left it shredded. Bobby had my class ring, too. I worked two jobs to buy that thing. It had an azure stone, the color of Zach's eyes. Everybody knows how important it is to me. I can't figure it out. Bobby and I were friends. Why would he lie to Zach?"

"And why would Zach believe him," Jessie murmured.

"That part I finally get." Francie sounded bitter. "The bottom line, he wants out." Her chocolate brown eyes filled with tears. "And that's not the worst of it. I'm pregnant. He doesn't love me or want me, but when he finds out, he's going to insist on marriage."

"You could say no," Jessie suggested, gently.

"I will say no," Francie said, her voice thick with despair, "but he'll never give up. Never. Duty is more important to Zach than anything, including his feelings. And mine."

While Francie dozed, Jessie joined Mabel Ruth, Millicent, and Maude in the small living room. They spoke in quiet tones.

"Mark my words, girls. Prendergast killed Letty for the same reason he killed Blanche," Millicent echoed Jessie's earlier thoughts. "They knew too much."

Mabel Ruth nodded, sagely. "This is all about the secret."

The secret. Jessie suddenly realized there was another secret the old ladies didn't know. She opened her mouth to tell them, but no words came out. How could she talk about sex to three elderly spinsters?

"What is it, dear?" Millicent asked. "You look like a startled codfish."

Jessie sucked in a breath. She needed to keep them in the loop. After all, they wanted to nail Blanche's killer nearly as much as she did.

She described the tryst, omitting some of the juicier details.

"Good goddess!" Millicent breathed. "The man's a married minister!"

"Of course. That's why he keeps the church locked," Mabel Ruth said, grimly.

"Were they just embracing," Maude asked, "or was it the whole hog?"

Jessie laughed. "It was most of the hog. We were really just ear witnesses."

"We?" Mabel Ruth looked intrigued.

Nuts. Her face flamed. But then, she'd done nothing wrong. Not really. They had been trapped together behind the stable.

"Luke was there. He'd heard me snooping around upstairs when he came in to put the tables and chairs away."

"That must have been a bit, well, awkward," Millicent commented.

Jessie appreciated the understated understanding. "It was."

Jessie's annoying ringtone interrupted them and she quickly answered the phone.

"Elf?"

She ignored the burst of excitement she felt and corrected him. "My name is Jessie."

He ignored that. "The chief called. I've got a list of stomach contents here. See if it means anything to Mabel and the others."

"Shoot."

"Chocolate, milk, flour, egg, oatmeal, and peanut oil."

Jessie let out a little shriek. "Murder by peanut oil."

The old ladies exchanged a grim glance.

"Looks like Prendergast bagged another one,"

Millicent said.

"Now, Mil, we don't know that for certain," Mabel Ruth reminded her.

"We know it," Maude said, with uncharacteristic fierceness. "But we need proof."

Francine emerged from the bedroom, still pale, but insisting she felt much better. Jessie was wild to start investigating Letty's death, but she'd promised to stay with her friend. Besides, she didn't know exactly where to start.

Apparently Mabel Ruth could read her mind. "There's only one place to get the answers we need," she said. "The horse's mouth. Francine, dear, where do you keep your board?"

Chapter Eight

Mystic Hollow had no public Fax machine.

He shouldn't have been so surprised. After all, a town whose market stocked only rot-gut beer, was a town stuck back in the '50's.

So, because of Mystic's retro ways and because he refused to drag his heels in getting the final loan for marketing his search machine, Luke found himself driving the twenty-five miles to Roanoke. It wasn't all bad. He got a good cup of coffee. Besides, it removed him from temptation.

It also removed him from his job as protector of that temptation.

Now it was early afternoon, and he was sitting in traffic on I-81. He stared broodingly, at the snowflakes that drifted onto his windshield. Maybe the Shenandoah Valley would have a white Christmas this year.

Christmas! He sat up straight. Surely Jessie Maynard would go home for Christmas. She had Norman Rockwell written all over her. It was already December Twenty-second. Would she leave today? Tomorrow? He told himself not to get his hopes up, but his spirit lightened anyway.

If Jessie would only go home for Christmas, he could leave Mystic Hollow for the last time. He could return to his unfurnished D.C. apartment. He could leave the emotional past behind and start fresh. Alone.

He frowned. The idea wasn't as compelling as it should have been. Naturally he'd have preferred a warm home and a welcoming woman, but it wasn't in the cards.

Crystal's "Dear John" e-mail had taken care of that. Bitterness erupted inside him, and he snapped on the radio. The flakes, it turned out, were a scouting party. The rest of the frozen troops were scheduled to descend tonight. His gut tightened.

He'd be snowed in tonight in a warm house with a wary woman; one he couldn't touch. He forced himself to focus on Letty Appleby's death.

He had a feeling he'd find an answer or two at the J. Mortimer Epps Mortuary: Embalming Specialty.

****

If he'd had his druthers, Dennis wouldn't have bothered with a three-thousand-dollar, coffin but he had to keep up appearances. Everyone knew Miss Leticia Appleby didn't approve of cremation. She'd made a big enough fuss about it after Blanche Maynard's death. So here he was, pretending to care about her final resting place when all he wanted to do was find a hole and throw her in.

"That one." He pointed to the first one he saw. Dark veneer with a blue lining. "Smith should release her tomorrow," he told the mortician. "You can pick her up at the M.E.'s office in Roanoke."

Mort nodded.

"We'll have the service tomorrow evening. I'd like to get it out of the way before Christmas.

Mort looked at him over the top of heavily rimmed glasses. "I would think so."

Dennis gulped. Christmas Eve would be a big day. The annual Christmas pageant was always the most important event in Mystic Hollow. There was also the matter of the much-anticipated payoff. Half a mil. This would be the last one, he promised himself. The deal had turned rancid. It wasn't worth the sleepless nights, the sense of always looking over his shoulder.

Mort slid a piece of paper in front of him. It was a form to release money from Letty's estate for burial expenses. Dennis didn't check to see whether he was authorizing anything else. Sometimes it was better not to know.

Their business completed, Mort accompanied him to the reception area.

"I'll be busy with an embalming for the next hour or two," the mortician told his wife before he disappeared down the darkened hallway.

Dennis looked at Lois. His anxiety level was so high he barely noticed the magical breasts. He knew he had to break it off with her.

"We have to talk," he said, in a low voice.

She came out from behind the desk, took his arm and squeezed it. "Sure," she said, "I know just the place. Lots of privacy."

He shouldn't have been surprised at his reaction to her heavy perfume and the jiggling flesh pressed against his side. Christ. He'd turned into one of Pavlov's dogs. Show him a mammary gland and he'd salivate. She drew him into the showroom he'd just left. The walnut box was still standing there with its lid up, a grim reminder of Letty's future. Everyone's future, he thought, glumly. Even his. He shook off the gloomy thoughts.

"We can't go on like this," he told Lois. Before he could finish his thought, she had her hands inside his charcoal velour shirt.

"Like what, sugar?"

Dennis tried to ignore the way her palms felt against his slightly convex naked chest. "It's too dangerous. We're playing with fire."

"Um-hmm." She was only half listening. Most of her attention was on his Italian leather belt. She loosened the buckle with one hand before he could protest.

"No," he mumbled. Lois ignored the protest and sought the thick flesh inside his pants. She began to stroke using the right amount of pressure to drive him insane. His eyes rolled up in his head.

"God, that feels good."

"And I can make it feel better."

She rubbed and squeezed until he groaned and then, without letting go, she tugged him across the room, a cow led to slaughter.

"What're you doing?" By now he was so turned on he didn't really care.

She stopped when she reached Miss Letty's open coffin.

"Lie down," she commanded. "Let's play Dracula."

****

Maude closed the living room curtains and turned off all the lights, while Millicent lit five fat white candles and set them on the card table that Mabel Ruth pulled out of Francie's closet. While the older ladies set everything up, Jessie helped Francine into a clean, burgundy colored sweat suit.

She couldn't resist a question. "Do you do this often? Consult the Ouija Board, I mean."

Francie smiled. "You want to know whether I believe in it. Well, I'll tell you. I don't know. My mom was my only family and she died nearly ten years ago. I think there are spirits or unseen hands or whatever you want to call them. They've sustained me on more than one occasion."

"Some people might call that God."

"Sure. And some would call it an overactive imagination."

"Mabel Ruth and the others seriously believe in magic," Jessie said.

Francie nodded. "That makes it more fun."

Moments later Jessie rested her fingers on the plastic planchette. Francine sat opposite her.

"I call upon the corners and the elements." Mabel Ruth's deep, pleasant voice rolled throughout the room. "I call upon the animals and the spirits, the goddess and her horned consort. We wish to speak with the recently departed."

Maude and Millicent began to hum like a couple of occult backup singers. Jessie and Francine exchanged an amused smile.

"Pierce the veil, Letty," Mabel Ruth chanted. "Come back one last time. What happened to you last night?"

The planchette was as still as a stone dropped in a quiet stream.

Nothing.

Crickets.

Mabel Ruth didn't seem to notice. With her eyes squeezed shut, she kept chanting, and Maude and Millicent kept humming, and finally, Jessie felt a faint vibration. Francie's brown eyes widened. She'd felt it, too.

The plastic pointer began to swoop and circle, like a skater feeling out the ice. The first circles covered the whole board, but they got smaller and smaller, as if zeroing in on a target. Then, as suddenly as it had started, the planchette stopped. Jessie shivered. Francine's cozy living room felt like the inside of a cave.

"S," Millicent called out.

Jessie concentrated on keeping her touch feather light. If Miss Letty was speaking to them she didn't want to interrupt. The planchette began to move again, this time fast and then faster. It barely paused over the letters, and Millicent rattled them off.

"S.Y.N.E.R."

The movement stopped.

"Synergy?" Jessie guessed, pleased with her powers of deduction.

"Sinner," Millicent corrected. "Spirits can't spell for beans."

The planchette moved again.

"R.A.T.H."

Jessie looked at Millicent.

"Wrath," the older woman interpreted. She sniffed, and her voice took on a chastising tone. "All right, Letty, stop being so judgmental. We know you're angry. Give us something we can work with."

The planchette started to spin and soar.

Letters appeared with lightning speed.

"B.O.S.I.M.L."

"Bossy Mil." Millicent frowned. "You were the bossy one, Letty. You turned into a regular old hag."

"Stop bickering," Mabel Ruth whispered. "And

you, Letty, stop beating around the bush."

"Obstinate," Millicent griped. "Just like she was in life."

The planchette whirled and swooped.

"E.G.G.S," Millicent read. She shrugged.

"Eggs?"

The five women searched each other's faces.

The planchette stopped in the center of the board, the temperature rose, and one of the candles flickered out.

"She's finished," Mabel Ruth said. "She's gone."

"She left us with eggs," Maude said.

"More like egg on our faces," Millicent grumbled.

Jessie stared at Francine. She knew she should be trying to figure out the message, but for some reason her mind kept drifting back to last night's surreal experience in the church closet. She felt the warmth of Luke's body around her. She heard his constricted breathing. She jumped as someone cried out. Prendergast at the moment of climax.

"I've got it," she said, in a too loud voice. "It isn't 'eggs.' It's 'Epps.'"

"Gracious Goddess," Maude breathed. "Does that mean Mr. Epps is the murderer?"

"Or it could be Lois Epps," Mabel Ruth said. "Letty didn't specify."

"Nonsense," Millicent huffed. "It's Prendergast. Prendergast killed them both."

Maude sighed. "Mil, just because he closed the library doesn't make him a murderer."

"Infidelity could drive a man crazy," Francine put in, quietly. "If he were already unstable, it could probably drive him to murder."

"Then wouldn't he kill the faithless wife?" Millicent asked.

"Not necessarily," Mabel Ruth said. "Perhaps he couldn't face the humiliation of having everyone know about her affair."

"I still think there's more to it," Jessie said, thinking hard. "Epps is probably involved in whatever is going on at St. Michael's. What we need to do is figure out where he was last night."

"You mean whether he could have gotten the peanut oil into Letty's system," Maude said.

"Exactly. I think a little visit to the undertaker is indicated."

"Jessie." Mabel Ruth's voice was sharp, authoritative. "I don't want you going there alone. There have already been two deaths."

Jessie nodded. She didn't want to lie to her aunt's best friend, but she didn't know how to explain her odd compulsion. For some reason it was important to do this herself. Excitement mixed with trepidation rocketed through her. The investigation was about to be well and truly launched.

****

Eleanor Prendergast sliced the baked chicken. Soon she would mix it with a special blend of olive oil and spices. Then she'd combine it with the vegetables she'd chopped into precisely equal bite-sized bits. Mushrooms, broccoli, carrots, leeks. It was a healthy recipe, one of several she'd developed to help in Denny's battle of the bulge. She herself didn't have a weight problem.

She'd lost her appetite years ago.

She glanced at the wall calendar she'd received

courtesy of the J. Mortimer Epps Mortuary. Only four days until Christmas. It was past time to finish up the details on the annual Christmas pageant and to decorate the church with fresh evergreens, bright red bows, and slim white candles. This would be her twentieth year as a pastor's wife. She'd spent a fifth of a century decorating churches, directing pageants, teaching church school, visiting the sick, and providing a home for her husband.

She had little to show for her efforts: A spic-and-span duplex that didn't belong to her, acquaintances but not friends, a life of service but no career of her own, a faithless spouse.

Eleanor paused, her paring knife poised in the air. She knew she was an object of pity to the people of Mystic Hollow, but it didn't bother her. This wasn't the life she'd have chosen, but she'd found satisfaction in it.

Eleanor pushed down on the knife and made a sharp, clean cut through a crisp carrot. There was always honor in a job well done.

A few moments later she slid the casserole into the oven and set the table for her husband's supper.

****

Lois Epps's breasts were hard to miss. They bobbed in the spandex top like a couple of buoys on the waves. She had a way of directing attention to them by slipping her finger under the fabric, taking in a quick little breath, slightly arching her back.

It was wasted effort. The breasts were a flagship and, probably, a business asset. Luke could imagine a newly bereaved husband so distracted he didn't notice the humongous cost of a funeral. Epps should have them insured.

The mortician's wife moved so close he could smell tic-tacs on her breath.

"It's Luke Tanner, isn't it? I hope condolences aren't in order."

He smiled faintly. "No. I'm just here to pick up a copy of Blanche Maynard's death certificate."

Lois's smile gleamed. Her teeth were slightly crooked, like pickets in an aging fence.

"I'll have to get permission from Mort, and he's tied up with an embalming. Maybe you'd like a tour while you wait."

She managed to make it sound like she was offering a roll in the hay. Maybe she was.

"Great."

She slipped her hand through his arm, as if she needed his support. One bulbous breast pressed against him. The movement recalled the feel of Jessie's resilient curves and he tensed. He could tell by Lois's smile that she knew it. What's more she'd taken the credit.

"I've heard business is good," he said.

"Yeah. Mort's doing a land-rush in the embalming business. Lots of times the family decides to use the churchyard here. It's kind of quaint."

The oversized breast squashed against him. Luke began to develop a little sympathy for Dennis Prendergast. The preacher's wife was nice but essentially sexless. In contrast, Lois was as lush as the Garden of Eden.

They'd just stepped inside the coffin showroom when the phone rang. Lois answered an extension but quickly put the caller on hold.

"It's a contract," she told Luke. "I need to handle it with the computer. Wait here for me?"

"Could you direct me to the men's room?"

Her eyes sparkled and she winked.

She probably figured he planned to duck in there and slip on a condom.

Chapter Nine

As soon as Lois's well-padded butt disappeared down the hall, Luke slipped into the showroom office. The top desk drawer contained individual keys, all but one identified by bits of tape. It was the unmarked key that he scooped into his hand.

He ducked back into the "L" shaped hallway and turned the corner. He walked past the embalming room, the office, the kitchen, the crematorium. The last door on the end contained no label. With his sixth sense screaming in his ear, he fitted the key to the lock, turned the knob, and walked into a tomb.

There were no windows, no lights, no air.

He moved his fingers along the wall and found a switch.

Suddenly the darkness exploded into a blinding, white-hot glare. Pain stabbed the backs of his eyes and forced them shut. He'd fallen into the sun. Or maybe this was Hell.

He opened his eyes gradually, wincing at the glare. After a moment, he realized the unsettling effect was caused by the brilliance of the megawatt overhead light as it bounced off shiny surfaces. He opened his eyes wider. It looked as if Epps had papered the room in stainless steel.

Everything was metal, all the countertops, drawers, cabinets, and tables. A refrigerator that could have supported half a dozen catering companies took up most of one wall.

He began to open cupboards and pull out drawers. Inside were an array of surgical instruments including scalpels, cutters, picks, sutures, and scissors. A cabinet contained lengths of pipe. Plumbing pipe?

What was the mortician doing? Building Frankenstein?

Luke pulled open the refrigerator door.

It was deep enough to hold a dozen bodies awaiting burial at sea. A dozen. Why on earth did J. Mortimer Epps need that kind of capacity? Was he storing corpses? For who? The mob?

Luke poked around the surgery a little more, but all he found was a second, smaller refrigerator, this one filled with soft drinks and a couple of sandwiches. Smelled like tuna fish.

A hissing sound behind him made his heart jerk. No one was ever able to sneak up on him. J. Mortimer Epps moved like a ghost.

"May I ask what you are doing in here, Mr. Tanner?"

Luke studied Epps's face. It looked like a skull with the hollowed out eye sockets, prominent bones, and skin the color of a winter moon. Luke's attention quickly shifted to the revolver in the mortician's hand.

J. Mortimer Epps was certainly not your garden variety mortician.

Luke indicated the sandwich. "Looking for lunch."

It was hard to read the mortician's eyes behind Coke-bottle lens set in dark frames, but Luke watched a muscle move in his ill-defined jaw.

"This isn't a cafeteria."

"I came to get your records on Blanche Maynard," Luke said, easily.

"Surely you didn't mistake this for my office."

"To tell you the truth, Mr. Epps, I am having as much trouble figuring out what this room is used for as I am understanding why you've got that weapon in your hand."

"None of your business."

Luke contemplated the other man. "Fair enough. I have some questions that are my business. Why, for instance, was Blanche cremated on the day of her death? What was the damn hurry?"

Epps's expression didn't change. "There was no reason to wait. There was no family to consult. We made an attempt to reach you, Mr. Tanner." The arrow hit home. Guilt sliced through him.

"You moved very fast."

Epps shrugged. "I'm a busy man."

Luke nodded at the refrigerator. "A busy man with a lot of business. You could fit several football teams in there."

"We harvest organs, Mr. Tanner, for donation. They have to be kept cool."

"What about the plumbing pipe? Surely that's not all for bathroom repair."

The muscle moved again in Epps's jaw. He fingered his lapel, his right hand moving nearer the gun. "Interested in mortuary science, Mr. Tanner? If so, I'll start the tour with the crematorium."

****

The Mystic Hollow Emporium was heavily geared toward winter in the mountains, so Jessie bought several oversized lumberjack shirts, a pair of overalls, a yellow slicker, black fishing boots, and a couple of Christmas-themed sweatshirts as well as hot chocolate mix, popcorn, cranberries, and a turkey. She might have to celebrate Christmas alone, but she'd do it up right. Besides, maybe Luke would still be around. They could roast chestnuts over an open fire. She imagined the two of them cuddling on Blanche's Victorian sofa, then she shook her head.

That wasn't going to happen.

Still, Christmas was Christmas. Jessie's spirits rose, and she stuck out her tongue to catch the first crystals of snow.

By the time she got her purchases back to the witch hat house, it was four p.m., and snow was falling steadily. She deposited her packages in the kitchen. She wondered if it was too late to drop in on Epps. She could say she needed Blanche's files or something. Hastily she shed the too-large parka and slipped into her boots and slicker.

It was time to get some answers.

The only person in the dimly-lit reception area was Lois Epps, dressed in some kind of bubble-gum pink leotard. Unorthodox choice of clothing for an undertaker's wife, but then, as Jessie had reason to know, Lois was unorthodox for any kind of wife.

The brunette nodded to take a seat while she finished a phone call. Jessie let her eyes wander the room looking for clues. She didn't know exactly what she expected to find. A half-opened bottle of peanut oil? She allowed herself briefly to admire J. Mortimer Epps. Death-induced by an allergic reaction. It was almost the perfect murder.

Naturally there was nothing in the room but

comfortable chairs, brochures about the business, a magazine titled "Rest in Peace." She shuddered and got to her feet. Lois's voice was hushed, but Jessie heard the tension in it. Was she talking to her lover? It was clear she was paying no attention at all to Jessie who took the opportunity to sidle down a narrow corridor. Either Lois would stop her or J. Mortimer's skeletal form would jump out of from behind a closed door and scare her to death or she'd get a chance to take a look around.

She could hear her heartbeat as she tiptoed down the silent hallway. The doors were open revealing an office, a small living room, a chapel, and a coffin showroom. The door marked "Crematorium" was closed as was a second, unmarked door. Jessie was pretty sure there was someone in the latter. She pressed her ear against it. Two men. One was clearly agitated, angry, even. The other was familiar. Her stomach clenched. Oh shit.

Luke was trapped with a murderer!

There was no time to formulate a good plan. She threw her fist against the door and shrieked at the top of her lungs.

****

It was all bravado. The mortician was trying to intimidate him, but Luke recognized the fear under the mask. He watched the pistol tremble in the other man's hand. He knew there was nothing more dangerous than a guy with a nervous trigger finger. It was probably time to get out, but he wanted some answers. He kept his voice quiet, calm.

"What's really going on here, Epps?"

The mortician took a step toward him just as a

banshee shriek tomahawked through the air. It was accompanied by door pounding worthy of the Gestapo.

"Lucas Tanner! I know you're in there. You come out here this instant!"

Luke's heart sank while Epps cursed and winced. What the hell was she doing here? Her hysteria was shredding what was left of the undertaker's nerves. There was no telling who he'd shoot. Damn Jessie anyway. How was he supposed to protect her? "Ignore that," Luke muttered.

"If only that were possible," Epps barked. He jerked open the door, and someone catapulted into the room.

It was the Morton Salt Girl.

She ignored Epps as she marched up to Luke and wagged a finger in his face.

"Lucas Tanner," she shouted, "How dare you stand me up?"

Epps's face twisted in fury. "Miss Maynard, this is a mortuary. We try to maintain a sense of decorum here."

She turned toward the mortician as if she'd just noticed him. Would he attack her? More likely she'd attack him. She was a warrior princess. Luke balanced his weight on the balls of his feet, prepared to intervene, but the elf surprised him. She flashed Epps a smile so bright it reflected off the stainless steel surfaces.

"I beg your pardon, Mr. Epps," she said, in a conciliatory voice. "I am so sorry for the interruption. But I'm sure you'll agree that I have a right to be angry. This guy"—she jerked her thumb at Luke without taking her eyes off the mortician—"was supposed to pick me up forty minutes ago. We've got an appointment to get our blood tests."

Epps frowned, apparently as confused as Luke. "Blood tests?"

"For the license," Jessie continued. "We agreed to get married the day after Christmas."

We agreed to get married?

Luke stared at her. He was uncomfortably aware her declaration had taken his mind off the real threat in the room.

"Unless," Jessie said, her narrowed eyes lasered on Luke, "you weren't serious. Promises in the dark are easy to make."

He wanted to tell her he didn't make promises he didn't mean which was why he didn't make promises. He wanted to scoop her up, throw her out into the snow, and roll her home. He knew they were in real danger. The guy was a mortician. He could shoot them, cremate them, and dump the ashes before anyone noticed they were missing. He had to get her out of the mortuary, and there was only one sure way to do it.

He looked at Epps as he moved toward Jessie and placed his big body between her and the gun. "Sorry, man. We'll have to continue our tour some time that's more convenient for my ball and chain." He grabbed Jessie's arm and dragged her toward the door.

"I'm sorry, too, Mr. Epps," Jessie called out over her shoulder, "but when a girl gets a live one, she can't afford to let any grass grow under her feet." She directed her next comment to Luke. "Think the jewelry store in Roanoke'll be open tonight? I can't wait to buy a ring."

"Just a minute," Epps said, blocking the door. "I want to know exactly why you were snooping around my business."

Jessie let out a peal of silvery laughter that startled Luke. "I'll let you in on a little secret," she said to the mortician. "Luke doesn't like people to know, but he's a writer."

Epps looked as confused as Luke felt.

"Mystery novels, you know. He was over here doing research."

It was lame. Weak. Luke didn't think Epps would buy it, but he never got a chance to find out. The door opened again and Lois, preceded by her breasts, stepped into the room.

"There you are," she said, batting her eyelashes at Luke. "I can finish giving you that tour."

He stared at Lois. "May I have a rain check? I'm tied up right now."

Epps looked from Luke to Jessie to his wife.

"They're getting married," he said.

"The day after Christmas," Jessie bubbled. "It's kind of last minute, but we hope you can both attend."

Luke knew the Mystic Hollow grapevine. Snowstorm or not, by tomorrow morning, everyone in town would think he was marrying Jessie Maynard. For real.

Luke didn't speak as they negotiated the steep, snow-covered steps from the mortuary's front door, crossed the church parking lot, jaywalked at the corner of Church and Cobblestone, and cut across Blanche Maynard's lawn. Luke didn't speak, and Jessie didn't stop chattering. His heart raced, his gut throbbed, and a vein beat in his forehead. By the time he'd closed the front door behind them, his adrenalin flow had reached critical mass. He grabbed her upper arms, shoved her against the door, and glared into the golden eyes. His breath came hard, causing her to blink.

"I'm sorry about the engagement thing," she said, "but it was all I could think of."

"God dammit Jessie!"

"This doesn't have to be a big deal," she reasoned. She obviously wasn't the least bit afraid of him. "We'll just say it was a mistake."

He ignored that. "What the hell were you doing at the mortuary?"

Her shoulders straightened, and her chin thrust out. "What was I doing? I was rescuing you, you dope."

Rescuing him.

He dug his fingers into her shoulders. "Listen to me. This isn't some kind of a game to distract you from your failed wedding. Two women are dead, and if you're not goddam careful, there'll be a third. Epps had a gun."

The color left her face. "I didn't see it."

"He kept it behind his back. You've got to keep your pretty little nose out of this business."

An expression came and went across her features, but she didn't back down. "I want to solve the murders."

He let go of her and thrust long fingers through his hair. He felt unutterably weary. "Jesus Christ, Jessie."

"This doesn't involve you, Luke. You're not responsible for me."

Only he was. That was his problem in a nutshell. He forced himself to take a couple of deep breaths.

"Let's get back to basics. Why did you go to the funeral home?"

She shrugged, a dismissive gesture that infuriated

him. "We got a tip."

"What do you mean 'we'?"

"From Letty. She talked to us through the Ouija Board."

"Oh my god." He wanted to thread his fingers through her snow-dampened brown curls. He wanted to haul her soft curves against him, tuck her under his chin. He wanted to slip his hands inside the slicker and feel her warm skin. He felt his body stir. Things were going from bad to worse. He forced his mind back to the cockeyed conversation.

"Jessie, Mabel Ruth and the others like the idea of witchcraft, but believe me, they're mostly in it for the jewelry."

"Maybe." Her soft slips spread into a grin. "But you can't deny Epps is a great suspect.

Maybe Letty decided to use the Ouija Board to finger her murderer."

****

Jessie poured homemade soup out of a plastic container, warmed it up, and poured it into two flat bowls. She set them on the table while Luke poured them each a glass of wine.

It was probably the quietest meal in the history of the room, especially in contrast to the supper Jessie had shared last night with the Tuesday witches. Luke was clearly upset. Because they'd narrowly escaped danger? Or because of the 'engagement?' Probably the latter.

"I really am sorry," she said. "That business about the blood tests was the first thing I thought of."

"You've got marriage on your mind."

She thought about Kit's call. She could erase the past few days as if they'd never happened. She could go home for Christmas, marry Kit in a quiet ceremony, and provide the solution to all her family's problems.

"Or maybe," Luke continued, unaware of the direction her thoughts had taken, "it's because of the chemistry between us. I think it's time to acknowledge that."

His frankness surprised her. "Okay."

"But this can't go anywhere."

His voice was surprisingly gentle, but it embarrassed her that he knew she wanted him. At least he didn't know she'd never felt this way before.

"No. Of course, not."

He frowned. Apparently he didn't like her answer. "Only because of the circumstances. If you were anyone but Blanche's niece, we could enjoy each other for the time we're here."

"Ships passing in the night."

His brows lifted. "Yeah."

The silence in the room was broken only by the sounds of spoons scraping against china and by the cloud of sexual tension.

"Was it like this with your fiancé?"

The question surprised her. If the funny look on his face was any indication, it surprised him, too.

"I thought we were going to avoid the subject of sex."

His eyes flared. She knew he was turned on. She felt an insane urge to crawl into his lap and slide her fingers under his sweatshirt.

"I'm just making conversation. So was it?"

She wasn't going to lie. "Not really."

"That why you ran?"

Maybe it should have been.

"I found him at the rehearsal dinner with his ex-wife's mouth attached to his genitals."

The green eyes reflected shock followed by anger. Anger, she thought, at Kit for hurting her. Something moved inside her chest. Luke Tanner had a strong protective streak. She wondered why he was still alone.

"The guy was an ass," he said.

Jessie wanted to change the subject. "You never told me why you were at the mortuary?"

He leaned back in his chair. He was an impressive specimen in his gray sweatshirt printed with the word "Army." His shoulders were as wide as the Shenandoah, and she already knew how safe a woman could feel sheltered against his hard torso.

Of course "safe" was a relative term.

"I was snooping, too. Even without the benefit of words from the other side, I figured out Epps was involved in all this."

Excitement warred with possessiveness. This was her investigation. Still, she couldn't afford to pass up any information. "And?"

"That room we were in. It's a fully-outfitted, state-of-the-art surgery. Like something you'd find in a hospital."

"Maybe it's where they do the embalming."

He shook his head. "Then it's overkill. There has to be some other reason a small town funeral director would spend tens of thousands of dollars on all that equipment."

She thought about that. "Maybe that's where they remove organs for donation."

"Epps mentioned that."

Jessie eyed him. "But you're not buying it."

"I think there's something else."

"What?"

He shook his head. "Don't know yet."

It was kind of a relief that he hadn't already figured it out. That gave her time.

"We should call some mortuaries out of the area," she suggested. "Find out if that kind of equipment is really necessary."

"Not a bad idea."

She grinned. "Maybe you could be my Watson."

He picked up her hand and studied it. It looked impossibly small in his big palm. Small but safe. He lifted it to his lips and her heart somersaulted.

"I want you to do something for me," he said, in a quiet voice. She caught a sudden vision of the two of them up in her bed, their bodies naked and sweaty, their breath short and fast, their cries filling the room.

"What?"

"I want you to go home."

She swallowed hard, her throat dry with regret. "I can't do that."

He didn't argue. He just got up and cleared the table. After they'd finished the dishes and wiped down the counters, he pulled a stack of clean towels out of a cupboard in the pantry.

"Sponge bath?"

"Funny girl. They're for Pye."

Chapter Ten

As soon as he was sure the cat was comfortable in the parlor, Luke beat a path upstairs to his bedroom. Pye wasn't in any hurry to deliver, and he needed a break from Jessie.

The elf was driving him crazy and not only because she insisted on throwing herself into danger. She heated his blood. He didn't understand it. He'd had plenty of sex in his day, but he'd never felt a woman's lure like this. Not since Crystal. It was probably the isolation and the fact that Jessie was off limits. Whatever. He was damn tired of being hard and helpless to do anything about it.

He polished off a couple of beers while he searched the internet on his laptop. He wished his own search engine was ready to go. He needed a lot more specificity than he could get from Google or Yahoo.

He was aware of commotion in the hall outside his door. He ignored it for a while, but curiosity won out. He stepped into the corridor to find her trying to balance a pile of cardboard boxes.

"What's all this?"

"Aunt Blanche's Christmas decorations. I figured I'd put them out."

"Why?"

She shrugged and didn't answer at once. He thought he glimpsed a suspicious gleam in her golden eyes. Of course. She was homesick. In exile. He refrained from suggesting the obvious solution.

"Give me the boxes."

After he helped her haul the stuff downstairs, he helped her unload it. Her delight in the old, somewhat shabby decorations was fascinating. Crystal had hated everything about the old Victorian house, including him.

Jessie looked more than ever like an elf as she cavorted around the parlor hanging a garland from the mantelpiece, arranging the crèche, setting out the ornaments that would go on the tree—if there was a tree.

"Oh, look at these," she exclaimed. She held up two red felt stockings with "Jessie" and "Jillian" spelled out in sequins. "She must have made these for us and saved them all these years."

He heard a tremor in her voice.

"I wish I'd made a bigger effort to come and see her. I don't know why the family stopped coming here for Christmas."

Luke had his own ideas on that. He suspected that Blanche, once she'd taken him in, had wanted to keep him away from the nieces. He'd been trouble cubed.

"She knew you cared about her," he heard himself saying. "She used to talk about you and your sister."

The bright smile on her face rewarded him. It also made him hot. He headed for the kitchen. "I need another beer."

He stood at Blanche's sink and stared out at the garden buried under the snow. Who would stake the tomatoes next summer? Who would pick the raspberries and turn zucchini into fragrant loaves of bread? He remembered the last time he'd seen Blanche. It had been here in this kitchen on Christmas Day two years ago. Crystal had started in on him about his plans to leave in the morning, and Blanche, in an effort to give them privacy, had taken the backstairs up to her room.

The sense of loss was almost unbearable. It seemed like he'd been alone all his life. It seemed like that would continue till he was six feet under.

Jessie's quick footsteps in the butler's pantry broke his bleak reverie. She burst into the room.

"Oh my gosh, Luke. You can't believe what I found. It's so perfect and beautiful. Here—" She flipped on the kitchen light and held an object up in the air. "Look how it reflects the light."

It was a tiny glass angel blown by an artisan so talented he or she managed to achieve an almost lifelike face and a slim, graceful body. Her wings were as delicate as those of a hummingbird and she held in her arms a newborn child.

He recognized it instantly, and a guttural cry ripped out of his throat. He heard the snap of shattered glass, heard her yelp of dismay and pain. He closed the distance between them and forced her fingers to open. Worms of blood wiggled across her palm. Needle-sharp shards stood rooted in her flesh.

Goddam it all to hell.

He took her good hand and dragged her over to the sink where he found the first aid kit Blanche had used on him so many times. He gripped her hand in one of his and extracted the shards embedded in her skin. She flinched but she didn't cry out.

"I'm sorry," she whispered.

He concentrated on the task. When he'd finished, he cleaned the wounds with warm water and dressed them with antiseptic. Then he wrapped a thin strip of gauze around the hand, between the thumb and forefinger and secured it with tape.

"We'll hit the E.R. in the morning."

Jessie put her unhurt hand against his face. Her eyes were soft and comforting.

"The angel was special wasn't she? She was a gift to Aunt Blanche?"

He didn't want her to stop touching him, and he hated himself for it. He knew his words would hurt her. "The angel was a gift to my wife."

"Your wife?" She looked around as if she thought Crystal might be hiding behind the trashcan or behind the refrigerator.

"Ex-wife."

"Oh."

She sounded what? Shocked? Relieved?

Disappointed in him? Probably all three.

"You're not together anymore."

"That's what divorce means."

"What was her name?"

"Crystal."

"Crystal. That's why you bought her a glass angel."

The elf's obvious emotion about his spoiled marriage was starting to get on his nerves. "I bought her the angel because I thought she'd like it. Crystal liked beautiful things."

"Was she beautiful?"

Surpassingly. "Yeah."

"Oh, Luke. What happened?"

He ought to tell her to mind her own business, but he didn't. He figured it was as good a time as any for a lesson in reality. He gave her his fiercest look.

"She divorced me, Jessie, because I was a terrible husband."

Jessie blinked. "That's not why."

****

Jessie leaned against the front of the Victorian sofa. Pye moved restlessly on the nest of blankets next to her. Jessie felt certain the birth was about to begin. She wondered if she should go get Luke, but surely he'd check on the cat. A minute later he opened the glass doors that connected the parlor with the foyer.

He kept his gaze on the animal. Jessie heard him murmur something, and then he was building up the fire. He knelt on the stone hearth and poked twists of paper in between the logs. Then he took a long match out of a box on the mantelpiece and started the blaze. Tongues of fire lit the harsh planes and angles of his face. Jessie thought she'd never seen a man so appealing, or so alone.

He'd loved and trusted someone enough to get married. He'd wanted a picket fence and a golden retriever. She wondered what could have possessed the beautiful Crystal to divorce him. There was nothing in this world or the next that could induce her, Jessie, to leave a man like Luke. Not if he loved her.

The truth hit her like a bolt out of the blue. It wasn't just chemistry. She was falling in love with a man who no longer believed in it.

She sure knew how to pick 'em.

He turned to her, tall, fit, impossibly masculine. Jessie wondered what he would say.

"Why," he asked, "does it smell like toothpaste in here?"

She blinked. "It's a peppermint candle. The scent is supposed to be soothing. I read about it on a Lamaze website."

His gaze glanced over the bowl of ice chips and at Blanche's old radio which Jessie had turned to a station playing Christmas carols.

"You do remember she's a cat."

"A special cat. She told you she was cold, didn't she?"

His green eyes glittered at her. She dropped her gaze and noticed, with a shock, the bulge in his pants.

"Maybe you are a witch, Jessie Maynard," he said. Their gazes held for what seemed like forever. He wanted her, but he wasn't going to do anything about it. For some reason the realization was unbearably disappointing. She looked down at the cat. She peered more closely at the slimy, dark object the size of a miniature Baby Ruth.

Was that what she thought it was?

"First one out of the chute," he said.

"Oh my god," Jessie cried. "Do you think I could touch it?" She looked at the cat. "May I?" Pyewacket blinked.

Luke knelt next to them. "Nice job," he said.

The green eyes glittered.

"I think she said 'fuck you.'"

"The cat version of it."

"Well, that's normal for laboring moms."

He held Jessie's gaze. "Good to know."

By the time five kittens had been born, Luke was feeding ice chips to the cat. He'd punched up the fire several times, always returning to the feline's side. His strong fingers were gentle when he stroked Pye's head. Jessie's heart melted even as she worried about the mother cat. How long could all this writhing and birthing go on? "How many do you think there are?"

"Nine," he said.

"Did she tell you that?"

"I did a little weight ratio calculation. It's an estimate."

"Nine. Wow. Think she'll be all right?"

"She'll be fine." Luke's voice was confident, easy. Jessie stared at him. "What?"

"You're a good birth coach. You'd make a good dad."

He shook his head. "You are such a hopeless romantic. You've known me two days."

"Well, I might be a witch. And I've always had good instincts about people." She remembered Kit. "Usually. My ex wants a second chance."

She didn't know why she'd confided that. He couldn't be interested in it.

"You gonna give him one?"

She shook her head. "Would you give your ex a second chance?"

"It's not the same. She left me."

"But if she came to her senses. If she came back."

A resigned look came over his face. "Crystal left me because I failed her, okay? I am not the knight in shining armor you think I am."

It was humiliating to have revealed her feelings. She wanted to deny what she'd said, but that would be even more humiliating.

They waited for the rest of the kittens in silence.

****

Dennis Prendergast pushed himself away from the kitchen table after the second helping. He could have handled a third, but then he'd have to redouble his weight loss efforts to make up for it. Not that he'd mind. His mind drifted back to this morning's coffin sex. Lois was a sexual genius. How could he have even contemplated ending the relationship? A satisfied smile crawled across his face. It soon disappeared when he thought about all the complications.

The deaths were already stirring people up. Folks from outside would start showing up, including the county sheriff's department. The powers that be at the synod who usually left regional churches to themselves had started to call him to report complaints.

He was scared to death of his partner in crime.

Yeah. Intellectually, he knew it was time to move on, but Holy Smoke. He'd miss Lois's talented tongue.

They'd stay till the pay off on Christmas Eve. Maybe a day or two more. It might be awhile before he found someone like Lois. He imagined her skillful hands on him, and he moaned. It might be a long time.

"Are you feeling well?"

His wife's words of concern brought him back to the present. He smiled at the milk-pale woman across from him. She'd been a perfect wife for him. He reached across to touch her cold fingers. "Great meal," he said. "As always."

She got up, carried their plates to the sink, and began to scrape bits of food into a bin. She spoke without looking at him.

"Denny, do you ever want something more?"

He looked at the back of her head. The pink and

white scalp showed through her thin strands of graying red hair.

"Never," he said. "I have everything I need."

She looked up and smiled. He felt a flash of discomfort when he realized how seldom he saw that smile. Maybe she wanted something else. Well, he'd buy it for her. This last payoff would be a big one.

"The world's our oyster, Ellie," he said, expansively. "And you are my pearl."

"When will you hold the service for Letty?"

"Tomorrow afternoon, weather permitting. I don't know as we'll be able to dig a hole in all this snow. Might have to let Mort keep the body a day or two longer." He chuckled. "At least she's finally shut up."

"Denny!"

He winced at the sharpness in her tone.

"Letty Appleby was a human being. One of God's creatures. Her death isn't something to joke about."

It was as close as she'd come to lecturing him. Of course she had no idea what he was up to. He hoped she never found out.

"We'll give her a good send-off," he promised. "Could you get me a toothpick?" He dug at the food between his teeth for a minute while she watched him.

"You left your cell phone here this morning."

He grimaced. "It's heavy. I didn't want to stretch out my good wool slacks."

She pulled something out of the pocket of her apron. It was a small, gaily wrapped gift. She placed it, shyly, in front of him.

"What's this?"

"A Christmas gift. An early one."

"Aw, El, you shouldn't have." He ripped open the

package to find a small, sleek cell phone.

"Fantastic!"

"Your pants are safe," she said.

Not only that, he could start over. No more stored phone numbers that someone might find.

"You're the best," he said.

****

"I'm worried about Jessie," Mabel Ruth told the two women sitting at Millicent's Formica topped table. The trio had gathered on Pine Street in the kitchen of the anorexic brownstone that was the Underhill family home.

"She seems to be thriving in Mystic Hollow," Millicent pointed out. "She's made friends with Francine."

"And she seems to be getting along with Lucas," Maude said. "You know that's what Blanche was hoping for."

A long, heavy pair of earrings bearing the images of the sun and the moon tangled with Mabel Ruth's long hair as she shook her head. She found she couldn't shake off her concern. "Lucas hasn't made peace with the past."

"Perhaps we could help things along," Maude suggested.

"You know that isn't kosher, Maudie," Mabel Ruth admonished. "No tampering with matters of the heart."

"Perhaps it isn't as serious as you think," Millicent offered.

Mabel Ruth shook her head. "I've seen the way she looks at him."

"What way?" Millicent asked.

"The same way he used to look at Crystal

Wetherington."

"You mean Crystal Tanner," Millicent said, heavily.

"Blanche always said Luke was a one-woman man," Mabel Ruth replied. "I'm afraid Jessie is going to get her heart broken."

Chapter Eleven

The eight black kittens in the toilet paper nest looked less like bite-sized candy bars than like dark chocolate Easter eggs, Jessie decided. Either way, they were adorable.

It had been a long night, longer for some than others. Pye was exhausted. Jessie had fortified herself with three beers—two over her limit—out of anxiety for the cat and agitation at Luke's proximity. The room was mellow and hazy as she leaned back against the sofa. There was room for another person between her and Luke but she could still feel heat and it wasn't coming from the fire.

She felt curiously content, and she sighed drawing his attention.

"What?"

She covered her mouth as if to impart a state secret. "I think the beer is making me horny."

She knew instantly it was a mistake. His face hardened with a familiar tension. "So," she said, grabbing the first topic that came to mind. "I never heard the story of how you wound up with my great aunt."

His gaze shifted back to the fire.

"What happened to safe subjects like religion or politics?"

She tilted her head to one side and squinted at him.

133

"I'd guess you are a lapsed Protestant and socially conscious, fiscally conservative Republican."

A reluctant smile stretched across his face.

He leaned his head back and closed his eyes.

"I got in some trouble. She heard about it. Blanche could never resist a challenge."

Jessie tried to picture a teenage Luke. He'd have been heart-stoppingly attractive with his nearly black hair, his green eyes, his athletic build, the rebellious chip on his shoulder. Great-Aunt Blanche had been a brave woman.

"Were you in the foster system a long time?"

"Nine years. Nine homes."

Pain sliced saber-like through her heart. So many partings. So much rejection. Maybe his wife had left because he'd never learned to bond with people. She glanced at the fingers stroking the cat's head. He did just fine with animals.

"What kind of trouble?"

"Petty stuff at first. Shoplifting. Weed. Joyriding."

"And when Aunt Blanche found you?"

The green eyes met hers. "I got a girl in trouble. Her dad hauled me into court."

Her heart twisted.

"Aren't you going to ask if it was my baby?"

Her answer was instinctive. "I know that if it was you'd take responsibility."

"Jesus, Jessie." He palmed the back of his neck.

She wondered if he was stiff.

"Take off the rose-colored glasses."

"What happened?"

He looked away. "Nothing. She got an abortion."

Jessie wondered if he was even aware of the regret she heard in his voice. "Hero," she whispered.

He moved quickly like the athlete he'd been. All at once she was on her feet, her body pressed against his so tightly she couldn't tell whether the drumming heartbeat she heard was hers or his. She tried to tell him he could take his time, that she wanted this, but the minute she opened her mouth his came down over it. The kiss wasn't gentle. Instantly he was in full possession, and she felt completely dominated. Her body melted like butter, and she ground herself against him with all her strength. He ripped his mouth away, panting.

"Jesus, Jessie."

"You said that before," she murmured.

His big hands came up to her face, and he held it still as his tongue, his clever, talented tongue, tasted her lips and explored the moist warmth behind her teeth. Her knees trembled.

"Put your arms around my neck," he suggested in a husky whisper.

Brilliant idea. The move gave him free access to the skin under her sweater. His hands—strong, rough, calloused—gently abraded the soft flesh, caused a heaviness in her breasts.

"Higher," she murmured. "Harder."

He let out a choked sound and deftly unhooked her bra. How much experience had he had with this? The question died when the masculine fingers found the undersides of her breasts, found the tightly furled tips. Every stroke triggered a small explosion inside her. She gasped. "Oh! Oh! Oh! Oh!"

Jessie's response seemed to galvanize him. He

snaked one hand up her back while the other continued its tantalizing work. She felt surrounded by this man, owned by him.

"Wait," she puffed.

He froze. "You don't want this."

She held his gaze while her hands found his belt. "I want this and more."

Her words sent a tremor through his body.

Or maybe it was her action. He seemed to hold his breath while she fumbled with his belt buckle. "I'll do it," he bit out.

An instant later she lifted him in her hands. He was heavy, hot, pulsing with need. She ran her fingers up and down the hard length, marveling at the thick vein, the smooth stretched skin, the velvet tip, and the heavy sacs underneath. He was fiercely male, and at the moment, he was all hers.

He endured the exploration at first but need seemed to crash in on him and he thrust heavily into her hands.

"Jessie," he moaned.

She had a sudden, irresistible urge to pleasure him. Without letting go she dropped to her knees and cautiously took him into her mouth. His fingers tightened in her curls, and he breathed another curse. A sense of power ignited her and she sucked. Hard. His cry didn't mask the other sound in the room, a cat's frightened whimper. Jessie felt a moment's regret then all her attention centered on the animal. She quickly detached herself and moved closer to Pye.

Pyewacket's sides bellowed in and out like an overworked racehorse. Her beautiful green eyes were slits in the feline face.

Fear replaced lust, and tears gathered behind

Jessie's eyes. Was Luke's cat going to die?

"I'm going to call a vet," she said, even knowing Santa Claus himself couldn't get out in the storm.

"Wait." Luke, with his pants still unzipped, focused on the patient. His fingers worked over her swollen body, his voice was gentle, soothing.

"You can do this, girl. Just one more."

He kept up soft, encouraging words in a way that made Jessie's heart melt. She was sure no female would be immune to his tenderness, and as the seconds passed and Pye's pitiful whimpers eased, it looked like she was right. Luke continued to massage the cat, but he muttered to Jessie. "Sing. It'll divert her attention." Sing? Sing what? Inna Gadda Davita?

She watched Luke push on the cat's belly. If he could do that she could sing. She opened her mouth then heard an off key melody and the words of an old song.

"What's new pussycat? Whoa, whoa, whoa, whoa…"

The last kitten dropped. Its fur was pale gray.

"Busted," Luke whispered. "Now we know the papa is that old tom of Maude's."

The tenderness in his deep voice filled Jessie's eyes. She hid the emotion by offering Pyewacket an ice chip. The small pink tongue licked at it a few times then Pyewacket closed her eyes and went to sleep. They checked the newborns and leaned back against the sofa.

"Thank God that's over," Luke murmured.

"You saved her. Hero."

He lifted one dark brow. "Don't you ever learn?"

She held his gaze. "Hero, hero, hero, hero, hero."

And then she was on her back on Blanche's thin

carpet. This time the clothes were shoved out of the way without any words. He rose up over her, wide shoulders blocking the glow of the fire, his fierce expression disappearing as his mouth took hers in a thrusting, searing kiss. His fingers dropped to his swollen flesh, and he surged into her. The entry was tight but slick, and Jessie's hips came up to meet him. A harsh groan rumbled up through his rib cage and shook her. His muscles stiffened and he lifted his head. She felt the pleasure zephyr through him and her heart swelled.

"I love you," she whispered.

Even in the midst of the climax his face twisted.

It was the wrong thing to say, but it was the truth.

He didn't allow himself to collapse on her. Instead, he held himself away, his arms trembling, his breath expelling in rough bursts, his kryptonite eyes harsh, unforgiving. As soon as he collected himself he got to his feet.

"What a disaster."

Was he referring to the too-speedy execution? "I liked it," she replied.

He scrubbed his hands down his face then he glared at her. "Don't you ever get tired of sacrificing yourself? Christ. You need some self-preservation skills."

"Teach me," she said. She'd meant it as a joke, but he wasn't laughing.

"Ah, Jessie. Haven't you figured it out yet?
You'll never get anything from me."

****

A faint scent of cedar mixed with vanilla filled the room as Great-Aunt Blanche stretched out her arms and hovered over the bed. Jessie strained to hear, but she couldn't distinguish any words. Apparently spirits had as much trouble with enunciation as they did with spelling.

Jessie's eyes popped open. The room was empty. Had Blanche been a dream? An apparition? Had she been trying to tell Jessie something? Warn her?

A quick, hot memory of twisting bodies—hers and Luke's—slammed into her. Her body throbbed with a need that wouldn't be satisfied. She knew Luke regretted what had happened downstairs, but she didn't. He was wrong about her.

Okay, the marriage to Kit was a dumb idea, but making love with Luke, well it was the high point of her life. He'd shown her possibilities.

He'd shown her how good sex could be when love was involved, even if it was only on one side.

She threw her legs over the side of the four poster and walked to the window. She should have been cold in her peach and green negligee, but she wasn't. She reminded herself she'd come here to regroup, and she'd taken on the murder investigation. This stuff with Luke was a bonus. She grimaced as she remembered the wedding photo and the crystal angel. Luke was clearly still hung up on his ex-wife.

Could Jessie help him get over Crystal?

Maybe. If she had enough time.

She crossed the room, sat on the chintz covered window seat, and gazed out at the snow-saturated, sleeping town. How quiet it was after a storm. In only two days she'd gotten attached to the town, its people, and Blanche's house. For the first time in her life, she'd really opened her heart to those outside her family. It felt scary but good. The window seat shimmied under her weight. Curious, she ran her fingers under the edge and found a latch.

A moment later she extracted a musty smelling, leather-bound book from the cupboard inside the seat. Jessie's heart beat faster. There were no words on the cover and there was no name inside but it clearly belonged to Blanche. She recognized her great aunt's neat handwriting in the words written on the flyleaf.

My Book of Shadows.

A witch's diary! Would it contain spells? Recipes for magic potions? Would there be a clue about who killed the two old ladies?

Would there be secrets about Luke's marriage?

She scowled. She probably shouldn't be reading something as private as a diary at all, much less hoping to unearth secrets Luke obviously didn't want her to know.

On the other hand, maybe Blanche had left the book here. The ladies seemed to think Blanche expected her.

A shiver wriggled down her spine. She'd better take a look at this in bed. As soon as she stood, something slipped out of the book and landed face down on the floor. It was a snapshot of a bride and groom. Jessie picked it up, slid back into bed, and turned on the bedside light.

She examined the Polaroid. It had been taken under Blanche's arbor out front but instead of dead vines, the lattice work was covered in rich green leaves. It was a perfect backdrop, but Jessie suspected no one ever appreciated it. The newlyweds commanded all eyes, especially the statuesque bride, with her flaxen hair sculpted into a smooth, elaborate up-do, her photogenic features, her swan-like neck, and model-sleek figure outlined in white satin. Her eyes, framed by thick, dark lashes, were a startling amethyst color as she smiled at the photographer. Next to her the dark-haired groom looked elegantly masculine in a black tuxedo, a sprig of lilies of the valley in his collar. It wasn't possible to see his eyes, but Jessie knew they were a sparkling emerald green. His face was in profile as he gazed at the woman who had just become his wife.

It was a perfect picture of a couple in love. Luke's eyes glistened in a way they never had with Jessie. Jessie's heart ached for his loss and for her own.

She leafed through the book and found another photograph. This one was taken earlier but also in front of the witch hat house. Three teenaged boys stood together, their arms resting on each other's shoulders. Luke stood on the left, his green eyes ancient in his young face. Zach Reeves was on the right. There was a serious expression in his sky blue eyes. In the center was a blond, young man whose eyes crinkled at the corners and whose grin lit the picture.

Jessie glanced at the writing on the back and her heart clenched at time's inevitable changes. The third boy was Mystic Hollow's golden boy, the late Bobby Ray Russell. Just for a moment Jessie sympathized with Zach. Bobby Ray would have drawn any woman's eye.

Jessie looked at the heart wrenching pictures for a long time. Finally, she put them down and started to read. Jessie noted dates as far back as the 1950s. She knew Blanche had only taken up witchcraft in recent months. Had she changed the diary's purpose as well as its name? Jessie scanned the entries. It might as well be called A Social History of Mystic Hollow.

There was no way she could read it all. Not tonight. Jessie leafed through the book searching for the words, Prendergast, witch, and St. Michael's.

The church was listed in an entry dated more than thirty years earlier. Earl Russell had been engaged to Charlotte Stewart since high school, and the wedding at St. Michael's was set for October. That summer, Blanche noted, Earl began to spend time at the toy shop where pretty Judy Chatham worked with her father. Blanche noted that the wedding of Earl and Lottie went ahead as scheduled and a month later Judy married Karl Reeves. Five months later Zachary arrived.

"Some might blame me for recording this, but it is information that could be important someday. I hope not."

Jessie went very still. She glanced again at the photo of the boys. Was Zach Reeves really Earl Russell's son? If so, did Earl know? Did Zach know? How had the families lived all these years side by side with such a secret? Because whether Earl knew or not, surely Judy did and probably her husband, too.

Did the secret have anything to do with Zach's refusal to believe Francine?

"St. Michael's" appeared again in a heartbreaking note of a funeral. "Marie Tanner, a seamstress," Blanche wrote, "was killed in a hit and run accident. She leaves behind a seven-year-old son."

Jessie felt the little boy's pain. A tear dropped onto the yellowed page before she could stop it. She wiped her eyes. Eager to find what she sought, Jessie skipped ahead until she found Blanche's notation that she'd taken responsibility for Lucas Tanner. His behavior, she wrote, had been scandalous, but within a few months he'd settled down with her. Jessie smiled to herself. Blanche was proud of Luke. She wrote not of his football victories or his academic achievements, she wrote of his character.

"He's a good young man, only he doesn't know it."

Luke's marriage to Crystal was recorded with a date and the details of the wedding at St. Michael's. There was no comment on Crystal Wetherington Tanner, at least none that Jessie could see. Had Blanche worried about the union? Had she known Crystal would break his heart? She paged ahead and found the divorce recorded three years later, again without comment.

Jessie leaned back into the pillows exhausted after the emotional walk down memory lane. It was like reading a heart-tugging novel only it hurt more because she loved the main character.

After a few minutes Jessie got back to work. She searched for some mention of the problems at the church, Reverend Prendergast, and the mortician, but she found nothing. The pastor's wife, though, rated a paragraph.

"I can't help sympathizing with Eleanor Prendergast. I have met with her several times and find her a pleasant, unassuming woman, dedicated to the church and her husband, but heart heavy. Perhaps she wanted a child and was unable to have one. She has not confided in me."

Great-Aunt Blanche had a lot of insight. Eleanor Prendergast bore the burden of an unfaithful spouse, one whose infidelities, if they were discovered, would look larger than life to the residents of Mystic Hollow. Jessie felt sorry for the woman, too.

She never did find anything about the secret at St. Michael's, but the last entry grabbed her attention. She read it through several times.

"I helped Lottie go through Bobby Ray's things over at the Russell's. I found an envelope that contained correspondence addressed to Bobby Ray in Iraq. They were typed and signed by Francine. Each appeared to be a love letter, and I did not understand as Francine has long been in love with Zachary Reeves. Perhaps I shouldn't have pried, but I confess I did."

"In the final paragraph of each letter were penciled lines under every fifth word. It was a code. Something compelled me to decipher that code, and I discovered a sad truth."

"Bobby Ray was carrying on with Crystal."

Jessie felt the heaviness in Blanche's words.

"Lucas must never find out. It no longer matters as he is divorced from the woman, but the knowledge of the *affaire de Coeur* would break his heart all over again."

Jessie turned out the bedside light and stared into the dark while she tried to decide what to do. This information would be invaluable to Francie and Zach. It would set them free to have the future they'd planned. On the other hand, Jessie knew Blanche had been right. It would devastate Luke.

Jessie weighed the matter for a long time, but in the end, there was no real choice. She turned the light back on, ripped the page out of the Book of Shadows, and ripped it into tiny shreds. She left them in a little pile on the bedside table to throw away in the morning. She turned out the light, but just as she was settling back into the bed, the door opened.

He leaned against the frame, backlit by a faint light. His broad chest was bare, his arms folded over it. Long, muscular legs were encased in half-zipped jeans. The thick dark hair was rumpled. She couldn't make out his features, but she knew they were set in a hard expression. She knew the emerald eyes were glittering.

The poster boy from hell.

There was no mistaking his purpose. Adrenalin shot through her system, and she felt her lips stretch into a grin.

"Merry Christmas to me," she murmured.

Chapter Twelve

It had been a mistake. A fatal mistake.

He'd betrayed Jessie. He'd betrayed Blanche.

And he'd betrayed himself.

God dammit all.

The minutes crawled as Luke shifted and tossed on sheets damp from his sweat. He didn't know which was worse, knowing he'd hammered the last nail into his coffin or knowing he'd do it again.

Finally, he got to his feet and paced the room. Despite the winter cool and his bare chest, he was suffocating. He thrust long fingers into his hair and rubbed the back of his neck. Every muscle was knotted, and blood poured into his lower body like a raging river. He stopped in front of a window and scowled at the snow.

How had it come to this? He hadn't felt this urgency, this desperation since he was a teenager and got his first look at the ice queen. He'd lost his head. And he'd lost his pride, too. Hell, the instant he'd slipped into her tight little passage he'd come like a bull. Damn.

He wore out the carpet as he reviewed his options. There weren't many. He might be able to walk away from the elf, but he couldn't ignore his debt to Blanche. Basically he had two choices, and one of those was divine intervention.

God dammit. There'd be no miracle. Hell, he didn't deserve a miracle. Not this time. He faced his future with a grim determination.

He'd have to marry Jessie Maynard.

It wasn't all bad. He liked Jessie. She'd have made a good friend. And she was a surprising lover. His body stirred as he realized his decision meant they could have all the sex they wanted. Luke felt his body harden.

Goddam. Maybe they'd be okay as long as she understood. Luke could give her his name, his worldly goods and his body, but he couldn't give her his heart.

He pictured her sleepy-eyed, warm and welcoming in the four-poster bed, and his jeans tightened. It was uncomfortable, but it wouldn't be for long.

When he opened the door of her room the light from the hallway revealed the dark gold of her eyes. She was awake. She said nothing as he moved toward the bed but he could see the shock on her face and the response of her body under the filmy fabric of her nightgown.

His voice came out in a husky growl. "Your nipples are hard."

****

Jessie couldn't get enough oxygen. Fire exploded in her belly. Hot liquid pooled between her legs preparing her for entry. His entry. He wanted her, too. She couldn't miss the excitement in his kryptonite eyes or in the impressive bulge between his legs.

He sank onto the bed, and the warmth of his body engulfed her. He reeked of restlessness, his hair disheveled, a sheen of sweat on his muscled torso. She should probably ask why the change of heart, but she didn't. It was enough that he was here.

His palm grazed the underside of her chin, and her heart thundered. She leaned toward him like a daisy seeking the sun. Her hand moved to his lap.

"Is this a gun in your pocket, or are you just happy to see me?"

His hand pressed against hers, and she felt the thrusting masculine flesh imprisoned in denim.

"You figure it out."

His breathing roughened, but the moan came from her.

His other hand gently cupped her barely clad breast, and she arched, craving more. And she got more when he pushed the negligee out of the way and took one aching nipple into his mouth. His other hand shoved aside the covers, and his fingers stroked her, inside and out, over and over. She felt invaded, possessed. Desire turned to need, and she felt herself tightening and twisting moving toward a promise of paradise. She wanted him to come along with her. She reached for him, but he angled away. The rejection was harsh, brutal, and short-lived.

"If you touch me now," he breathed, "it'll be all over before it begins."

Her lashes fluttered shut, and she focused on his touch. Soon she started the spiral. She clutched at dark curls on his chest, felt the slab of hard, hot muscle under her fingers, turned her face up to find his mouth.

"Who knew," Luke whispered as she rocked against his hand, moaned against his mouth, "elves were so sexy?"

The pleasure ambushed her, and with a broken cry, she shot into the stratosphere. Afterward she couldn't stop kissing him, his cheeks, his ear, his neck, the flat hard plain of his stomach, and then she came to the half-open zipper. His big body spasmed.

"I want to kiss you," she said.

She took his strangled growl as a yes, and she shifted into a more comfortable position with her knees straddling his legs. She put her hand on the zipper, bumping against his erection, and she began very slowly to unzip. After each half-inch, she pressed her face against him. She felt him tremble with need.

"You're killin' me, Elf."

She lifted her head. "I just want you to enjoy this gear for a while."

He dug his hands into her curls. "If I enjoy it much longer, I'll have a stroke."

A sense of power flooded her. She, plain Jessie Maynard, was giving him pleasure, this man who'd probably made love with dozens of women, who'd been married to a virtual goddess. She opened his pants, stroked the bulging vein in the thick shaft, caressed the testicles pulled up tight against his body, and took his fierce arousal into her mouth.

Luke groaned heavily, arched up, and exploded. She yelped and gagged.

"Jesus Christ," he said, when he could talk again. "I thought I'd suffocated you."

Chagrin swamped her. Way to spoil the moment. "I was just surprised."

He was silent a moment, and then he sat up and took her face in his hands. He searched it for a moment. "Not something you usually do?"

"Not so much." Make that, not ever.

"Did it bring back bad memories?"

Her eyes widened. Trust Luke to make the

connection with her disastrous rehearsal dinner. Of course he was wrong. She'd been thinking of nothing, and no one besides the man who'd bewitched her. She touched his hard cheek.

"I'm sorry I spoiled it. Could I have a do over?"

His chuckle warmed her from the inside out. "Give me a few minutes. And for the record, Elf, it was the best I've ever had."

An exaggeration, she decided, but still nice to hear.

He pulled her against him and flipped the quilt over them both. She curled against him, loving the way his heart pounded, rhythmic and hard, loving the way he stroked her back, loving him.

"Christ," he said, sleepily. "If we're gonna keep this up, I better buy some condoms."

****

Jessie slid under the bubbles in the claw footed bathtub.

Much as she hated to admit it, Kit had been right. She'd spent her life rescuing her family, guarding her heart. Making love with Luke had felt somehow transcendent. She was a new woman, a powerful, self-assured, desirable woman. She wasn't, however, a woman who was loved. Nobody got everything they wanted. She accepted that. But that being the case, there was no way she could indulge in a do-over. Luke would just have to use his soon-to-be-bought condoms on somebody else.

The water lost its heat, and she hefted herself out and into a fluffy towel. She didn't examine whether her shiver was from the cool air on her wet skin or on the disappointment she refused to let herself feel.

Luke was wrong. She did have some self-protective instincts, and they were screaming a dire warning in her ear. She wanted to run away again, but this time she wouldn't do it. This time she'd stand her ground. She just hoped she didn't have to stand that ground too long. Who had murdered Blanche and Letty? She'd focus all her efforts on the investigation. She'd forget that she'd fallen for the wrong man. Again.

Luke wasn't the wrong man, Jessie immediately corrected herself. He was a man too wounded to return her affection.

Jessie gazed into the oval mirror over Blanche's washstand. She looked the same—hazel eyes, untamed curls, a slightly irregular nose, lips that were a trifle too thin, and a chin that was a trifle too strong. She wasn't the same though. She no longer lived on the surface of her emotions. Blanche's green-eyed, bad seed of a foster son had opened her heart. Maybe she could return the favor, teach him that it was safe to love, safe to trust. She wrinkled her nose. She was jumping the gun by a mile. They'd just had a one-night stand. He wasn't asking her for a life-changing relationship. He wasn't asking her for a relationship at all.

It was something she'd do well to remember.

She dressed quickly in a butter-colored turtleneck with a pair of green corduroy overalls. She looked more like Rebecca of Sunnybrook Farm than Mighty Aphrodite. It was a good disguise. The cell phone interrupted her musings. It was Mabel Ruth. The witches had gathered at Bell, Book and Candle and they needed her.

****

Luke sat alone at the breakfast table. There were a

million things to think about, like the fact that Jessie probably wouldn't like his drab, unfurnished D.C. apartment, and the probability they'd be fighting like cats and dogs by the time they moved there just like the last time. Doubts crept into his mind. He shoved them aside. He'd figure out the right time and he'd ask her to marry him but he was through tempting fate. He shrugged into his leather jacket and headed for the drugstore.

There was no way he'd spend another night in this house without a box of condoms.

Hattie Bexler's eyebrows disappeared under her wispy gray bangs as she rang up his purchase and handed him the bag. "Thanks," he said, with a smile that didn't reach his eyes. He knew she'd be on that old rotary phone before he hit the street. She'd think it her duty to tell Blanche. He froze for an instant as pain pierced his heart.

Not Blanche. Not on the phone. But wherever she was, Summerland or heaven, Blanche knew about the condoms and Jessie. He could almost hear her voice. "Just make it right, lad. Just make it right."

****

The sign was lettered in an old English font. Bell, Book and Candle occupied a narrow storefront on Main Street between Molly's Bakery on the west and a narrow alley that separated it from the pharmacy.

A bell heralded Jessie's arrival as she stepped from the snowy sidewalk into the warm shop filled with hanging crystals, crocks of wands and brooms, shelves containing bottles of tinctures and herbs, racks of galaxy-studded clothing, and displays of silver necklaces, bracelets, and earrings.

One side of the shop was reserved for locally made items sold on consignment: stacks of baby sweaters, carved animals, homemade quilts, and sweet grass baskets.

"Jessie, is that you? The tea is ready, dear." Mabel Ruth's voice floated out from a back room.

Jessie stepped behind the cash register and through a beaded curtain. Millicent and Maude sat at a cloth-covered table in a small, dark storeroom. Maude held up a slightly gnarled willow stick.

"Francine found me a new wand. How do you like it?"

Jessie imagined Maude dancing around the room, waving the willow branch and singing,

"Bibbity, bobbity, boo."

"Very nice."

The bell on the door sounded, and Francine arrived. Jessie felt a quick guilt pang about the information in Blanche's Book of Shadows. She told herself she'd find a way to help Francie and Zach, a way that wouldn't involve Luke's heart.

"Jessie," Francine said, "I don't believe you've met Eleanor Prendergast."

Eleanor's pale face went straight to Jessie's soft heart. The woman didn't deserve to have a philandering husband who very well might be a murderer, too.

"We met at Miss Letty's house," Jessie said and wondered how she stayed warm in that thin, cloth coat.

Eleanor flinched.

"You look tired, dear," Maude said to Eleanor. "Can I get you a cup of tea?"

Eleanor shook her head. "No, thanks, Maude. I'm letting folks know Letty's funeral is tonight at five. We hope you'll be able to make it."

"Whoever heard of a funeral in the evening?" Millicent's mutter was low, but Eleanor heard and interpreted it.

"Interment will be in the morning," she explained, "but we didn't want to hold the services on Christmas Eve. There's the pageant, you know."

"Francie has always put on a first-rate Christmas pageant," Mabel Ruth told Jessie, "and for the past two years Eleanor has helped her."

"Immeasurably," Francie said.

"Perhaps we should cancel it this year," Mabel Ruth said. "Neither of you look healthy."

Eleanor gazed at Francie's pale face. "I don't want you to exert yourself if you're under the weather, but I can't bear to disappoint the children, and what with one thing and another, I think the community needs the pageant this year more than ever."

"I agree," Francie said, "and I'm fine."

Eleanor Prendergast left, and the older ladies moved to the back of the shop where a card table was covered with a white cloth.

Jessie looked at Francine. "More Ouija Board?"

"This time it's tea leaves."

In spite of her smile, new lines were carved into Francie's face, and there was a sadness in the chocolate-colored eyes.

Guilt snaked around Jessie's heart. She had to find a way to help Francie, and she had to find the murderer. On the latter point she needed more information. She looked at the cups Maude was placing on the table. Before she'd come to Mystic Hollow, she'd have viewed reading tea leaves as a parlor game. She'd changed. There were plenty of things in the universe she didn't understand.

And she now knew firsthand there was magic.

They took their seats and Maude poured tea into their cups but before they could drink it the phone rang.

Francine answered and then nodded at Mabel Ruth. "It's for you. Hattie."

A few minutes later Mabel Ruth returned to the table, a grim expression on her wide face.

"Forget the tea leaves," she said. "We're holding a hand fast instead."

Jessie blinked at her. "A hand fast? Isn't that like a wedding?"

"It's exactly like a wedding, dear," Maude said. "But why are we holding one?"

Jessie felt Mabel Ruth's eyes on her. What was going on?

"Lucas and Jessie are getting married." Her tone was flat and did not invite discussion.

Maude clapped her hands. "Thank goodness. Blanche would be so happy."

Jessie's eyes sought Francine. "What's going on?"

The redhead gave her a sympathetic smile. "I think the question is what went on last night. Luke must have given it away when he stopped at the drugstore."

Jessie remembered his concern about condoms. She closed her eyes and dropped her head.

"Oh, no."

Chapter Thirteen

Dennis Prendergast pulled a bottle of scotch out of his locked bottom drawer, splashed some into a shot glass, and threw it back. He was supposed to be preparing remarks for Letty's service, but he couldn't seem to concentrate. He needed something for his nerves. He couldn't shake the unsettled feeling that had grown stronger and stronger in the past few days. His hands shook as he filled the glass again.

The shrilling phone shredded his already tattered nerves, and a cold fist of fear closed around his heart. He gripped the arms of his chair while he listened to the terse message.

"Things are getting too hot. Tomorrow's the end of it, last delivery, last pay off. If you can't get the old lady in the ground tonight, we'll take shifts."

Shifts? Coffin-watching shifts? Who on earth would try to steal a peek into Letty Appleby's coffin? He didn't ask the question. There wasn't any point.

"We need special equipment when the ground's hard like this. I can't get it 'til morning." On top of which it was bad form to hold an interment at night. Dennis didn't say that, either. He stifled a groan. He was freaked enough without having to mount a ghostly vigil for Miss Letty.

He hung up and downed another shot. He'd been a fool. He'd blown the money from Ellie's dad on horses and women. Country parsons didn't make much, especially not the ones who didn't stay in one place. Mort had dangled an expensive carrot—a cool million—just to keep the church locked during the week, but after a while there were more favors and directions. Things got darker, and he got in deeper.

Now he was in up to his neck. He leaned back in his chair and closed his eyes. What he wouldn't give to run away. He pictured himself lounging in a hammock, a well-stacked native girl leaning over him, trailing long, red fingernails down his naked chest, over his washboard stomach, and under his swim trunks. He groaned and pressed a hand over the hardening flesh.

He'd sacrificed a lot for sex. Sometimes he wondered why. It wasn't the only thing in the world. He massaged himself and groaned again.

But it was far ahead of whatever was second.

****

Luke walked out of the drugstore. On impulse, or maybe because he was stalling, he turned down Western Street and followed it to a tidy garage—Carl's Automotive Repair.

The boots protruding from underneath the '79 Mustang were large, dusty, and familiar. The car was even more familiar. He and Zach had logged a lot of miles in that buggy. They'd felt up their girls for the first time in there, learned to soul kiss, and had even lost their virginity.

The car ought to have its own shrine.

"Hey," he called out.

Zach slid out from under the chassis. He got to his feet, grabbed a damp rag, and worked some of the oil off his hands.

"You fixing the car for yourself?"

"No. It's Jake's now."

Jake Reeves was Zach's seventeen-year-old brother.

"Doesn't he use your truck when you're overseas?"

Zach's squint kept Luke from reading his eyes.

"I'm not going back."

The side door opened, and Jake appeared. His hair was darker than Zach's, and he wore it long and loose. A gold hoop glittered in one ear, just the way Luke's had a decade earlier. The teenager looked like a younger, more rebellious version of his dad while Zach had their mom's blue eyes and dirt-brown hair.

"Hey, Jake."

The teenager grunted. That was new. Back in the day Jake had been attached to Luke, Zach, and Bobby Ray like a stubborn barnacle.

"He's pissed about the truck," Zach explained.

"This old piece of junk isn't cool," the teenager said.

Luke's surprise wasn't feigned. "This is a damn babe magnet. We had some mighty nice times in the old buggy."

Jake's chin, ragged with fledgling whiskers, stuck out.

"That where you did Crystal while my brother was humping Francie?"

Zach's fists clenched as Jake slammed the door and disappeared.

"Hey," Luke said, "calm down. He's just a kid."

"A mouthy kid."

"Same thing. So you changed your mind?" Zach nodded.

Luke let out a long, relieved breath. "Glad you came to your senses. I assume you're marrying Francie."

Zach hauled out a pack of cigarettes and lit one up. "A baby needs a father."

"A baby? Francie's pregnant?"

Before Zach could answer, the door opened again. This time it was Karl Reeves. Zach's dad, like Bobby Ray's dad, had attended all the ball games. He was quiet but a devoted family man.

"Mister Reeves," Luke said.

"It's time for you to call me Karl. Good to see you." He looked at Zach. "Tell your mom I'm going for parts. I'll be back before the Appleby funeral."

"No problem." Zach's tone was polite.

Karl, still agile, jumped into the pickup. He cranked the motor and backed out of the driveway.

Luke studied Zach. There was something wrong. The Reeves were the all-American family. Where was all this tension coming from?

"You gonna tell me what's going on?"

Zach took a drag then held the cigarette between his thumb and forefinger. "Karl's not my dad."

"What're you talking about?"

"Judy was pregnant when she married him."

"Judy? You mean your mom?"

Zach's eyes narrowed into slits. "You asked."

Luke knew it was a testament to their old friendship that Zach had even answered the question. Luke waited.

"She admitted it. Karl is Jake's dad. Not mine."

Luke thought about the older man's devotion to Zach. He'd offered to pay Zach's college tuition even though he'd have preferred to have Zach stick around and help with the shop.

"Who told you?"

The arm holding the cigarette dropped, and Zach stared at the cement floor. Luke realized he hadn't had to ask. He knew.

"Bobby. How the hell did he know?"

"He found out from his dad," Zach said. He sounded as bitter as he looked. "My dad."

Luke believed him. Bobby could be a jackass and he wasn't wedded to the truth but he'd always known how to stick it to someone. But he'd been Zach's friend. He'd have had no reason to lay this on him unless it was true.

"Bobby was a jackass for telling you."

"He was also my half-brother."

And Zach felt guilty because he'd lived while Bobby died.

"This have anything to do with you and Francine?"

Zach's face was impassive. He blew out a long breath. "No."

"It does." Luke's sixth sense told him he was right. "You feel betrayed by the Reeves and Russells, and you've let that poison seep into your relationship with Francine. She's different, man. She loves you."

"Shit. She wasn't even gonna tell me about the baby. I intercepted a phone call from the hospital."

"You can't blame her for that. You've been pretty unapproachable."

Zach's eyes lifted. His gaze was unfocused, as if he were looking into a dark abyss.

"Don't do this, man. I mean, marry her, but don't spend the rest of your life together making her pay.

This is what you've always wanted."

He saw Zach's fingers curl into fists crushing the cigarette, but his voice was defeated. "Yeah. Be careful what you wish for."

Minutes later Luke headed for Bell, Book and Candle. He figured Francie could use a shoulder. He opened the door with too much force and knocked the little bell onto the floor. He picked it up to find five women eyeing him speculatively.

Damn Hattie Bexler anyway.

"Just in time," Millicent said.

Maude swept the room with her wand, and he noticed a makeshift altar in the center of the store. Mabel Ruth and Millicent were knotting a thick rope.

"Are we having a hanging?"

"A hand fast," Mabel Ruth said. "You are getting engaged to Jessie." He looked at the elf.

"I can't seem to talk any sense into them."

Her golden eyes looked confused, and her hair tumbled in every direction. She looked cute as hell. The ruddy cheeks and swollen lips were his work. He felt a strange mixture of shame and pride.

And inevitability.

"You look like you've just plowed the back forty."

She grinned. "Just call me Daisy Mae Duke."

"Soon to be Daisy Mae Duke Tanner," Francine murmured. She sent Luke a wry glance. "Guess this is the season for shotgun weddings."

"We're not getting married," Jessie assured Luke in an overly loud voice. "No way. I mean I'm not even dressed for it."

"Nothing wrong with plain clothes," Maude said, cheerfully.

"Anyway," Millicent added, "it's time to pay the piper."

Jessie looked helplessly at Luke. "They heard about the condoms."

"I figured."

"It doesn't matter why people get married," said Mabel Ruth, a lifelong spinster, "that's only the beginning. You two will be happy together, and it would please Blanche to no end."

Now. It would please Blanche now that he'd defiled her great-niece.

He wondered at himself. He'd known that if he bought the condoms at her store, Hattie would jump to the conclusion he'd slept with Jessie and that she'd make sure Mabel Ruth was informed. Had he done it on purpose? Did he want to be married to Jessie Maynard? Was it because she was related to Blanche?

"Blanche always thought you and Jessie would suit, Lucas," Mabel Ruth said. "It's not just about last night."

Luke felt blindsided. Was it true? Had Blanche wanted him to marry Jessie Maynard? What about his marriage to Crystal? He knew Blanche had felt reservations about the union, and they'd turned out to be on the money. She had to have known though, that he'd never been serious about anyone but the amethyst-eyed beauty. A niggling suspicion raised the hairs on the back of his head.

Had Blanche engineered this meeting with Jessie? Had she thought her great-niece could take the place of his ex-wife? He reminded himself it didn't matter.

He knew his duty.

****

Jessie thought about life's little ironies while she and the others ate the "wedding" brownies Maude brought over from Molly's. A few days ago after she'd broken an engagement, she'd vowed to stay away from marriage. Then she met Luke and fell in love—real love. She should have rejoiced at a proposal from him, but she was, once again, fighting her way out of another convenient marriage.

Luke's eyes fastened on her. He couldn't fool her. He was determined to do right by Blanche's niece, but he didn't want to marry Jessie. He didn't want to marry anyone.

"You're a stubborn little thing," Luke grumbled.

"I think she's awesome," Francine put in.

Jessie thought she heard tears in her voice.

"She knows what she wants, and she doesn't let anybody push her around."

Jessie was pleased with the praise, but she felt compelled to be honest.

"It's not the same thing as you and Zach. You have a history together. Luke and I have known one another for a handful of days."

"That's the whole point, Jessie," Millicent said, with a touch of asperity, "you've known each other."

"The world has changed," Francie pointed out. "Just because a man and woman have sex, the woman doesn't expect marriage."

Jessie felt the heat flood into her cheeks. She felt Luke's eyes on her. She knew he was willing to marry her because of Blanche.

It was an even worse reason than her first engagement.

"I appreciate the thought," she said, including

everyone in her comment. "I'd have liked to see a hand fast ceremony."

"What if you're pregnant?"

Luke's words had the effect of a rock coming through the plate-glass window.

"It's very unlikely," Jessie said, after a long minute. "It was only the once."

"If you won't get married," Mabel Ruth said, "I feel duty bound to ask you not to tempt fate."

"She's right," Luke said, his voice gravelly. His eyes held Jessie's, and for a minute, she was lost in a sensual memory. "If you won't marry me, we can't use these." He took the crumpled bag out of his pocket and set it on the table.

"Hostage condoms," Francine said. "I like it."

Later, as Luke and Jessie walked home together across the snow-covered Green under a later afternoon pink sky, Jessie wondered if she'd made a mistake. Once again she wondered if Luke could learn to love her. It might have been worth the risk for the wedding night of hot, heavy sex. She felt heat explode inside her.

"What're you thinking about?"

She couldn't tell him how badly she wanted to plunge her hands into his hair, to feel the naked length of him thrusting against her thighs, to experience that euphoric release and the unparalleled pleasure of lying in his arms afterwards.

"Stuff. Expectations. Circumstances. The whole strange business of binding yourself to another person."

He nodded. "It's absurd to think a person can promise his or her feelings won't change over the course of a lifetime."

He sounded so bitter. She stopped and laid her

palm against his chest. His heart thrummed in a comforting beat.

"It's not absurd. You'll feel that way again." She struggled with the next words, but she knew she had to say them. "Maybe even with your ex-wife."

He shook his head. "Even if I were interested she's not. She made that pretty clear in her 'Dear John' e-mail."

Jessie's heart ached for him. "Then she's a fool."

Luke smoothed his thumb over her bottom lip. "Does that make you a fool, too?"

She didn't reply. It wasn't the same, and he knew it.

****

Maybe it was the still afternoon or the confused state of his senses, or maybe it was just a perverse reaction to her refusal to marry him, but he couldn't shake the feeling he was missing out on something great. Jessie Maynard was full of love and life and laughter. He could have done a lot worse in a marriage. Hell, he had done a lot worse.

"C'mon, Elf. Forget your doubts. Let's get married."

He hadn't intended to say that. She grinned at him as if she knew it.

"Ask me enough and I might take you up on it. Then where would you be?"

Heat flashed through him. Suddenly he was hard and ready. The lust must have shown in his eyes because she stepped away from him.

"Forget all this talk about marriage," she said, lightly.

He didn't tell her it wasn't marriage he was

thinking of, it was bed.

"It's the night before the night before Christmas, and we've got a funeral to attend. Think the murderer will be there?"

"Pink elephants and lemonade, dear Jessie, hear the laughter running through the love parade." A smooth masculine voice floated on the winter air.

"Oh no." Jessie's small figure went as tense as a hunting dog. "Kit."

Luke followed the trajectory of her eyes, but all he could see was a box truck emblazoned with a sign, Fusco's Frozen Foods, Chicago's Best, parked on Cobblestone Lane. The man seemed to come out of nowhere. His gelled blond hair gleamed in the glow of the street lamps. His teeth flashed, white and straight. He wore what looked like a cashmere overcoat and a soft white muffler. Mister Blowjob.

The intruder scooped Jessie into his arms with easy familiarity. He twirled her around.

"Put her down." Luke barked the command, and the man froze. He didn't put her down, though, and he didn't lose his smile.

"What's the problem?"

"She gets airsick."

"That's new," Kit said.

Luke waited for Jessie to contradict him. It was oddly satisfying that she didn't.

"Luke's right," she said, mildly. "I really prefer to keep my feet on terra firma."

When he obeyed, Luke decided to let him keep his teeth a little longer. "Luke, this is Kit Carstairs."

"Jessie's fiancé." The blond flashed his irritating smile and stuck out his hand.

"Ex-fiancé," Jessie corrected.

Luke stared into light green eyes that crinkled in the corners. The guy was loaded with confidence borne of good looks and an easy manner. No wonder he had a harem.

"Luke Tanner," he said, dryly. "Jessie's current fiancé."

Three jaws dropped. Luke didn't know who was more surprised, Carstairs, Jessie, or himself.

"So you weren't just blowing smoke, Tinkerbell." He chucked her under the chin. "I should have known. You've always been a stickler for the truth."

Luke found himself grinding his teeth at the man's inappropriate familiarity. He hated that BJ had a history with her. Anyone could see the clown wasn't right for her. That's why he'd bent the truth.

"Listen, bro," Carstairs said to Luke. The blue eyes glowed with confidence. "I'm here to let you off the hook."

A scent drifted on the air. It was delicate, expensive and familiar. Luke's gut churned. Chanel Number Five. Crystal's perfume. He spotted a tall, slim blonde rounding the corner of the truck. He nearly lost his un-wedding brownies.

Chapter Fourteen

It wasn't Crystal.

He knew it because he didn't get that constriction around his heart. He was still breathing normally.

The leggy blonde, clad in a black cashmere coat and fashion boots grabbed Jessie and wrapped her in a bear hug. At first glance they looked like polar opposites, but when he saw them side by side, Luke saw the family resemblance in the small straight noses, the sprinkling of freckles, and the glow in their faces.

Jessie couldn't stop talking. "When did you get here? Is Mom here? What about Dad? How did you get here? Why did you bring Kit?"

He'd like an answer to that last one himself.

The woman laughed then she looked at Luke. He recognized the feminine appreciation in her eyes. He returned her smile even as he wished she and Mister Blowjob would disappear.

"We've been here about half an hour. Mom's in the house. Dad's coming by plane. We borrowed the Fusco's truck so we could haul all the wedding stuff including the stations-of-the cross ice sculpture, and Kit is here in case you've changed your mind."

Jessie gaped at the truck. "She didn't bring mushroom cloud wedding dress did she? Because I'm not wearing it."

Luke stared at her. He couldn't believe she was

arguing wardrobe.

"You're not wearing anything," he said, irritably. "You're not marrying this guy."

"Ah," Gillian said, looking from one to the other. "So that's how it is."

Luke didn't bother to correct her. The least he could do is protect Jessie from that blond sleaze ball.

Suddenly Jessie seemed to remember her manners.

"Luke, this is my sister, Gillian. Gillian, Luke Tanner. And, as you know, this is Kit Carstairs." Her eyes narrowed on her ex. "Don't take this the wrong way, Kit, but I was really hoping not to lay eyes on you again."

"I screwed up, princess," he said.

He sounded contrite and sincere, and Luke wanted to knock his perfect white teeth down his throat.

"I'll do anything if you'll give me another chance."

It was time to intervene.

"Jessie's moved on."

"In three days?"

It did sound ridiculous. He wondered how he could have become so attached to the elf in such a short time.

"Sounds like a rebound. You need to take time to grieve."

"You didn't die, Carstairs, you cheated on her."

"It's all right, Luke," Jessie said. "I can handle this." She turned to the slick-haired ex. "I'm not interested in a reconciliation, Kit. I told you that on the phone."

They'd been talking on the phone? When?

"You can't tell me you're engaged to this guy,"

Carstairs said to Jessie. "I heard he's a bad seed."

"We're not really engaged," she assured him. "I mean,

we've talked about it and, oh, it's complicated. Luke and I are friends. That's as much as you need to know. And you heard wrong. He's a good seed."

Luke didn't know where the next words came from. "If you think I'm such a good seed, why won't you marry me?"

Carstairs laughed. "Looks like I've still got a chance."

God. He hated this guy.

"Jessie, dear." Another blonde rounded the truck. She looked exactly like Gillian down to the cashmere coat and boots except her face was a little older and she wore diamonds in her ears the size of a pair of dimes.

"Hi, Mom." Jessie hugged her mother. "I'm sorry about the wedding and all."

"No harm done. We've got all the trimmings and the license is still good. That is, if you've changed your mind."

Jessie put her arm around her mother. "I know you're disappointed, you and Dad. We'll find a way around this. Another way."

"Oh," Monica said, "I almost forgot. Someone named Mabel Ruth called. She said what with all the hand fast and confusion she was afraid you'd forget about the funeral."

Carstairs and Gillian spoke at the same time. "Funeral? What funeral?"

"Thank goodness Gillian and I wore black.

Christopher, did you bring a dark jacket?"

"You want to attend the funeral?"

"Of course," Monica said, surprised. "I imagine it's the event in Mystic Hollow tonight."

Luke looked at the trio of newcomers. No wonder

Jessie had been looking for sanctuary. "Did you really bring all the wedding food?" Her mother nodded.

"Good. We'll have something to contribute to the wake."

****

Jessie, Luke, and Kit carried large platters of cookies into the side door of the church near the kitchen. Eleanor Prendergast, as pale as ever, accepted the offering. If she had any qualms about serving the pink hearts scripted with "Christopher and Jessie" at Letty Appleby's funeral, she didn't mention them.

The Maynard party took up all of one pew. Jessie found herself in the wind tunnel between the men, each of whom was six feet tall. It wasn't that she really minded being the focus of all that testosterone, but their sheer size made it hard for her to get a good look at the other mourners.

Since they were only three rows from the front she couldn't find any of her friends but she had a good view of the reverend, draped in a solemn black robe with a white stole, and J. Mortimer Epps, who hovered near the casket like some kind of secret service agent.

Lois Epps sat in the front row on the opposite side of the church, and as the congregation rose to the organ strains of "Blest Be the Ties That Bind," Jessie could see the woman's awe-inspiring chest swell with song. Just as the congregation finished, Eleanor slipped in a side door and took a seat near the mortician's wife.

Reverend Prendergast's eulogy was long and effusive. It seemed to wander down one path and then switch to another. Jessie stopped listening. Now that her mom and Gilly were here, she realized how much she'd wanted to spend Christmas with them. At the same time, she regretted the loss of her private time with Luke even though she knew it was just as well.

His left arm rested against her right one, and she felt his hard warmth through the thin fabric of her dress. A lump collected in her throat when she remembered the way he'd tried to protect her from Kit. She'd thank him later even though it hadn't been necessary. He'd already protected her. She was a completely different woman from the one who'd agreed to marry Kit Carstairs. She'd never make a mistake like that again.

Jessie resisted the urge to rest her head against Luke's muscular shoulder. Just for an instant she allowed herself to pretend they were a couple, that they'd been married for several years. Since it was her fantasy, she gave them a couple of kids.

"Jessie."

His whispered voice made her jump. She hoped he couldn't read her mind.

"Epps is guarding that coffin like it was a cub and he was a mother bear."

"I noticed."

The obvious question was why? Why was he treating Letty's corpse like some kind of treasure? Was it because it was a treasure? Had they incinerated Letty and planted a treasure in the box? But why? Whatever was in there was going into the ground in the morning.

How could a buried treasure do Epps and Prendergast any good?

The case was frustrating. She wasn't even close to an answer. Of course she'd been a little distracted in the past twenty-four hours. Heat surged into her face.

Luke leaned against her. "Hot?"

She gave him a repressive look. No matter how

little she wanted to, it was time to put aside the hormones and solve the murder. She forced herself to list the thing she knew.

Number one: Blanche had died suddenly in bed. Epps had gotten a death certificate signed by a half-blind octogenarian doctor and cremation took place before the family was notified.

Number two: Letty Appleby died when an allergic reaction cut off her air passages. This time there was an autopsy, but the county medical examiner found nothing suspicious. The old lady accidentally ingested the peanut oil.

From everything Jessie had heard, she believed Miss Letty had been much too sharp for an accident like that. Mabel Ruth and the others believed Blanche had been killed to shut her up.

Had both old ladies been killed over a secret? And what was it? The reverend's affair? Or something worse. Something that had caused Prendergast to lock the church and to carry a gun. Epps carried a gun, too. No. This wasn't just about an affair. Jessie was certain of that.

And then there was number three. Why did Epps need an elaborate operating room at the mortuary? She'd meant to follow up on that. Tonight she'd go online and see what she could find out. There had to be some reason Epps was hovering around that casket like a mother hen.

Prendergast seemed to be winding down. Jessie tuned back in.

"Letty Appleby was a pillar of the community. She was the last living branch of a family that has been here in the Shenandoah Valley for nearly two hundred years.

Letty and the Applebys will live on in the pages of Mystic Hollow history."

Something tickled Jessie's memory. Some word. History? Pillar? Branch? Pages? Yeah. That was it. Pages. But why? Had Letty been mentioned in Blanche's Book of Shadows? Pages. Pages of time. A headline swam in front of her eyes.

"Local Man Named in Macabre Celebrity Scandal."

She placed it. The top paper on the stack of periodicals in Miss Letty's parlor. The newsprint was yellow and worn. Why had she kept that clip? What significance did it have? Jessie wished she'd taken the time to read the story. She'd find that online tonight, too.

She wished she could get a look inside that coffin. She had a gut feeling the coffin was at the center of this whole business. She knew it wouldn't be buried until morning. An idea leapt up inside her. It was bold, daring, and scary as hell, but it might help her solve the murders. And that's what she wanted. To solve the murders and get back to her real life.

****

Dennis slipped out of the social hall and sought the sanctuary of his office. He removed his robe and stole and hung them neatly in the closet. Between Lois's flirtatious smiles, and the danger he felt from Mort, he was near collapse. He'd been a fool to seduce the wife of his partner.

Especially a partner with access to a crematorium.

Chills chased up and down his spine like frantic squirrels.

He half sat, half fell into his comfortable chair.

Downstairs, the church was emptying out. The citizens of Mystic Hollow had paid their respects to one of their oldest, if not dearest, neighbors. Now they could head back to their comfortable homes in good conscience while Letty's remains and Dennis himself were left behind in the echoing church.

He shivered again.

He unlocked his bottom drawer, pulled out his pistol, and the bottle of Scotch. He filled a shot glass and drained it. Then he filled another. He couldn't believe his life had come to this.

Bodyguard to a corpse. He should've gotten out of town weeks ago.

A sickening click snapped in the quiet, and he nearly jumped out of his skin. Sweat poured down the inside of his white shirt. The liquor, comforting only a minute earlier, gave him heartburn. Who was up here? Epps? His blood ran cold.

"Hey, sugar."

Lois. Dennis sagged in his chair then got up to unlock the office door. His shirt felt clammy, sticking uncomfortably to his skin.

She slid a hand down her ample hips and leaned toward him. The movement caused her breasts to ripple under the fabric of her black wool dress. The movement reminded him of cold Jello and hot sex. His lower body flared to life, and he felt a tidal wave of relief.

He needed oblivion and what better to get it than some hot church office sex?

Lois held his gaze while she dropped a hand to his crotch and began to massage. Dennis moaned. She picked up his gun and pressed the barrel against his rapidly swelling fly.

He twisted and moaned, the fear factor upping the ante on the sex. She climbed in his lap, and her breasts swayed pendulously against his face. It was like making love to an airbag. She removed the necessary clothing so she could join their bodies.

"Ride 'em cowboy," she said, swinging the gun in one lifted hand.

"Be careful with that," he rasped. "It's loaded."

She jerked and twisted with practiced skill but she was heavy and he was on edge. After several long minutes she stilled.

"I haven't come yet," he protested.

"You're taking too long."

It was the anxiety, the fear, but he didn't want to admit it.

Lois got to her feet. "I'm hungry. I'll be back in a little while."

Dennis's mouth dropped open as he watched her saunter out the door. He wanted to grab his gun and shoot someone.

He didn't much care who.

****

"It was a very nice funeral," Monica said, as she helped herself to a glass of punch made out of a punch base, pineapple sherbet, and Sprite. "I like your friends a lot, Jessie." She nodded at the Tuesday witches who were standing in a circle with Luke and Gillian.

Jessie realized they were her friends—Mabel Ruth, Millicent, Maude, Francie, and Zach. She'd miss them when she left.

"I am a little surprised though at the lack of seasonal decorations. Why, there are no greens at all in the sanctuary. Not even a sprig of holly." She took a bite of a rich, chocolate brownie. She looked around the social hall. "There's nothing here, either."

Jessie found herself wanting to defend the Mystic Hollow. "The town's been preoccupied with the murders."

Monica munched, thoughtfully. "I like the way you've decorated Blanche's."

"It's just a start. I'll get a tree tomorrow."

"That will look lovely, dear. Something tall and bushy for the bay window."

Jessie smiled at Monica. The sins of the canceled wedding were truly in the past. If her dad arrived, the Maynards could have a real Norman Rockwell Christmas.

"Where is the reverend, Eleanor?" Jessie heard Hattie Bexler's distinctive voice behind her. "I wanted to tell him what a nice service that was. Letty would have appreciated it."

"He felt a migraine coming on," Eleanor apologized. "So he went home to bed. He wants to be in good shape for tomorrow."

Jessie was almost certain she'd seen a robed figure slip around the corner and up the stairs. Lois Epps was missing, too. Did Eleanor know about the affair? Was she lying to protect her husband?

A harsh crash cut her musings short. It was followed by a collective gasp and an instant of shocked silence.

****

One minute Francine was carrying a nearly empty crystal-cut punchbowl back to the kitchen for a refill, and the next the yellowish liquid stained the linoleum floor of the social hall. Half the broken bowl rolled under the serving table, and the other spun in place. Every eye was on the man who'd knocked the punchbowl out of her hands. Everyone heard his angry growl.

"That's too heavy for you to carry."

For a moment Jessie was touched by Zach's concern, but when she saw Francie's chocolate eyes flash with fury, she realized it was something else.

"You mean because I'm pregnant?"

Francie's response was loud and clear, and everyone in the room froze. Except Zach. He didn't appear at all embarrassed.

"Yeah. Because you're pregnant."

Francine kept her head high as she walked past her stunned friends and neighbors, the townspeople who had been her extended family since her mother's death. She marched into the kitchen and returned with a mop and a bucket which she thrust into Zach's big hands.

"Looks like you've got some cleanup."

No one moved as she headed for the door. Jessie caught up with her in the parking lot. She put her arm around the taller woman.

"He's trying to force my hand," Francie sobbed.

Jessie felt a strong male hand move her gently aside. She watched as Zach settled his leather jacket around Francine's shoulders. His voice was so tender Jessie barely recognized it.

"I'm sorry, Frannie."

Francie looked up at him. "Then why'd you do it?"

Jessie watched him pin Francine with a hooded gaze. The scene was so intimate and she had no business being there but excusing herself would be even more intrusive.

"I did it because I didn't want anybody thinking your baby belongs to someone else."

Fresh tears coursed down Francie's pale face, but her tone was matter-of-fact. "No one would think that, Zach. No one but you."

Zach didn't let go of her. "Come on," he said, stiffly. "I'll take you home."

Jessie was thoughtful as she watched them go. They cared deeply about one another but Zach was stubborn and Francie was proud. Maybe in time they'd talk this out and live happily ever after. Jessie hoped so.

****

Ignoring her conscience, Jessie sent Luke, Kit, her mother, and sister back to the witch hat house while she helped Eleanor clean up the kitchen. Finally, she convinced the older woman to leave, too.

For about ten minutes, Jessie puttered around the industrial kitchen that had once been used for community potlucks. She wanted to make sure there were no witnesses when she left the side door unlatched.

The instant she stepped into the darkened parking lot, she inhaled a woodsy scent, and her heart jerked crazily. Luke stepped out of the shadows.

"You came back for me?"

His grin was crooked and so appealing. "I figured it was the least I could do. If things had gone differently, this would have been our wedding night."

Her reaction was predictable. Heat suffused her body.

He took her arm. "C'mon, Jess. You've gotta admit we've got chemistry."

"No argument. But that's not a good enough reason

179

to marry."

"I agree. Marriage is just the cost of doing business in Mystic Hollow." The cynicism hurt.

"Besides, I think we'd do pretty well together."

Not really the proposal she was looking for, but she was determined to let it go. It was, after all, the night before the night before Christmas. She linked her arm in his. "I'd like to get a tree tomorrow," she said.

"A tree."

She nodded. "A ten-foot white pine. It would look perfect right there." She pointed to the bay window as they approached the house. Luke's silence didn't surprise her. Luke Tanner didn't seem like a man interested in Christmas trees, white pines or otherwise.

He paused on the porch just before he opened the door. Then he took her in his arms and pressed his lips very gently against hers. The kiss was so sweet it made her want to cry but not as much as his next words.

"You're an interesting woman, Jessie Maynard. If a tree will make you happy, we'll get a tree."

She touched his face and then stepped back as he opened the door. All the lights were on. The house was warm and welcoming, and the sound of laughter drifted into the foyer. The Maynards had gathered in the parlor.

Jessie caught the sound of a familiar baritone.

"Dad!" She dashed through the French doors to the parlor and into his big, comforting arms. She'd always had a special relationship with Howard. He'd always seemed indestructible until last year's heart attack. She remembered now why she'd agreed to marry Kit.

"Merry Christmas, baby."

"When did you get here?"

He paused. "A few minutes ago."

"Good trip?"

"Just a short snow delay at O'Hare. I rented a car in Roanoke."

When they stopped talking, the room seemed unnaturally quiet. What had happened to all the talking and laughing? She stepped out of her father's embrace but stayed by his side. Her gaze riveted on Luke. He looked different somehow. His dark features were frozen into an expression of wonder, as if he'd just witnessed the Second Coming.

Jessie realized then there was another person in the room. Her stomach clenched and at a gut level she knew, even before her brain processed it, who it was. The woman from the wedding photo but so much more beautiful in person. Jessie gasped as she took in the tall, willowy figure with the shining blonde hair, the high cheekbones, the perfectly proportioned nose and the full sensuous mouth. Rosy lips. Most striking of all were her eyes. They were the color of light purple jewels, amethysts.

Frankly, she didn't look like a real person. She looked like an angel. Or a goddess.

The introduction came from an unlikely source.

"This is Crystal," Howard said. "I gave her a ride from the airport."

Jessie blinked and studied the woman.

Crystal clearly bought into the image of herself as a goddess. She wore a loose-weave white wool sweater paired with a white wool, ankle-length skirt. Everything about her was light, silvery, crystal-like. Incandescent.

Jessie looked at Luke and saw him jerk his gaze away from the beauty. It felt like someone had stomped on her soul.

"It's nice to meet you," she said, finally. "Welcome to our home."

Crystal's smile was blinding, but one of her delicate eyebrows lifted in question.

"Our home," Luke said, firmly.

Jessie thought she detected a bit of hoarseness in that deep voice.

"Jessie's and mine. We're engaged to be married."

The smile didn't waver. "Congratulations," she said. She glided up to Jessie and bussed her lightly on each cheek. "I guess this means we're related."

Jessie didn't see how an ex-wife and a fake fiancée equated to family, but she held her own smile. At least she held it until Crystal went close to Luke. She twined her long arms around his neck and rubbed her cheek against his. Jessie felt a spasm of pain when she saw Luke's hands on the goddess's narrow waist. The kiss the two shared looked like a scene from a film. That final scene, when the couple comes together for happily-ever-after.

Finally, just when Jessie thought she couldn't stand it another minute, Luke broke the kiss.

Crystal turned to the gaping Maynards. "I've come a long way to see Luke," she said, in a quiet voice. "If you'll excuse us, we have some unfinished business."

Luke shook his head. "No," he said.

"Yes," Jessie said.

She knew what had to be done. She grabbed Luke's hand.

"We'll be right back," she said. She was half afraid he'd break loose, but he didn't. He followed her down the hallway to Blanche's study. When they got there, Jessie peered into his face. It was a mask of confused emotions.

"I didn't know she was coming," Luke said.

"You have to talk to her."

"No."

"Don't you want to know what she wants?"

"No."

She knew he wanted to avoid spending time alone with Crystal because he was still vulnerable to her.

"How long were you married, Luke?"

"Three years. A little less."

Jessie swallowed and said what she had to say. "She's right, you know. You and Crystal do have unfinished business."

****

Blanche's study welcomed him the way it always had. He loved the heavy walnut desk, the ceiling-high stacks of books, the faint scent of vanilla that reminded him of the old lady. He snapped on the green-shaded desk lamp. It cast a low light in the room. Crystal sat in a chintz covered loveseat while he took a facing chair. He hadn't felt that old destructive magic yet, but there was no sense taking chances.

He stared at the incomparable features across from him. The face that had broken a thousand hearts. He'd wondered, during the hell he'd lived and relived after the divorce, why beauty made such a difference. Was man just wired to respond to full lips, a narrow waist, long legs, and artistically arranged features? What was it about a pair of glands in a well-constructed push-up bra that had men salivating? And the eyes? That made more sense. If they were the windows to the soul, Crystal's soul was clear, pure and rare.

It wasn't true. Eyes were just eyes. Breasts were

just breasts. Lips were just lips. Every woman had 'em.

He had to keep his mind on that fact. "I'm glad you came."

She smiled her goddess's smile.

Chapter Fifteen

Blanche Maynard's parlor was filled with holiday scents and sounds from crab puffs to laughter. Everyone seemed to be having a great time. Howard and Monica Maynard, while occasionally joining in the general talk, spent many minutes together on Blanche's Victorian sofa, their foreheads touching, their voices low.

Kit was the master of ceremonies, freshening drinks, encouraging the fire, and telling funny anecdotes that had Gillian rolling on the floor. Pyewacket and her offspring dozed in the warm room, apparently not minding the invasion of humans. Jessie sat in Blanche's rocker. She didn't allow herself to pace or fret or reveal in any way that Luke's *tete-a-tete* with Crystal was tearing her heart out.

When Kit excused himself to make a new batch of eggnog, Gillian moved closer to Jessie.

"You worried?"

"I just don't want to see him fall into her clutches again."

Gillian made a sympathetic sound. "Ah, Jess. You know, I figured if you ever fell for a guy you'd be a head-over-heels kind of girl."

"It's not that. Well," she had to be honest, "not just that. She's not good enough for him."

"You mean under that breathtaking beauty beats a

185

heart of pure evil?"

Jessie smiled as Gillian had meant her to. "She broke up with him in a 'Dear John' e-mail. She was cheating on him with one of his best friends. Need I say more?"

"Geez." Gillian shook her head. "But you saw the way he looked at her."

"Yeah."

"In all fairness, Dad and Kit looked at her like that, too. I imagine all men do."

Jessie shook her head. "This is different.

Luke married her."

"What happened to the 'best friend?'"

"That's just the problem. He died recently. I think Crystal wants to try a reconciliation."

Gillian appeared to consider that. "He seemed awfully interested in you. At least he did before she arrived."

It was a dispiriting reminder. "Between us, that's mostly duty with a little chemistry thrown in."

"Maybe you represent a fresh start for him," Gillian offered. "A future without a lot of baggage."

"Maybe I was safe. If he's committed to me, he never has to really examine his feelings about her. He can just bury them."

Gillian glanced down the corridor toward the study. "Wonder what they're 'examining' now."

Jessie thought of the exquisite creature undoubtedly making overtures to Luke. He wouldn't accept them because of her, Jessie. Not that there were strings between them, but Luke had a very strong sense of honor.

It wasn't sex she feared. She sighed, heavily.

"Love is hard to kill off." As she was just beginning to discover.

One divorced couple, Luke and Crystal, still hadn't reappeared when the other divorced couple, Howard and Monica, excused themselves for the night. Jessie knew they'd stay together because there were only a limited number of rooms. And because Howard held his ex-wife's hand as he led her up the stairs.

Jessie and Gillian watched them go.

"You know," Jessie said, thoughtfully, "maybe this trek to Virginia is less about my wedding and more about getting a chance to get Dad away from the office."

"Let's hope they get re-hitched," Gilly said. "That way at least we'll be able to make use of that ice sculpture."

The women joined Kit in the kitchen where he was cleaning up the dishes. He stood at the sink, a dishtowel tied around his waist.

"You'll make someone the perfect wife,"

Gillian joked.

Kit glanced at Jessie. "I am available."

Gillian and Kit bantered while the trio cleaned up, and then Gillian excused herself.

Kit moved close to Jessie and placed his hands on her shoulders. "You all right, honey?"

The genuine concern in his voice touched Jessie. The shock of his betrayal had knocked all the good qualities out of her head. She remembered now. He always had been a decent guy. They just hadn't been in love.

"I'm fine. It's nice to have you here," she said, impulsively. "I'm just going to lock up and turn in."

The blue eyes held her for a long moment. "You're not gonna change your mind, are yo Jess?"

"No."

"And it's not just about that fiasco at the Happy Taco, is it?"

She shook her head. It was a relief to have him understand.

"I'm so incredibly sorry," he said, as though he meant it. He pressed a light kiss on her forehead. "See you in the a.m."

Jessie sat down at the wicker table after he'd left. It felt good to have things straightened out with Kit. It felt good to have her family here for the holiday.

It did not feel good to know Luke and Crystal were apparently going to "talk" all night. She reminded herself that it wasn't her business, but it didn't help. A weight, as heavy as a coffin, pressed against her heart.

A coffin. She'd forgotten all about her plan to re-visit the church tonight. Somehow, the idea of peeking into a coffin had seemed more doable in the early evening, when she was surrounded by people. But she thought about the goal she'd set out for herself. They weren't any closer to nailing Blanche's murderer than they had been three days ago. What if the definitive clue was lurking in that box? What if, as she suspected, Epps and Prendergast were using corpses to ship drugs or other contraband and the box was empty?

There was only one way to find out.

She got to her feet, trying not to listen to the silence down the hall. This time she armed herself with a flashlight. At least she'd be able to see in the dark. If there was anything to be seen.

****

Luke looked into Crystal's perfect face, and he listened to her musical voice. She'd missed him, longed for him, made a terrible mistake, could he ever, ever forgive her? Yada, yada, yada. He waited until she'd presented her case which consisted, pretty much, of describing her own unhappy state of mind.

"Nothing would be different," he said. "I couldn't make you happy before. Nothing has changed."

"But it has," she said, eagerly. They were sitting on a small loveseat near the front bedroom window and she leaned up against him. "You're not overseas anymore. You've come home."

"I still have to work a lot of hours. The business takes all my time, and I'm in debt."

A shadow flitted over those exquisite features. People always asked Crystal why she hadn't pursued a career in modeling. She had a variety of answers depending on the questioner, but Luke knew the truth.

Modeling was hard work, and Crystal was essentially lazy.

"You'll make a lot of money, Luke. I know you. You'll make a success of your business. It's just a matter of time."

He wondered if she even knew what his business was. "Thanks for the vote of confidence."

She pursed her full, lush lips. How had he ever considered that expression sexy? How had he never comprehended the extent of her self-centeredness? The answer was sobering. He had known. He'd wanted her anyway.

"I know I hurt you," she said. "I wish I could take it back. I don't even know what I was thinking. It was just that you were gone so much, and after we were married, it wasn't the same."

It hadn't been the same. He hadn't felt the same. He'd stopped worshipping her, and on some level, she'd known it.

"Do you hate me?"

He shook his head. The passion he'd felt for her had died long before the marriage, but he hadn't laid it to rest. He felt a surge of gratitude to Blanche for bringing him home and to Jessie for making him face the demon.

Crystal inched closer. She was offering him a closer look, a touch. Incredible he'd never figured this out before.

"If you don't hate me," she whispered, bringing her lips close to his, "then you must love me."

She'd never been deep. She'd never been rejected either. Trust a goddess not to know that the opposite of love wasn't hate it was indifference.

"I've made a commitment to Jessie," he said.

She waved her hand, dismissively. "She won't hold you to that."

Crystal was right. Anyway the commitment was more implied than spoken. "Maybe not, but I plan to hold her to the commitment she made to me."

It didn't end there, of course. Crystal Wetherington was used to getting what she wanted. She argued and pleaded, cried and pouted. By the time she'd run out of words, they were both groggy with fatigue.

"Let me stay in your room," she said.

"Fine." They went up the back staircase. She sprawled on his bed, already half asleep. He took off.

"We'll talk in the morning," she murmured. When he heard the soft, even breathing and knew she was asleep, he shed his suit. He slid into a pair of jeans. He might be exhausted, but he and Jessie had some serious talking to do. His pulse raced at the prospect of waking her. She'd be tousled and drowsy and warm and, he hoped, welcoming. He let himself out into the hallway. The quiet of the upstairs was broken by an unmistakable "click."

Luke's mouth set into a grim line. Someone was coming in or going out, and it didn't take extra sensory perception to figure out who it was. He flew down the stairs, threw his leather jacket on over his bare chest, and snagged the hook of her slicker before she'd made it through the arch.

"Where," he asked in a low, but deadly voice, "do you think you're going?"

****

Emotions warred in Jessie.

She did not appreciate manhandling, and her business was none of his business. But his scent, as always, made her knees weak and his green glare held her captive. Besides, when all was said and done, she didn't really want to visit Miss Letty alone.

"Going to check something out at the church."

His eyelashes flickered. She loved the way they swept his high cheekbones.

"The coffin?"

She nodded, waiting for a reprimand or an out and out order that she not go. It didn't come.

"Wear something else."

She blinked. "I can't believe you're arguing about wardrobe."

"The yellow is too easy to see." He sounded impatient.

He had a point. He opened the front door, and she found a dark cashmere coat. Kit's.

"Not that."

Jessie shivered. Was that jealousy in his voice or was he afraid she'd trip on the coat? He reached into the closet and brought out a navy blue jacket with an oversized "MHH" embroidered on the pocket.

His letter jacket. He helped her into it, and she transferred the flashlight and her cell phone into the pocket.

"Does this mean we're going steady?"

"Yeah."

The walk to the church at eleven p.m. was cold and lonely. Clouds scudded across the sky alternately revealing and obscuring the moon.

Despite the lighted tree on the Green, it looked less like Christmastime than Doomsday.

Jessie kept her head down. She decided not to ask about the rendezvous. It was hard to talk over the noise of the wind. Besides, she knew what he'd say. He was finished with Crystal. He wanted to start over with Jessie. Her heart twisted. He would do what he thought was right.

Her discretion lasted until they reached the side door of the church.

"You give any thought to how we're going to get in?"

She answered with a question of her own.

"Did you enjoy the stroll down Memory Lane?" His scowl goaded her.

"You guys must have had a lot to catch up on. You were together a long time."

"Crystal fell asleep."

"I'm surprised you left."

He blew out his cheeks and let out a long, harsh breath. "It's been a long day. Could we discuss this at a later time?"

Jessie was appalled. What was she doing? She didn't have the right to interrogate Luke on his personal relationships. "No problem."

"Great. Now, about the door."

She reached passed him and turned the knob. It opened easily.

"Luke," she said, "how come you're not yelling at me about snooping around?"

"We need answers. This seems like the quickest way to get 'em."

The look they exchanged assured Jessie they were on the same side in the investigation. She rationalized his involvement. Even the Lone Ranger had had a partner.

****

Dennis Prendergast slipped a baby blue cashmere sweater over his dress shirt. It was damn cold in the drafty building. It was getting harder and harder to get out of his comfortable office and make his way through the barely lit corridor down to the parlor. Mort had told him to check the coffin every fifteen minutes, but over the past three hours, nothing had changed, and he started to extend the intervals. Damn Letty. She was as much trouble dead as she'd been alive.

Dennis knew this wasn't about protecting the corpse. Epps was afraid someone would figure out the scam. Probably not Ezra Smith. More likely Blanche's nosy little niece or that green-eyed devil who lived with her. Two more days and Dennis wouldn't care who knew what, but he couldn't leave now. Tomorrow was Christmas Eve, and people expected him to be in the pulpit.

Besides, there was the last payoff to collect.

The big payoff.

Dennis ground his thumb and forefinger into his eye sockets. Another hour and he could leave. All he wanted to do was go home, dive under the cream-colored down comforter Ellie had given him last Christmas.

He let out a grunt. It was time to do the rounds. His steps slowed as he approached the open door. The parlor was like a small living room attached to a kitchenette. Bible studies were held there, book groups and committee meetings. At least they'd been held there until Mort ordered the church locked. Now the place smelled musty, stale. He glanced at the coffin. It was still there, of course, propped up on the church truck and surrounded by a velvet skirt. He thought he heard a sound, and his heart sling-shot in his chest. It wasn't the coffin that drew his attention, but a door at the back of the room. The door that connected St. Michael's with the Epps Mortuary.

Everyone in town believed the door was locked on both sides, but it wasn't. Mort controlled the door just as he controlled the whole operation. Dennis shivered again. He'd learned his lesson. Next time he'd forego the easy buck. Next time he'd stick to sex.

A phone rang. He jerked back like he'd been hit, and his heartbeat tripled. It was Mort. Had to be. He searched his pants pocket for his cell, then he remembered. He'd stopped carrying it because it stretched out his pants. The irritating ringing was coming from his land line. He sprinted down the hall, panting with the exertion by the time he got to the receiver.

"I'm recovered, sugar," the voice drawled. "And I'm ready to make all your dreams come true."

****

Miss Letty Appleby's coffin sat in the middle of the shadow-filled room like a guest at some phantom birthday party.

Jessie shone the flashlight on the smooth coffin surface. There was no latch.

"It's pressure sealed."

"Like Tupperware?"

He turned to look at her, a glint in his emerald eyes.

"You can get in; you just can't get out. It keeps the elements from getting at the body, and when the earth shifts, the coffin doesn't pop open."

Jessie shivered as she imagined being buried in the shifting earth. Luke read her mind.

"It'll come to us all eventually."

Death was a deep subject, a rich subject, and any other time, her imagination would have embraced the subject, but not now. Not with Luke's long, blunt-tipped fingers on the coffin. They looked powerful against the smooth wood. They were powerful. And gentle. Jessie longed to feel them on her skin.

Then the lid creaked open. Luke stared into the dark.

"Is she in there?"

"Yeah. Wanna take a look?"

"That's okay. I believe you."

"Let me know if we get company."

195

"What're you going to do?"

"Check things out. Stop talking."

She waited for a few minutes. He leaned into the coffin. She thought he was feeling around the body or maybe under it. Not a good image.

"Luke."

He twisted around. "Patience, Grasshopper."

She surveyed the room, circling it with her eyes. The door was open to the hallway. She'd hear if anyone approached. She started to get antsy. What if somebody caught them there?

"How much longer?"

He grunted something unintelligible. She crossed her arms across her waist and moved a few steps to the left. Anxiety gathered in her stomach and formed a knot in her throat. Her hands began to shake. She had the strongest premonition that they should leave.

She drifted closer to Luke. His big body drew her, and she reached out to touch him through the leather jacket. He was solid, dependable. She kept her hand there and noticed the trembling eased.

She started to relax and almost didn't hear the faint scrabbling sound. It could have been a mouse, but she didn't think so. Her eyes riveted on the door at the back of the room. Someone was there.

A single thought cut through the panic.

Luke was a sitting duck.

She hurled herself at him. Off-balance already, he toppled onto Miss Letty. The lid wobbled for an instant then dropped. Jessie dropped, too. She flattened herself against the floor and bit back a moan.

She'd locked Luke in the coffin.

Chapter Sixteen

Jessie was horrified.

The intruder might figure out someone was in the coffin. If so, it would be like shooting fish in a barrel. Luke would be a dead duck.

If not, Jessie squeezed her eyes shut and willed her heart to slow down. If not, when morning came, Luke would be buried alive.

Of course, if he survived, he'd probably kill her.

All she knew for sure was she had to save him. But how? If she moved she could get shot. But then, maybe the intruder didn't have a gun, didn't mean any harm. Or, maybe, she'd imagined that rustling sound.

Another sound, soft and furtive, reverberated through her like a gunshot. Oh God. She pressed herself against the floor, hoping, praying, but an instant later she knew her prayers would go unanswered when the floor underneath her vibrated as if someone were crossing the room, or walking over her grave.

Holy shit. A second vibration triggered a horrified shudder. She pictured a jackal stalking a sheep. For a moment she was paralyzed with fear, but she fought it off. She'd dragged Luke into this right from the start. He was only in this predicament because he'd been watching out for her. She couldn't just lie here and wait for the axe to fall.

She had to save Luke's life even if it meant he'd

spend the rest of it with the blonde goddess.

She tried to focus on the enemy. Who was it? Epps? Prendergast? Neither prospect was consoling. They were definitely up to something. They both packed heat. And if either or both had killed Great-Aunt Blanche and Miss Letty, they wouldn't hesitate to shoot a couple of snoops.

She reviewed her options. She could provide a distraction by jumping up and racing across the semi-dark room out into the hallway, but she couldn't outrun a bullet. Without her, Luke would be left to an unthinkable fate.

Or she could wait here with her heart ricocheting off her ribs and use the element of surprise. After all, unless he was a bat, the intruder couldn't see much in the unlighted room.

The next vibration was as light as a caress, but it seemed to explode inside her. The danger was so close. If only she could leave a message. She thought of her cell phone sitting, uselessly, in the pocket of her yellow slicker. There was no pen or paper, no lipstick or blood with which to scrawl a note. She was, literally, Luke's only chance.

Sweat gathered under her armpits and dripped between her breasts. Making as little noise as possible, she pulled her feet up under her so she was ready to pounce. She felt another vibration. Her heart was pounding so hard and so fast she wondered if she'd pass out. Oblivion beckoned but she couldn't respond.

Tears built up behind Jessie's eyes. She didn't want him to die. She didn't want to die, either. She wanted them to live. Together. For an instant she forgot about Crystal and all the reasons they couldn't have a happily-ever-after. She wasn't just fighting for their lives. She was fighting for their future. She positioned her flashlight so she could bring it down hard on the intruder's head.

Of course she wouldn't be able to reach his head. She'd have to settle for his chest or his stomach or— that was it. She'd aim for his groin.

She felt the ground shake again just before she heard an ominous click. She pulled back her arm, sprang to her feet, and swung the flashlight as hard as she could just as a gunshot cracked. She swatted at the air, her momentum carrying her in a circle and knocking her to the ground. The shooter missed, too, but he wouldn't a second time. Now he knew she was there, sprawled and panting on the floor. She heard the click again. She just hoped someone caught the bastard after she was dead. And Luke. He'd be buried alive.

"He's in the," she croaked, but her words were cut off by a shriek followed by the clacking of stilettos on linoleum.

"Oh my god, Denny! I heard a gunshot in the parlor!"

The vibrations started again. They were quicker and faster. Would the gunman shoot Lois? The door opened and closed, softly. No. The intruder had slipped back into the silence of the mortuary.

"C'mon, baby, that was just the cork from that bottle of bubbly." Dennis Prendergast's voice was slurred.

He and Lois were at it again. That left only one reasonable conclusion.

The stalker was Epps.

Jessie lay on the floor, visible from the doorway if

either of the lovers had gotten that close. She willed them to go back to their business.

"It sounded like a gun," Lois maintained.

"C'mon back here, hon. I've gotta gun just waitin' for you."

****

Luke could hear Jessie gasping and puffing as he dragged her through the empty streets. Fueled by adrenalin and rage, he ran full-out, allowing no quarter for her much shorter legs.

He vaulted up the shallow steps to Blanche's front porch. He stopped so fast she slammed into him as he dug out his key. He cursed. The instant they were inside, he pinned her shoulders against the door.

"Goddammit," he bit out. The golden eyes held no fear, only contrition and something else that reached into his chest and under his heart. Her lips parted, and he wanted to drill into her hard enough to split her in two.

Need clawed at him like an animal trapped in a box. He didn't care if the rest of them woke up and sold tickets. No way he'd make it upstairs. He had to have her. Now. Her hands were on his face, her tongue in his mouth. Thank God she felt the same.

Desperate to feel her soft skin, to lose himself in her warmth, to possess her. Desperate to get inside her, his fingers tangled with hers over the snaps on his old letter jacket. Finally, it was open. "Shit," he growled. "Overalls."

His gut spasmed, his erection throbbed. Frustration slammed into him.

"I've got it," she breathed. She shoved the straps off her shoulders and down her body. The boots stopped her, but her eagerness had given him fresh resolve. He stripped off her boots and clothes, ripped open his jeans, and thrust into her. Christ. He was wound as tight as a rubber band.

Goddammit all to hell. Mabel Ruth had confiscated his condoms. It wasn't going to stop them. He was already thrusting. She was dripping, moaning. He felt her fingers dig into his hips as she arched up into him. The pleasure was so great it was almost pain. "Jessie," he gasped.

She read his mind and fought him. "Don't stop."

He didn't think he could stop. He wanted her the way he'd wanted Crystal back in high school; mindlessly, hopelessly, relentlessly. His jaw clenched with desire and resentment. He didn't want to lose control like this but, damn, he wanted Jessie.

They strained against each other, slipping on the hardwood floor. He retained just enough sanity to stroke her, and he felt her tighten, tighten, even as he pounded into her.

"Ow!" she yelped and he paused, stricken. "What?"

"My head. Think I hit the coat rack."

Jesus. They'd slid across the hardwood floor, and he hadn't even known.

"Luke," she pleaded. "Don't stop."

He closed his eyes and touched her again. He knew he couldn't hold out long enough for her to catch up. His body, squeezed by her tight passage and her writhing hips, thrust wildly. The climax rushed at him like a speeding train. He shut his eyes and buried his face in her shoulder to keep from yelling his relief. Her body convulsed, and her cry seemed to explode in the quiet house.

He jerked his head up in time to see the flush on her face and the self-conscious look in her beautiful golden eyes.

"Sorry," she breathed, "we'll get an audience." He lowered his lips and kissed her softly.

"We'll probably get a baby, too. I should be shot." Her eyes widened in shock, but she gave him a potent half smile that made him harden all over again.

"The damage is done," she murmured. "Let's do it again."

With his jeans still open he carried her upstairs and settled them both on the four-poster. He kissed one resilient breast and stroked the other.

"Luke?"

Reluctantly he lifted his head.

"Could you take your clothes off?"

The lust was rising hard, but he paused to smooth a curl behind her ear. "Anything you want, baby. Anything."

She grinned at him. "I want it all. And I want it naked."

They didn't stop until first light. He pulled her against him, spoon fashion, and buried his face in her curls. "Marry me," he murmured.

"You got it," she said.

****

Jessie woke up in a cave. A hot cave. It took her a minute to realize the heated, granite-like body that ran along her back was Luke. The hair on his chest tickled her back, and his warm breath soughed over her neck. She let the feelings of happiness wash through her. He'd released the passion she hadn't even known was buried inside her. She felt as strong as a warrior princess and as invincible. She was close to discovering a murderer and a real life hero wanted to marry her.

On top of that, her family was united.

Oh yeah. And she was in love for the first time. And the guy seemed to want her, too.

Life just didn't get any better than this.

There were no guarantees. Jessie knew that.

Luke was still fighting the remnants of his feelings for his ex-wife but, in time, he'd let go of those old dreams. She hoped. She'd give him a home and a family and he'd forget the past.

A family. She flinched. She'd kind of lied to him about that. A sin of omission, but still a lie. He'd conscientiously bought the condoms, surrendered the condoms then worried about not having the condoms, and all the while she'd been safe. She probably should have told him she'd only been off the pill a week. Less. Why hadn't she? The thought was troubling. Was she testing him? Trying to find out whether he'd step up to the plate in case of a possible pregnancy? She knew he would. He had. The thing was, did she really want him that way?

The truth was she wanted him. He might not be in love with her now, but he could learn to love her. The hurly burly of love at first sight wasn't the kind of love that lasted. Was it? And they had passion going for them. Just thinking about last night made her face flush and her core melt. She closed her eyes and drifted on the sensuous memories.

Married to Luke. Yeah. She could do that.

****

Luke woke up hot and hard and horny. He needed

to get away from Jessie so he could think. He slipped out of the bed and grabbed up his clothes.

He'd been hit by an asteroid. It was the danger, of course. And the fear. Good God, the woman was impossible. She'd tried to hide him in a coffin. The feel of Miss Letty's still form beneath him was nothing compared with the fear he'd felt about Jessie's safety. He shook his head. He should have wrung her neck. Instead, he'd come apart in her arms.

He thrust his fingers through his hair and stared into Blanche's bathroom mirror. There was no going back now. She might be pregnant, and if she wasn't, she would be soon. He couldn't keep his hands off her. Wouldn't. This was it. His lips straightened into a grim line. Like it or not, they were getting hitched.

He hoped it was what Blanche would have wanted.

He picked up the coat rack in the foyer and a shiver of anticipation twisted down his spine. He frowned. He'd just spent hours having sex with Jessie. He should be over it. He spent a few minutes with Pyewacket and then crossed the dining room and walked through the butler's pantry. He had a half-formed plan in the back of his mind, but he forgot it, temporarily, when he walked into the kitchen and got the shock of his life.

It was Crystal. But a Crystal unlike anyone he'd ever known. Her long, corn silk hair drifted around her face, and she'd given up the expensive white wool suit in exchange for a red-and-white checked blouse and a pair of blue jeans on her long legs. A makeshift apron was tied around her slender waist and she was—he had to take a second look—she was cooking? He looked from the chagrined expression on her face to the burnt toast on the plates. The eggs were burning, too.

The amethyst eyes filled.

"I wanted to make you breakfast."

He strode across the room, removed the skillet from the burner, and shoveled the eggs onto the plates. As he forked them up he realized he was hungry. Starved.

"Okay," he said, when he'd finished. "Who are you and what have you done with my ex-wife?"

Her smile was tentative. "I was trying to tell you last night. I've changed."

He met her gaze head on but didn't speak.

"I made a mess of things between us, Luke. I was so used to getting and so unused to giving."

He nodded. Beauty like Crystal's definitely had its downside.

She sucked in a deep breath. Confession might be good for the soul, but it was obviously hard for her. He felt a grudging respect.

"I've been working on these changes for a while now and I wouldn't have bothered you, but when I heard you were here, in Mystic, I just found myself on a plane."

He could read between the lines. "You heard I was with another woman."

"Yes."

"From whom?"

"Mabel Ruth."

That didn't make sense. Mabel Ruth seemed like Jessie's biggest fan.

"I don't think she contacted me because she wanted to see us together," Crystal explained. "She thinks you can't move on until you confront your past." Her lovely face took on a pleading look. "I don't want you to move on. That's it. Plain and simple. I love you, Luke, and, under the anger, I think you still love me."

He was surprised at her insight. He thought she was right about Mabel Ruth.

She seemed to take courage from his silence.

"There's something else." She looked down at the table and her long, thick lashes swept her lovely cheekbones. "I want to be honest with you.

I got involved with Bobby Ray." He held still for a long moment.

"Say something, Luke."

"When?"

"A few months before our marriage ended. I was unhappy because you were gone so much and he, well, he pursued me."

Luke believed that. For all his undeniable charm, Bobby Ray had been trouble. "Is that why you wanted a divorce?"

The amethyst eyes reflected disbelief. "I thought you'd fight it. I thought you'd come riding in on a white horse and snatch me back, but you didn't."

Such a response hadn't even occurred to him. Now he wondered why.

"Afterward I kept up the clandestine thing with Bobby. Why not? You were gone."

A bell rang in the back of his brain. "Are you involved in the troubles between Francie and Zach?"

The color drained out of her face. "That wasn't our intention. You've got to believe me. We did use—I used her name as a cover on my letters. I mean, it made it more fun."

There it was. That self-centeredness. Crystal and Bobby had ruined the happiness of two innocent people just because it "made it more fun."

"You have to tell Zach. If you don't, I will."

"Of course." The light returned to the beautiful eyes. "Do you think you can forgive me?"

He studied her face. Crystal's problem wasn't cruelty. She hurt people without even realizing. Somehow, that seemed worse. Lucky for him, the confession of infidelity felt more like a shallow bruise than a crater in his heart. Lucky for him he'd met another kind of woman.

"Sure. For what it's worth. I forgive you."

The eyes lit with a celestial fire. She launched into full seduction mode. With his forgiveness she thought there was a chance for reconciliation.

Luke wondered when he'd become immune to the beauty. He'd probably never know, but he knew what he wanted; he wanted a woman he could count on and that reminded him.

"I've got to go get a tree," he muttered.

Crystal's eyes lit up. He knew she was remembering two years earlier when she'd dragged him through the snow in search of the perfect white pine.

"Can I come?"

He started to decline but changed his mind. He was going to marry Jessie, but he wasn't planning to be a lapdog. Not this time. "Sure."

****

Jessie woke to see the sun streaming through the arched window. She could smell Luke's tantalizing scent, but she knew she was alone in the big bed.

She stretched like a contented cat.

She inhaled the scent of testosterone and lovemaking on the sheets. She felt a sudden, urgent need to see him, to touch him, to assure herself that his proposal was real.

She hopped out of bed. A quick shower later, she pulled on a pair of green corduroy jeans and a red sweater embellished with a decorated Christmas tree, ran a brush through her curls, and took the backstairs two steps at a time. She had a busy day ahead, but for the first time in a long time, she had a partner.

She hugged the secret to herself.

They'd get to use the stations-of-the-cross ice sculpture after all.

Chapter Seventeen

Monica and Gillian sat at Blanche's wicker kitchen table bathed in the swath of light created by the morning sun. The cheerful room smelled of cinnamon and coffee and something else. Evergreen?

Jessie hugged her mother and sister. "Merry Christmas," she caroled.

"You, too, sweetheart," her mother said.

"Ditto that," Gillian replied.

Jessie gazed from one to the other. "What's with the long faces? We're all here together, and it's Christmas."

Two sets of sky blue eyes exchanged a glance. Jessie thought she understood.

"Mom, if you're self-conscious about last night, I mean I know you and Dad shared a room."

A pretty flush brightened Monica Maynard's cheeks, and Jessie's heart sang. This Christmas just got better and better. "Does this mean you're reconciling?"

"No," Monica said. "Dad hasn't promised to retire and until he does, nothing will change."

It was a reminder to Jessie that she'd screwed up the plans. If she'd been able to marry Kit, Howard Maynard could have retired and her parents' marriage would have been saved.

"This isn't about you," Monica said, reading her thoughts. "You have to make your own decisions. You have to live your own life."

"Guess you're fired as the family's guardian angel," Gillian quipped, but there was no twinkle in her eyes.

Jessie put a hand on her sister's forearm. "What's wrong?"

Gillian laid her own hand over Jessie's as the door from the butler's pantry swung open. Kit entered. He wore an expensive sweater and slacks, and he smelled of the outdoors and his cheeks were rosy, as if he'd just finished a snowball fight.

"It's about time you got up, sleepyhead." He grinned at Jessie. "Come on out here and see your surprise."

"You shouldn't have," Jessie said, meaning it. She didn't want her ex to have any false hopes.

"Don't worry," he said, grabbing her upper arm and tugging her along, "I didn't."

Jessie looked over her shoulder. Her mother's smile was wooden and Gillian looked positively grim.

What on earth was going on?

An instant later she knew. She stopped dead in the double-door entrance to the parlor and gazed at the Currier & Ives scene. A ten-foot white pine filled the bay window. A lean, dark-haired man stood on a stool arranging a string of lights while nearby his beautiful blonde wife directed and advised. A perfect *pas-de-deux*.

Right out of Christmas in Connecticut.

Right out of The Nightmare Before Christmas.

It was the tree she wanted and the man she wanted.

She remembered that old saying Be careful what you wish for.

Luke and Crystal were absorbed in their project, absorbed in one another. Listening to their conversation was like plunging a dagger into her own heart.

"Shift that one string up a couple of inches. It's all about spacing and color. We don't want a red light next to a Santa light, do we?"

"Why," Luke grumbled, "am I getting such a sense of *déjà vu*?"

His tone was playful, familiar, as if they'd done this many times before. As if they'd do it many times in the future.

Jessie wrapped her arms around her waist. They looked so right together. It wasn't as bad as seeing Kit's dalliance with his ex-wife. It was ten times worse. A hundred times. Because this time she was in love with her fiancé.

Kit's arm came around her shoulder. She barely felt it.

"Isn't it perfect?"

"Perfect," she echoed.

Luke's head lifted and his green eyes met hers. She masked her sense of betrayal. He couldn't help loving someone else.

The doorbell chimed.

"Who's that?" Jessie asked, even though she didn't really care.

"It'll be Ezra," Crystal said. "We called him from the truck. Mabel Ruth, Millicent and Maude, too."

They'd gone out to cut the tree together. Of course.

"Jessie," Luke said. They heard Crystal greeting the visitors.

"Let me go see about the coffee," she said.

****

Chief Smith settled into Blanche's rocking chair. Mabel Ruth and Maude sat side by side on the Victorian loveseat while Monica, Gillian, and Millicent shared the sofa. Luke had brought a pair of chairs from the dining room. He straddled one. Crystal took the chair across from him. She was in Luke's direct line of vision. It was a good strategic move. If Jessie had been one-tenth as beautiful as Crystal, she'd be into staging, too. She dropped down to the hearth and scratched Pyewacket behind the ears. She looked up to see Luke's green gaze on her, and something inside her cracked. The pharmaceutical companies were missing the boat, she thought. There ought to be an over-the-counter pill for heartbreak. She heard Luke's voice. It took a minute for her to realize he was talking about their midnight adventure.

"We thought the coffin might be empty," he said. Everyone gasped. "Jessie had a theory, a very good one, I might add, that Epps was smuggling drugs in carcasses and burying the coffins to allay suspicion."

"So was Letty in there?" It was Millicent.

Luke rested his lean, muscular arms against the back of the chair. The sight of those powerful thighs and competent hands catapulted her back to the pleasure of last night. She forced herself to listen to his answer.

"Most of her."

"Most of her?" Monica Maynard sounded shocked. She and Howard stood near the glass doors.

"Her bones had been replaced with lengths of plumbing pipe." Luke's eyes met Jessie's. "That's why Epps keeps it on hand."

The old newspaper headline flashed before her.

Epps wasn't smuggling drugs. "He's corpse looting," she murmured.

Horrified gasps filled the room.

Luke nodded. "Corpse looters harvest bone and tissue and sell it to tissue banks, hospitals, and individual doctors. The buyers need the body parts for transplants, and they don't realize the parts were illegally obtained. Epps undoubtedly forges signatures granting permission, and he falsifies the certificates if the donors are over age or have been seriously ill."

"There's a strong risk of infection for the recipients," Jessie explained. "There was a lot of publicity about the scandal involving Alaistair Cooke. His body parts were looted up at a funeral home in New Jersey."

Smith frowned. "Alaistair Cooke?"

"The host of Masterpiece Theater," chorused Mabel Ruth, Millicent, and Maude.

"I think Miss Letty suspected," Jessie said, soberly. "I read a headline in one of her old papers. I think it was about the Alaistair Cooke story."

"Blanche must have found out," Mabel Ruth said, in a sorrowful voice. "She probably confronted Epps. She never had any fear, not when she knew she was right."

Jessie watched Luke's eyes find those of his ex-wife, and her heart twisted in pain. It was her first real experience with jealousy. It really was the green-eyed monster.

"But what about the reverend," Millicent asked. "We know he was in cahoots about Blanche's death."

Luke rubbed his hand over the bristles on his face and chin. He hadn't taken time to shave before he'd gone off to buy the tree. With Crystal.

"My guess is Epps paid Prendergast to keep the church locked," Luke said.

Maude looked confused. "But why?"

"A precaution," Jessie said. "He probably wanted as few people as possible near the mortuary." She thought of something else. "Focusing attention on the church diverted attention from the funeral home." Her eyes flew to Luke's. "Epps might even have engineered the tryst between Prendergast and his wife to throw more suspicion on the reverend."

Luke nodded. "That occurred to me, too."

"I still believe the reverend killed Blanche," Millicent said, stubbornly. "Letty, too."

"There's something else," Luke said. "Someone came through the door that connects the church and the mortuary and shot at Jessie last night."

All eyes flew to Jessie.

"What?" her mother cried.

"Where were you?" her father demanded.

Luke kept his eyes on Jessie. "She heard someone coming, I didn't. She protected me by tumbling me into the coffin, then she formed a plan to attack the newcomer with a flashlight."

"Oh my god!"

"I missed," Jessie said. "Mister Epps missed, too."

"How do you know who it was?" Gillian asked. "Could you see his face?"

Luke and Jessie exchanged another look.

"She knows," Luke said, "because Prendergast and Lois were down the hall. They actually scared off the intruder."

There was a brief shocked silence.

"The reverend said last night that Miss Letty would be buried this morning," Crystal said, slowly. "If Jessie had been killed, Luke would have been buried alive."

Misery and guilt flooded Jessie. How could she have been so careless with Luke's life?

"I'd have gotten the lid open," Luke said. His green eyes were warm on her. "Jessie risked her life to save mine. She's a hero."

Everyone murmured words of praise, but they didn't console Jessie. She wasn't a hero, and anyway, she didn't want Luke's gratitude.

"My goodness," Monica murmured.

"Mysterious deaths, grave robbing, illicit sex. Sleepy little Mystic Hollow has turned into a regular Peyton Place."

"I'm glad for Eleanor's sake," Millicent said. "She's had enough misery from that husband of hers. At least he's not a murderer."

"I wonder if Sweeney Todd sliced up your Aunt Blanche," Kit put in.

Jessie saw Luke flinch. "Aunt Blanche was cremated the same day she died, remember? Epps wouldn't have had time to, you know, work on her."

"Probably couldn't take a chance on someone finding out how she died," Millicent said.

"And Mister Epps knew Aunt Blanche had powerful friends," Jessie added. The elderly ladies appeared pleased with her comment and her heart warmed. "He was probably afraid of an investigation. After all, it's because of your suspicions we've discovered the murderer."

The chief flattened his beefy hands on his solid thighs and pushed to his feet. "I think it's about time to have a little look-see over at the mortuary. I'll have to drive to Roanoke for a warrant." He looked at Luke. He obviously wanted the younger man's help.

"I'll ride along if it's all right with you," Luke said. "Jessie should come, too. It's her investigation."

She shook her head. She didn't need to be in on the arrest, and she couldn't bear to spend time with Luke knowing it was over between them, that he'd be looking for a good time to tell her. She decided to ease his path by setting the time herself.

"I'll stay here and help with the Christmas preparations," she said. "You can fill us in after the pageant."

Chapter Eighteen

For Reverend Dennis Prendergast, Christmas Eve was a slam dunk. The church service consisted of beloved carols, a Bible story, and a pageant guaranteed to please all of the parents in the congregation.

The whole thing required little or no pastoral effort. If only everything in life could be just like Christmas Eve.

He enjoyed their personal traditions, too, his and Ellie's. On December Twenty-fourth, his wife abandoned her efforts to lower his cholesterol and blood pressure and prepared a brunch worthy of the gods.

This year the menu consisted of quail's eggs and *pâté de foie gras*, hash browned potatoes, strawberries and cream, crisp bacon, imported cheese, pink champagne, and his wife's specialty, quiche a la Ellie. The rich food and bubbly drink warmed his insides, and for an all-too-short moment, he relaxed and allowed his natural optimism to surface.

This would all work out. Today was not only Christmas Eve, it was payday. It marked the end of his unholy alliance. By tonight, when the children of Mystic Hollow were tucked all snug in their beds, the pastor of St. Michael's would have much more than sugar plums in his head. He'd have a cool, tax-free million dollars in his hands.

Even better, he'd be free of his Faustian bargain.

From now on, he'd tread more carefully. This caper had turned him gray. Not that it showed. Thanks to a wonderfully clever colorist next to the tanning salon in Roanoke, what was left of his hair still gleamed a burnished gold.

He leaned back in his chair and groaned. He rubbed at the slight ache in his overfull stomach. Something brushed his arm and he flinched. Ah. It was only Ellie. His nerves really, really needed a vacation.

She set a parfait glass in front of him. It was rain bowed in citrusy colors. Dennis thought he'd hurl if he had to eat one more bite.

"Are you all right, Denny? You look a little peaked."

"Fine." He smiled at her. "You really pulled out all the stops, Ellie." He glanced at the dessert.

"Not sure there's any more room at the inn." She looked resigned but only for a second. She'd never pressure him. He knew that. On the other hand, she'd worked hard on the whole meal. The least he could do was eat it. He picked up his spoon. "Looks delicious." It was delicious. Light, easy to swallow.

"There's more to this than lemons, limes, and oranges," he said, thoughtfully. "Secret ingredient?"

"Kiwi. Makes it a little tart."

He leaned back to accommodate the mound of his stomach. "Another triumph," he said, sleepily, "a symphony in culinary success."

She smiled, rose, and started to clear the table. He should offer to help, but he couldn't seem to keep his eyes open. Naturally she noticed.

"Why don't you take a little nap? We've got a

couple of hours before we have to be at the church."

A nap sounded great.

He pushed back his chair and lumbered to his feet. He moved to give her a hug, but her hands were full of dirty dishes. "Thanks again, Ellie. You always make Christmas Eve the best day of the year."

"Don't forget to take your phone with you, dear," she said, as she moved toward the sink. "Just in case we need to touch base at the last minute."

Dennis pulled the little phone out of his pocket and held it up.

"I never go anywhere without it," he quipped. "It was a great surprise, Ellie."

He had a surprise for her, too. Tomorrow, they were getting the hell out of Mystic Hollow.

****

On the drive to Roanoke to pick up a warrant, Ezra and Luke talked for a few minutes, but soon both lapsed into silence. Luke's eyes burned from lack of sleep. He realized he hadn't slept more than a few hours a night since Jessie had arrived.

Jessie. Something was bothering her. Luke was no expert on the female psyche, which probably accounted for his divorce. But he was observant. He'd left a sensuous, satisfied woman in bed, but she'd seemed tense and brittle this morning. The question was why? He'd gotten her the tree she wanted. Had she felt threatened by Crystal's participation? He frowned. Shouldn't she have been satisfied with his proposal? He'd thought Jessie Maynard was different, that she wouldn't succumb to petty jealousy.

He tried to see the situation from her point of view. Crystal was an intimidating act to follow, but hell, he'd proposed to Jessie. If she was waiting to hear an endless litany of reassurances and professions of love, she'd wait a long time. He wasn't going out on that emotional limb again.

Not ever.

Not even for a woman who kept trying to rescue him.

Maybe she was torqued that she wouldn't be present for Epps's arrest. He knew she felt possessive about the investigation. But she could have asked to go along. She hadn't. It was something else. He let out a long breath. He'd have to track this down tonight. Heat curled in his stomach. Yeah. They could work this all out tonight.

In bed.

Luke shifted in his seat. Just thinking about Jessie made him hard.

"I appreciate all you kids have done on this business," Ezra said. "What're your plans now? Heading back to D.C.?"

Chief Smith glanced at him. Luke must have looked startled because the older man explained. "Blanche kept us informed about your doings. That woman was so darned proud of you."

Luke said nothing. He was pretty sure Blanche wouldn't have been proud that he'd seduced her great-niece.

"I may stick around," he said. The words surprised him. "I'm going to marry Jessie Maynard."

The chief kept his eyes on the road, but he nodded his head.

"Good decision, boy. I believe this time you've got it right."

****

The witch hat house was starting to look like the set from a Christmas television special. Garlands of evergreen decorated the mantelpiece and twined around the banister. A string of colored lights outlined the large oval mirror in the parlor. Red and green ribbons were tied on the individual lamps in the chandelier in the dining room. The air was full of cinnamon and pine.

Monica bought the last fresh turkey at Ferguson's along with the fixings for creamed onions, stuffing, squash and corn relish, and cranberry sauce. Early Christmas Eve afternoon, while Luke and Chief Smith were out chasing down a warrant, Jessie, Monica, and Gillian baked pumpkin and mince pies. Kit, dressed in a stained apron, was stringing cranberries while Crystal kept him company.

When Monica went out to the parlor to put up her feet, the younger people gathered around the table for hot chocolate.

"I love Christmas," Crystal said. "It's such a romantic time."

More romantic for some than for others, Jessie thought. But she held onto her friendly smile.

"Ah, romance," Gillian said. "The year I was nineteen," Gillian said, "I spent Christmas in Paris and fell in love with the Louvre Museum."

Crystal laughed. "It was Paris. You should have fallen in love with a man."

"Oh, I did that, too," Monica said. "It's just that my relationship with the museum lasted longer."

They all laughed.

"I remember the year I fell in love with Rags," Kit reminisced.

"Rags?" Crystal's lovely lips tilted into a smile.

"He was a beagle. I was ten." He smiled at Jessie. "What about you, Jess?"

Jessie thought about meeting Luke, how she'd fallen in love so fast and so absolutely and how she'd realized, too late, he still loved his ex-wife.

"Jessie's in love with the holiday itself," Gillian said. "This is the first year she didn't play Santa for kids on the south side of town."

"Why not?" Crystal asked.

Jessie was ashamed of herself. She'd completely forgotten her favorite Christmas tradition. "Got too tied up in wedding arrangements," she muttered.

"Christmas is a time for weddings," Crystal said. "I got married on December Twenty-fourth." But you left him. You wanted a divorce.

"So this is your anniversary," Gillian said.

Crystal nodded. Her amethyst eyes looked dreamy. "Everyone said it was the most beautiful wedding ever held at St. Michael's."

Jessie believed the claim. She'd seen the photo. Most beautiful wedding. Most beautiful bride. Most besotted bridegroom.

Howard Maynard appeared at the door, and he motioned to Jessie. Fresh from a nap he looked rested. Jessie's mood lightened. She'd wanted her dad healthy and her family together. It was all good. They walked down the hall to Blanche's comfortable study. Howard took the big desk chair while Jessie sat on a small sofa.

"I just wanted to take a minute to apologize, sweetheart."

"Apologize?"

"Your mother and I saw your marriage to Kit as a

way to solve our problem. In all fairness, I believe he's a fine young man. It seemed like a good match for you, but that doesn't excuse our selfishness."

Jessie shook her head. She couldn't let him take all the blame. "I apologize to you for all the time and money spent on the wedding. I thought Kit and I could make a go of it, but it never would have worked."

"I see that now," he said. "You were always more friends than lovers. I never saw that desperate passion on either of your faces."

She smiled. "Is that how you feel about Mom?"

He nodded. "She's my life. I'm glad you finally found someone you could feel that way about."

Jessie's face burned. She'd been too obvious. Now her folks would be disappointed again. "What about you and Mom? Will you remarry?"

He grinned. It was a satisfied expression she hadn't seen on his face in a long while. "We haven't discussed it. I haven't told her I'm retiring in January. Gonna let Kit run the show. If he does well, I'll sell him the business."

"What about Grandad's legacy?"

"I've learned an important lesson through the heart attack, the divorce, and your canceled wedding. You can't spend your life taking care of someone else's dream. You've only got one chance, Jess. Do what you want to do."

Jessie stayed in the study after her father had left. She thought about his words. She thought about all the efforts she'd made to hold her family together, to protect her dad's health, to be the daughter her parents needed instead of the woman she was.

She'd started to pursue her own dreams down here

in Mystic Hollow. Here, in Great-Aunt Blanche's home, in her town, Jessie had finally found a place where she could be herself, a place that felt like home. She'd become her own person. She knew it wasn't the quaint house or Blanche's friends or even the murder investigation that had wrought the change. Love had made her see beneath the surface, made her feel alive. She thought about Luke, and her heart squeezed. The metamorphosis had come with a high price, but even so, she wasn't sorry. And she vowed not to be bitter. If Crystal could make Luke happy, she wanted him to have her.

That's what love was all about, wasn't it?

She leaned back in the chair and closed her eyes. The noble sentiment faded when she remembered the feel of Luke's body on hers, the tickle of his breath at her ear, the sense of oneness she'd never experienced with anybody else.

She was lying to herself. She didn't want Luke to reconcile with Crystal. She wanted the man for herself. That thought gave rise to a more painful one. She still had secret knowledge that would help Francine and Zach. She needed to use it without hurting Luke and there was only one way to do that. She headed for the kitchen in search of Crystal.

When the women were back in Blanche's study with the door closed, Jessie didn't know where to begin. She decided just to plunge in. "I read some of Blanche's," she hesitated then chose a word, "diary. She knew you were getting together with Bobby Ray and using Francine's name to hide behind."

Jessie knew her tone was accusing. She thought she saw remorse on the other woman's face and she tried to lighten up.

"In any case, Zach and Francine are going to get married. They're going to have a baby." For an instant she felt like a gossip, but everyone at Miss Letty's funeral had heard about it.

"Good for them," Crystal said. She didn't sound sarcastic.

"They're getting married," Jessie continued, "but they're still estranged. He believed the lies your late boyfriend told him."

Crystal lifted her slim shoulders. Even her shrug was pretty. "We did it to protect ourselves.

Well, me, mostly. I didn't want Francine to get hurt."

"She did get hurt."

The beautiful face twisted. "Bobby probably rubbed Zach's face in it. He was charming and he knew it but he had a mean streak."

"What about you? You risked hurting your husband."

"I couldn't get his attention. He was always so busy, so focused on school and work and making a living. I just wanted him to notice me."

"I doubt there's a man alive who wouldn't notice you," Jessie said. She noticed Crystal took the compliment in stride. The woman knew her own power.

"He wanted me. They all wanted me. But it was physical. Luke never treated me like an equal. He wasn't interested in what I thought."

Sympathy nipped at Jessie. Crystal sounded like one of the women who'd married to avoid taking charge of her own life. A woman like Jessie had been just last week.

"Bobby was trying to stick it to Zach," Crystal said, shame coloring her voice. "They are half-brothers. Zach was a war hero, and Bobby was jealous of his dad's admiration for that." Half-brothers. That explained a lot.

"First Bobby hit him with that, then with the business about Francine. Once Zach had confirmed the fatherhood thing with his mom, it was only logical that he believe Bobby on the other."

"And he was vulnerable to betrayal," Jessie murmured. Poor Zach.

"You need to talk to Zach," she told Crystal. "Straighten things out." She stepped closer to the other woman. "And there's one more thing, Crystal, you can't, under any circumstances let this get back to Luke. It would break his heart."

Crystal looked at her strangely. "Would it? You're awfully anxious to protect him."

Jessie was uncomfortable with the other woman's scrutiny. No doubt everyone could see she was in love with Luke. She wasn't putting it into words. "I'm protecting his interests. They're my interests, too. Don't forget, we're getting married."

She'd meant the words to sound mercenary, but they unlocked something deep inside her.

Joy.

She was getting married to Luke.

She barely heard her buzzing cell phone.

"Your phone," Crystal murmured. Jessie picked it up.

"Hello?"

"Jessie," Mabel Ruth said, "can you come over to Maude's?"

****

Mort's face was as white as the bleached bones of a skeleton left too long in the desert. His left eye twitched noticeably as he eyed the briefcase on the floor. It contained a couple of million dollars. He longed to touch the money, fondle it, spend it.

He knew he wouldn't get the chance.

How stupid he'd been. Of course there couldn't be any witnesses. He deserved his fate.

"Your gun."

He handed over his weapon. What else could he do? There was a loaded gun barrel not five feet away. He found himself staring at the face opposite him. It was ruthless, implacable, a face the public would never see. The face of a cold, calculating killer.

"Let's take a walk."

The words were uttered in a bland voice, but Mort felt the fire. Sweat poured out of him. His plastic glasses slid down his long nose and fell to the floor. He let them go. He wouldn't need them.

Ann Yost

Chapter Nineteen

Maude lived in a brownstone Victorian. Her kitchen, like Blanche's, was big, square, and inefficient. An old-fashioned mangle iron filled one corner.

The ladies motioned for Jessie to join them at an oak farm table that was too big for the kitchen.

"Have some chamomile mint tea," Maude urged. "You look a little stressed."

"Thanks," Jessie said, accepting the cup. She turned to Mabel Ruth. "Is there something going on?"

"Several things," Maude said, vaguely.

"Let me tell her," Millicent interrupted. There were two bright spots on her pale face. "Maudie took a nap a little while ago, and she had a visit from Blanche."

Jessie nodded. She'd had the same sort of dream the other night. Right before Luke showed up, sinfully sexy in those unbuttoned jeans. Heat flashed through her. The chemistry between them had to mean something. She knew he didn't love her but love didn't always come at first sight. She thought he could be happy with her.

She was sure she could be happy with him.

"Jessie," Mabel Ruth interrupted, "you seem a little flushed."

Jessie found a smile. "Just the excitement of Christmas, and everything."

"Here's the thing of it," Maude said, her blue eyes

as round as saucers. "She told me she wasn't murdered at all."

"She?" Jessie had lost the thread of the conversation.

"Blanche, dear. No one killed her. She just went to sleep and didn't wake up."

That couldn't be right. "But we've been so sure there was a murder."

"There was a murder all right," Mabel Ruth said, grimly. "Blanche told Maude that Letty's food was doctored with peanut oil. Someone wanted her out of the way."

"I still say it was Reverend Prendergast," Millicent put in. "Letty probably discovered his liaison with Lois Epps."

"Now, Mil," Mabel Ruth said, looking down her nose at her friend, "the reverend may be a philanderer, but it wasn't he who shot at Jessie last night."

"So Aunt Blanche didn't mention any names?"

"She was vague," Maude confessed. "Spirits can be vague."

"And bad spellers," Millicent put in.

"Or perhaps I wasn't concentrating," Maude admitted. "It was just so nice to see dear Blanche."

Jessie knew there were many who would discount information that came in a dream to an elderly lady, but she wasn't one of them. Whether the dream was an actual visitation or the product of Maude's experiences, Jessie thought it was legitimate.

"That's all we learned from the dream," Mabel Ruth corrected. "We have other information, too."

Jessie felt a flicker of excitement. "What information?"

"Hattie Bexler called me this afternoon," Millicent said. "She wanted to let me know my cod liver oil had come in."

"It's wonderful stuff," Mabel Ruth put in.

"It cleans out the pipes," Maude added. "If you know what I mean." Jessie smiled.

"Anyway," Millicent continued, "Hattie has chronic insomnia and it flares up in the winter."

"I'm sorry to hear that."

Mabel Ruth took up the narrative. "When Hattie's awake at night, she paces her upstairs hallway. She lives above the pharmacy."

"So she has an excellent view of the Green," Maude said.

"Now the point," Mabel Ruth said. "Last night she saw someone."

"Mister J. Mortimer Epps," Millicent said, with a pleased smile. "Hattie says he suffers from insomnia, too, takes pills for it. When they don't work, he walks around the town."

"What time was this?"

"Eleven fifteen," Mabel Ruth said. "Right around the time you and Lucas were in the church."

"I remember checking my watch just before we left the house," Jessie said. "It was a bit after eleven. We must have been there ten or fifteen minutes."

"Could Mister Epps have shot at Jessie and then hurried out onto the Green?" Maude asked.

Jessie wondered. Epps's "alibi" depended on the accuracy of Hattie Bexler's observation, but there was a little leeway timewise. But wouldn't the mortician have stuck around to see if anyone else came to check out the coffin? Would he have squeezed off a shot and then paced the streets of the small town?

Maybe. If he needed an alibi. But how could he be sure Hattie or anyone else would see him at that time of night?

"If it wasn't Epps," she said, slowly, "and it wasn't Prendergast whose footsteps I heard, who was it?"

No one spoke. All three elderly faces looked tired, wilted. Oh no. The suspect was a friend. All at once she knew.

"There's a short list of people who had access to the church and mortuary," she said, slowly. "If we can account for the whereabouts of Dennis Prendergast, Mortimer Epps and Lois Epps that leaves only one person."

Maude's sigh was shaky. "Poor Eleanor."

"She never has had any luck," Millicent added.

"Save your sympathy, girls," Mabel Ruth said, bracingly. "If she didn't murder Letty she doesn't need it. And if she did kill her, she doesn't deserve it."

Sensible words, Jessie thought, but they ignored the strings of friendship.

"If Eleanor Prendergast was the shooter," Jessie said, slowly, "she must be involved in the corpse looting."

"I imagine so," Mabel Ruth said, heavily. "She lives next to the mortuary, and well, her late father was an undertaker."

It occurred to Jessie that she'd been a little distracted. She should have found out the background on everyone involved in this business.

"We can't let her hurt anyone else," Jessie said, suddenly. "Let's call Chief Smith."

"We tried. His phone is turned off," Mabel Ruth

explained. "And Edna's not answering at the house."

"I imagine she's at church by now," Millicent pointed out. "It's nearly time for the pageant to start."

"That's right," Maude said, "at least we'll know where Eleanor is for the next couple of hours."

Jessie looked her question.

"Eleanor reads the Christmas Story," Mabel Ruth explained. "She and Francine co-chair the Pageant Committee."

Jessie wondered if it was the first time in history a Christmas Pageant co-chair had murdered someone. She suspected not.

"We need to get over there," Jessie said, jumping up. "We may need the element of surprise to catch her."

The social hall at St. Michael's looked like the floor of the New York Stock Exchange. People buzzed here and there, greeting neighbors, trading holiday wishes, stuffing their children into costumes, and setting up the cookies for the post-pageant reception.

Jessie waded through the crowd and up the stairs. The sanctuary was already filling up. She saw her family, including Kit and Crystal, sitting near the front on the right side. Eleanor Prendergast, wearing an ill-fitting gray suit, sat quietly near the lectern. The pulpit was empty. Zach leaned against the wall in the narthex. He never took his eyes off Francine who was working as a troubleshooter, soothing hurt feelings, creating angel costumes out of shepherd's garb, and lining children up for the processional down the aisle.

The redhead looked as if she might drop. Jessie figured there was nothing she could do about Eleanor Prendergast at the moment. They didn't have any proof, and she couldn't exactly make a citizen's arrest. She studied her pregnant friend. And then she looked at Zach's glowering face. Had Crystal had a chance to talk with them? The least Jessie could do was help out now. She crossed the room to Francine. "Need some help?"

"Lord, yes." Francie's smile didn't reach her eyes. "Eleanor usually helps with this part but she got here late and she's had to take her place at the lectern."

Jessie wondered where the pastor's wife had been. And where was Prendergast himself? Dead in an alley?

"Where's the reverend?"

"I believe he's in his office getting robed," Francie said. She seemed a little distracted, too. "Are you okay?"

Francie grimaced. "Zach and his mother and father are watching me like hawks. He must have told them about the baby."

She opened her mouth, but the redhead interrupted.

"Listen, could you put on that hooded bathrobe? The Sanderson's golden retriever, Bosco, is supposed to play Rudolph."

Jessie glanced at the big yellow dog with a pair of felt antlers on his head. He grinned at her.

"Bosco's pretty well behaved, but I don't want to take any chances."

The assignment was perfect. She'd have a legitimate excuse to go right up to the front. She could keep a close eye on Eleanor. If the woman was innocent, well, no harm done. If she was a killer, Jessie would make sure she didn't hurt anyone else.

****

"Damn."

Dennis scrambled out from under the toasty comforter. Why hadn't Ellie wakened him? He felt

233

groggy and slow and now he'd have to rush. He hated to rush.

He pulled on his gray wool slacks, shouldered into a fresh white shirt, buttoned it, clumsily, then tried to knot the Christmas tie she'd left for him. It was mauve and cream with Christmas tree outlines fitted together like an Escher puzzle. Very tasteful. He glanced at his Rolex. The pageant was set to start in twenty minutes. She must have left a good hour earlier.

Dennis barely had time to style his hair, grab his topcoat and his new phone, and hurry out the back door. Thank God he only had to cross the parking lot.

He noticed Eleanor had left her seven-year-old sedan in the driveway. She always parked next to his late model BMW. She must have been in a helluva hurry.

Maybe she'd fallen asleep, too.

He glanced into the backseat window on his way past. Then he stopped and took a second look. He grinned at the box constructed of carbon fiber and aluminum. A Henk. It was the Rolls Royce of suitcases and something he'd mentioned he'd wanted. So that was his real present. Dear Ellie. She knew he'd missed out on gifts as the son of a parsimonious pastor. She always came through with good presents, but this year she'd outdone herself. He patted the pocket that held the light-as-a-feather cell phone.

He was late enough that the social hall had virtually emptied. He slipped past it and up the stairs to his office. Someone, probably Ellie, had unlocked the door for him. All he had to do was climb into his robe and stole. If he forgot about Mort Epps, he could really enjoy this Christmas Eve.

Dennis hung up his coat, replaced his sweater with a robe, and had just started to work the zipper when he heard someone clear their throat. His pulse jumped, and he clamped down on the cry that made its way up to his throat. Mort.

The head that appeared over the top of the sofa facing away from him, however, was female.

"Hello, lover," she said.

"Jesus, Mary and Joseph," he exhaled. "You scared me to death."

Lois pulled the cord of a small lamp. The light allowed him to get a good look at her. The dress was Christmas red, and it barely covered her nipples. Her breasts mounded like foothills in the Appalachian mountain chain.

"Jesus," he breathed again. He felt the blood rush to his groin, felt the rush of need. He was barely aware of a leather briefcase in Lois's hand.

"Mort told me to come and give you this," she said.

The money. Hall-le-lu-jah.

Lois set the case down and moved closer. He could see a faint sheen of sweat between her breasts. The flesh quivered under his gaze. He tried to be sensible.

"There isn't time."

She smoothed her hand over the rock hard flesh beneath his zipper.

"Feels like we'd better make time."

She was right. He could barely remain standing.

He let her push him onto the sofa and unfasten his pants.

Lois was good. It took less than a minute. Still breathing hard, he tucked himself back into his pants and got to his feet. He zipped his robe and pulled the satin stole over his head.

"How's my hair?"

She smoothed the strands with the fingers of one hand. He watched her breasts expand as she breathed. He felt himself expand, too.

"Damn."

"What's the matter?"

"I'm hard."

"What'd you have for lunch, sugar? A Viagra sandwich?"

"Very funny." He placed her hand against him.

It took a little longer this time. He gathered himself for the climax that would bring him relief when he heard the organ swell. He frowned.

They'd started without him?

"What's that?"

"A hymn," he said. Her hands kneaded his erection. "O Come, O Come, Emmanuel." She giggled and paused.

Dennis was out of patience. "C'mon. I've got to get down there."

Minutes later he zipped up and dashed for the door only to make two dismaying discoveries.

The door was locked from the outside.

And he was hard. Again.

There was no way he could go downstairs even if he could get the door opened. He couldn't even call for help. Sweat began to roll down his face.

"Hey, sugar," Lois said, "does it seem like it's getting hot in here?"

****

They found nothing at the mortuary. The place looked the same, peaceful, if funereal, but empty. A search of the office revealed most of the files missing. An electronic search told Luke the computer memory had been erased.

Someone had known they were coming.

"We're too late," Ezra said, heavily. "He's skipped."

"Maybe."

Luke stepped out of the office and into the hallway. The place felt empty. His footsteps echoed as he paced the corridor. This time he didn't go into the unmarked door. This time his sixth sense took him in another direction.

He went into the crematory.

The pile of ash in the oven was still warm. Whose ashes? A client? Or was the answer more sinister? Luke flipped on the lights and looked around the room. There was something over there, behind the equipment. Chief Smith poked his head in the room.

"Find anything?"

Luke pulled a rubber glove out of a box and put it on and picked up the object. He'd been slow on the uptake, distracted. He held up the plastic-rimmed glasses.

"Those look like Mort's," Ezra said.

"They are," Luke replied. He nodded at the pile of ashes. "We've been after the wrong person."

"Who's the right person?" Ezra's intelligent eyes met his.

"The last person to see Letty alive. Eleanor Prendergast."

Ezra stared at him then shook his head. "Hell," he muttered. "Never underestimate the fury of a woman scorned."

The pieces of the puzzle clicked together in Luke's mind. "The murders and the corpse-looting, they are only the first part of her plan," he said. "The *coup-de-gras* has got to involve Prendergast. My guess is she'll kill him tonight."

Ezra was already moving. "We'll pick her up over at the church, but we'll have to go slow. Everyone in town will be there."

Everyone in town. That meant the Maynards and Crystal and Jessie. Luke set his jaw. Eleanor Prendergast was a loose cannon. A premonition made him shiver. The pastor's wife had set everything up for tonight when she'd have a stage and a captive audience. What if her grand finale included fireworks?

He couldn't let that happen. The two men sprinted toward the church.

****

Jessie proceeded up the aisle with Bosco and a bevy of small boys dressed in bathrobes while the congregation sang, "While Shepherds Watched Their Flocks By Night." When the music stopped, Jessie stood near the stable. She estimated she was five to eight feet away from Eleanor Prendergast. The pastor's wife stood at the lectern waiting to read her next line.

"And, lo, an angel of the Lord stood before them and they were terrified."

From underneath her hood, Jessie scanned the congregation. Where was Luke? She wished she could warn him, wished she hadn't acted like a petulant child earlier. She glanced at the plywood stable and memories surged.

The congregation rose again, this time singing "Angels We Have Heard on High," while a dozen little girls in white nightgowns with tinsel haloes on their heads, danced up the aisle and across the front of the sanctuary. Jessie's heart jerked. All those innocent children. She prayed Eleanor would leave them alone. She had to be interested in the fate of one person and one person only. Her husband. Reverend Dennis Prendergast.

The congregation settled back into their seats, and a string of children dressed in satin and velvet, crowns crooked on their heads, processed up the aisle while Eleanor continued the gospel.

"In the time of King Herod, after Jesus was born in Bethlehem of Judea, wise men from the East came to Jerusalem asking 'where is the child who has been born King of the Jews? We have observed his star and have come to pay him homage.'"

****

Eleanor listened to the congregation warble five verses of "We Three Kings." It had to happen any second now. She knew him well. He'd hear the organ, panic because he was late, scrabble around trying to figure out how to get out of the room, realize there was no way and finally, finally he'd think to call her.

He was actually stupider than she'd thought. He should have made the call already, but then the Viagra she'd stirred into the citrus parfait had probably addled him.

It didn't take much.

She found she was holding her breath, and she made herself inhale and exhale slowly. She didn't want to blow the whole thing by hyperventilating.

Why the hell didn't he call?

She'd located a man who, for a hefty fee, had

inserted a tiny bomb into the new phone. It shouldn't kill anyone, but Dennis would lose his head. The congregation would rush to see what had happened and they'd catch him with a million dollars he couldn't explain, his cheap mistress, and his pants down. Her eyelids fluttered with anticipation. Finally, Dennis would get a taste of the humiliation he'd so heedlessly heaped on her all these years.

The revenge would be complete when he discovered it was she, his loyal, loving wife who'd lured him into a life of crime, who'd scared him to death, and who'd set him up. The only flaw in the plan was that she couldn't stick around and watch.

Someone in the front row cleared her throat. It was time for Eleanor to take up the story. As she took in a breath, she saw a movement out of the corner of her eye. A man was working his way up the outside aisle in the shadowed church. Luke Tanner. She felt his eyes on her, and she knew he was heading for Denny's office. He was going to ruin everything.

Fury erupted in her, constricting her breathing. She reached under the lectern for her pistol, but before she could use it, the bomb exploded. In the candlelight people screamed and scrambled to find their children. Eleanor, of course, kept her head. Luke was on the other side of the chaos, twenty feet away and he was moving but Eleanor was an excellent marksman. She knew she could hit him. She aimed the pistol and fired.

****

Jessie had one eye trained on Eleanor Prendergast, the other was assigned to watch the back of the church. Luke would come, and he'd have Chief Smith with him. What if they'd figured this out? Neither

Prendergast, Lois or J. Mortimer Epps was here. Had Eleanor killed them all? Would she stop at a cop and sidekick?

The sanctuary was dark, lit only with candles. Everything seemed normal. It was the same scene being replayed in thousands of churches across American tonight. Hopefully it was the only one that involved a diabolical corpse-snatching murderer. Jessie was staring so intently at the front door she wasn't surprised to see it open. She wasn't surprised to see Luke enter, his jaw set, his face grim. He moved toward the front of the church. She watched him over the heads of the standing congregation. When the hymn was finished and everyone sat down, he was clearly visible even in the candlelight. He was heading for Prendergast's office. Would Eleanor notice him? She glanced at the pastor's wife and saw her hand slide under the lectern.

A sudden explosion rocked the crowd. Women screamed, men shouted, kids started to cry. Jessie tore her eyes away from Luke and fixed them on Eleanor Prendergast. It all seemed to happen in slow motion after that. Eleanor palmed a small pistol, sighted it, and aimed. Jessie knew she couldn't stop the bullet. Luke was only a few steps from the door that would take him to Prendergast's office, but Jessie knew he'd never make it. Her best chance to save him, her only chance, was distraction. She filled her lungs and bellowed.

"Luke!"

He heard her and dove toward the solid oak baptismal font just an instant too late. The bullet hit, and while Jessie gaped in horror, his big body spun around. Some sixth sense had her looking back at Eleanor. The gun reported again, but the bullet thudded into the stable as Eleanor was knocked off her feet by seventy-five pounds of excited golden retriever.

Zach and his dad were on Eleanor in an instant. They pinned her down where she'd fallen. Jessie didn't have time to worry about Eleanor. She didn't have time to thank Bosco.

Jessie's mother, father, sister and Kit materialized around her in a protective fortress.

"Let me go," she yelled, desperately. "I've got to get to Luke."

"Take it easy," Kit said. He pulled out a handkerchief and dried the tears she hadn't even realized were coursing down her face. The ambulance driver, who'd parked outside to attend the service, wheeled the stretcher through the front door. Jessie twisted away from Kit.

"I have to go," she repeated.

Kit held her shoulders firmly but without hurting her. "Now isn't the time," he murmured.

As the crowd ebbed and flowed around Luke, she saw Kit's point. Crystal knelt next to Luke, her blonde head on his chest, his fingers buried in her hair.

In the candlelight Crystal looked less like a goddess and more like a beloved wife.

Chapter Twenty

Dennis stared at the soot-stained skin on his hands. He didn't understand what had happened. He only knew that Lois's shrieking was making him deaf.

"Can't you get her to shut up?" he asked plaintively.

His eyes burned, and he realized there was smoke in his office. A fire? No. An explosion. Right when he dialed "1" to call Ellie for help.

The door had been blown off its hinges and half a dozen people crashed into his office.

"Reverend," a masculine voice called out, "your pants."

What about his pants? They were fine wool, hand-tailored. Ellie'd given him the lightweight phone so it wouldn't stretch his pocket.

A short, squat man approached him. Ezra Smith. Denny wondered why middle-aged men neglected their appearance. How did they expect to attract lookers like Lois? Her bleating cries were really beginning to annoy him now.

He put his hands over his ears and closed his eyes. When he opened them, Ezra was standing in front of him. "What happened?"

Denny put his hands down. Luckily, Lois's caterwauling had drizzled into whimpers. Questions chased themselves through his head. Was she hurt?

Was he hurt? Where was Ellie? She should be here, taking care of him.

"Explosion," he said, finally. "It happened when I dialed my cell phone." He looked around. "I guess it flew out of my hand." His gaze settled on the briefcase by the sofa. He gave a start as he remembered. The money! He needed to grab it and get out of here.

Where was Ellie?

"What's in the case?" Smith asked.

"Papers," Dennis said. "Just some private papers."

"We'll have to take a look," the chief said. "This is a crime scene now."

Dennis panicked. "Okay, it's not papers. It's money. I can explain it though."

Smith nodded. "First things first. Your fly is open."

Dennis glanced down to the opening in his pants. The silk of his boxers rubbed against his erection.

"Oh my God," Lois said, in a cold voice. Apparently her hysteria was over. She pointed at his swollen groin. "I don't fucking believe that."

"What's the money for?" Chief Smith switched the subject again.

Suddenly Denny was trembling. He couldn't handle this by himself. He needed help. He answered Smith's question with one of his own.

"Where," he asked, "is my wife?"

****

The bones surrounding Eleanor's eye socket throbbed. She'd fallen hard on her face, and then a large man, instead of helping her up, had planted his knee on her spine. She could barely breathe.

Something had gone wrong thanks to the damn dog. She was supposed to be in the car en route to a small airstrip twelve miles outside of town. Despite the change in plans, she had no intention of panicking.

"Please let me up," she said. Her words went unheard in the chaos. The pain, she realized, was coming from more than her face. She'd fallen on something, too. She felt hard, metal ridges dig into her abdomen. She felt a flash of excitement.

The pistol!

They'd let her leave if they knew she had a gun. She was a crack shot, and she wouldn't hesitate to give a demonstration of her skill.

She probably wouldn't need to shoot. People tended to panic when faced with a weapon. Of course, most people were cowards.

Not her. She heard Ezra Smith's voice.

"Anybody find a gun?"

She felt a surge of satisfaction. No one knew where it was. She'd have the element of surprise working for her. She smelled a familiar cologne, and Dennis put his fingers on her cheek.

"Ellie?"

Rage exploded inside her. She could feel the heat rush to her face. What the hell was he doing here? The faithless bastard was supposed to be up in his office with his erection jutting out of his pants and his bimbo at his side.

He leaned down far enough so she could see him. The usually florid face was pale. He didn't look embarrassed though. He looked concerned.

Her heart flopped in her chest. It was all over. Her grand scheme of revenge had failed. The idiot didn't even know he was supposed to be humiliated. Eleanor closed her eyes and gritted her teeth against the despair.

"Ellie? Ellie, speak to me, honey."

Inspiration arrived like a gift from heaven. She could salvage this. She could still make her worthless tool of a husband suffer. A cold resolve formed in her chest.

"Denny," she said, in a pitiful voice, "I can't breathe."

"I'll take care of it, sweetheart." His voice took on the authority of the pulpit as he spoke to her captor. "Let her go. I'll take responsibility for her."

"She's under arrest," Ezra Smith pointed out. "She shot Luke Tanner, and we have reason to believe she killed Letty Appleby."

"Denny," she whimpered.

"You're wrong," Dennis said to Smith. "Tell him, Ellie."

"I would if I could breathe."

Smith must have given the okay because the pressure on her back eased enough for Eleanor to position the pistol in her hand.

She canted up far enough to gaze into Dennis's pale blue eyes, and she put the barrel of the gun in her mouth. He'd never expect her to shoot. He thought he knew her inside out.

The explosion threw her out of his arms. Dennis stared at the dead woman he'd been married to for twenty years. The woman he hadn't known at all.

"Ellie," he whispered. Then he threw up.

****

"You okay, Jess?"

Kit's voice insinuated itself into her misery. They were sitting in a pew bench, among the stragglers still in the sanctuary. She was far from okay.

Gillian appeared and took a seat on her other side.

"Luke is going to be fine," she said, in a soothing voice. "The ambulance attendant said it looked like the bullet nicked an artery, but they'll stabilize him in the ambulance and whisk him into surgery.

"I shouldn't have yelled."

"That shout saved him, as I understand it," Howard Maynard said. He appeared next to the pew, his arm around Jessie's mother. "He was literally able to dodge the bullet."

"I don't suppose anybody knows why Eleanor Prendergast would shoot Luke Tanner," Gillian said.

It was such a long story. Jessie didn't feel up to telling it. She didn't feel up to anything. Her thoughts were with Luke. She prayed he'd survive. She tried not to think about how much it hurt to see Crystal bending over him, to glimpse his fingers in her hair.

She forced herself to answer her sister. "She must have figured out he was heading for the office to rescue Prendergast and Lois."

"Rescue them from what?" Monica asked, puzzled.

"Let's continue this conversation at home," Howard said. "Jess needs to get out of here. And I need a Scotch."

Someone—Kit probably—stripped off Jessie's bathrobe and covered her with a coat.

"I don't want to go home," Jessie said. "I want to go to the hospital."

Fifteen minutes later the E.R. receptionist told her Luke was in surgery. The woman suggested that Jessie wait with Luke's wife who was here "all alone."

Jessie glanced around to see Crystal seated in a comfortable waiting room chair. There were five cups of coffee on the table next to her and a gaggle of young, male doctors hovering around. Jessie resisted the urge to point out that Crystal was hardly alone and that she was Luke's ex-wife. None of that was important right now.

The admiring physicians departed, reluctantly, when Jessie took a seat opposite Crystal. There was a look of determination in those amethyst eyes. Jessie had to hear everything.

"How was he in the ambulance?"

"Unconscious," Crystal said. "He's in surgery to repair a ripped artery in his thigh. Listen, Jessie. You can't marry Luke. He belongs to me. He always has. This whole thing, you and Luke, it's all about Blanche. She always wanted him to meet someone who wasn't me. She had a thing about you and Luke, and she tried to manipulate you into a couple by asking him to come here and look after you. She probably didn't know he'd be risking his life."

Jessie's eyes widened in shock. Was it true? Was this about Aunt Blanche. She focused on the last accusation. Crystal was right. In the past few days, Luke had been locked in a coffin, threatened with a gun, and finally, shot.

"He's a lot safer with me," Crystal added.

Jessie's eyes narrowed on the other woman. "Safer, how? You broke his heart."

The lovely eyes hardened for an instant, and then they shone with unshed tears. "I told you. I didn't intend to divorce him," Crystal said, in a soft voice. "I did it for us. I knew he loved me. I was just trying to get his attention."

"If he loved you so much, why did he walk away?"

Something flashed in the amethyst eyes. Uncertainty? "That's what I came back to find out. This time I'm in all the way. The picket fence, the golden retriever." She held Jessie's gaze. "The baby."

It was ridiculous to feel as though someone had cut out her heart. She stared at the other woman, unable to come up with a single word.

"I know he's made a commitment to you," Crystal continued, "but you're a smart woman. And a romantic. I know you wouldn't want to marry a man in love with someone else."

Jessie knew Luke would never back out on his commitment. So it was up to her. She could marry him, or she could set him free so he could marry the woman he'd always loved. At the moment neither option was appealing.

Their conversation was interrupted by the reappearance of a handsome young doctor. He nodded to Jessie but his attention was all for Crystal.

"Mrs. Tanner? We've set up a cot in your husband's room so you can stay with him tonight." The doctor glanced at Jessie. "No visitors tonight. Just family."

It was after midnight by the time Jessie left the hospital with Kit. He pulled up to the curb in front of the witch hat house. The windows were dark except for a small light in the foyer. Jessie's head lolled against the back of the front seat in the Fusco's truck.

"God," Kit said. "What a night."

Jessie gazed through the windshield at St. Michael's, still and dark as an abandoned tomb. Within the next few days, Miss Letty and Eleanor Prendergast would be buried in the churchyard. A new pastor would open the doors and let in fresh air. A new mortician would establish a respectable business. There was no more terror in Mystic Hollow. The community was starting to heal.

"You accomplished a lot," Kit said, clearly thinking along the same lines. "You've been here less than a week, and you shut down a corpse-looting ring and exposed a cold-blooded killer."

Suddenly she was unutterably weary. "All I did was get people stirred up."

"Sometimes that's all that's needed."

Her eyes swept the Green. The white lights on the gazebo twinkled in the opaque dark. She'd almost forgotten it was Christmas.

"Jessie," Kit said, shifting in the driver's seat to face her, "I know you think you're in love with Luke Tanner." His look was full of sympathy. He knew about the cot in Luke's hospital room. He squeezed her hand but she hardly felt it. "Come home with me. Let me show you I won't let you down again."

She looked into his light blue eyes. "Why?"

"I think we can make a good life together. We've always been friends and deep down I think you know we have similar goals. I care about you, Jess. And I think you care about me."

Jessie thought about the home she could have with Kit. They would have kids, dogs, a lovely home, lots of friends, and her parents nearby. They'd have all the things she thought she wanted until she found out there was more.

"There's no spark."

"It'll come."

It had come. She'd felt the spark. Just not with Kit.

She decided to follow a hunch. "Kit, have you ever considered dating Gillian?"

The look on his face was one of shock. "I'm in the middle of a proposal, and you're trying to fix me up with your sister?"

"Just think about it."

"That's your final answer? Because I won't ask again."

"I know."

She didn't know why she'd made the suggestion, but after she'd climbed into the four-poster, she began to think about a match between her sister and her ex. They were a lot alike, brash, funny, smart, sassy. They might do very well together. She closed her eyes and fought the image of Luke's hand in Crystal's hair. A deep aching chasm opened up inside her. It was as cold and lonely as the empty bed. She loved Luke Tanner. The question was, did she love him enough to let him go?

Chapter Twenty-One

On Christmas morning Jessie woke early, often and alone. Each time she checked with the hospital's information line. Luke was doing fine. It was an immense relief. She managed to restrain herself from asking whether Crystal was sleeping in his hospital bed. She'd trust her instincts on this. If she sensed he wanted out of their engagement, she'd let him go with her blessing. Maybe not her wholehearted blessing. She wasn't convinced Crystal would make him happy.

And Jessie wanted to try. She wanted to be the one to complete his life. She realized she'd never wanted anything in her life as much as she wanted to make Luke happy. It was a scary feeling.

Her bare feet hit the cold floor, and she hurried into the bathroom. She'd filled her life with her family's concerns. She'd never let another man anywhere near her heart. And now, within a matter of days, the green-eyed sorcerer had gotten under her skin. Her heart twisted. If she lost him, it would hurt. Still, she couldn't be sorry. She never again wanted to go back to that half-life.

She'd had a taste of love and nothing less than that would do for her now.

She decided to reward her own insight. She picked up the phone and punched in the number she'd long since memorized.

"His condition is the same as it was an hour ago when you called," the information nurse said.

There was some irony in her voice. "He's sleeping peacefully."

Yeah, but is he sleeping alone? Jessie found the fortitude not to ask the question.

****

Luke felt the searing pain before he opened his eyes. He struggled to orient himself. Why did his eyelids feel like they were weighted with rocks? Why did his thigh feel like it had been slashed?

He forced one eye open. He recognized the IV drip bag at the same time he became aware of the excruciating pain in his leg. Oh yeah. Eleanor Prendergast's shot had pierced his femoral artery. He took in shallow breaths and tried an old trick, one that had gotten him through the break-up. He visualized himself shoving the pain into a lock box and walking away.

The pain receded a bit, and he opened his other eye. There was an empty cot in his room. Jessie. She'd stayed with him. His heart lurched, and his body tensed all over again triggering the pain. It was less this time though. Jessie was here. He wondered when he'd started needing her like this. He couldn't put his finger on the moment everything had changed. He pictured her in the church last night, wearing that ridiculous bathrobe. Her warning scream had given him a split second to dive behind the baptismal font.

She'd probably saved his sorry hide. Again.

He frowned. He'd cure her of that risky habit once they were married.

Heat that had nothing to do with the injury shot

through his body. He planned to spend a lot of time instructing her in the future. He planned to spend a lot of time buried in her sweet warmth. He wondered if she knew he loved her.

He groaned as he lifted up to look around. A sense of anticipation dulled the pain and spiked his temperature. Any minute she'd come through that door, and her bright smile would light his heart.

The door opened and pain stabbed him.

Only part of it due to his leg.

"Where's Jessie?" He growled.

His ex-wife floated over to his bed and sat on the side of it, the picture of beauty and grace. She wore a white turtleneck and her lush, spun-gold hair drifted around her shoulders. Her makeup was, as always, perfect. She ignored his ill-tempered greeting.

"How are you feeling sweetheart? Can I get you some breakfast? Or maybe a kiss?"

He fell back on the bed. "A painkiller."

"I'll call the nurse." She leaned closer then flinched. "You could use a shower, too. And a shave."

He squeezed his eyes shut. He needed all his energy to fight the pain. The door opened, and his hopes rose again until a no-nonsense nurse strode across the room and checked the settings on his monitors. She hissed in a breath and flipped a switch.

"Good God. Your morphine drip isn't even turned on. I was told someone would stay with you last night."

"I couldn't really sleep on the cot. It wasn't comfortable," Crystal explained, defensively. "One of the interns let me use a bed in the lounge."

The nurse had one those bony, horse-like faces, but at the moment it was the most beautiful face in Luke's world.

"This patient is barely twelve hours out of surgery," she snapped. "The drip should have been at full force."

The next time Luke woke the room was empty again. At least the pain was manageable now. Where was Jessie? Had something happened to her? An accident on treacherous roads? Where were his clothes? His cell phone?

By the time Crystal appeared twenty minutes later, he'd worked himself into a state of high anxiety. He scowled at his ex-wife.

The amethyst eyes widened. "If I didn't know better, sweetheart, I'd think you aren't happy to see me."

His heart was pounding, and sweat broke out between his shoulder blades. A sense of mindless urgency drove him.

Where was Jessie?

"Crystal," he said, "I want you to call the house. Find out if everyone's all right."

"Sure, sure." She took her cell phone out to the hallway where the reception was better. Three minutes later she returned. "All present and accounted for," she said. "They're playing Yankee Swap."

"What?"

"Something about passing out random Christmas presents. Sounds like they're having fun. I heard a lot of laughter in the background.

Jessie says 'hi.'"

Jessie says 'hi?'""You talked to her?"

Crystal tilted her head to one side, a gesture which used to drive him crazy. She sat gingerly on the edge of

Ann Yost

the bed. "What's all this about, Luke?"

He didn't answer. He tried to process the obvious lack of interest. What had gone wrong?

"I know you told me last night that you were going to marry her," Crystal went on, "but, honestly, she doesn't seem like an in-sickness-and-health kind of a girl. I was the one who rode in the ambulance with you. I was the one who stayed all night."

"In the intern's lounge."

She laid her cool fingers on his hand. "So that's what this is about. I insisted on my own bed. Believe me, you have nothing to be jealous about."

He forced his jaw to unclench. He was taking his disappointment with Jessie out on Crystal, and it wasn't fair.

"I appreciate your being here, but we have to get things straight between us."

The conversation was interrupted when his surgeon came through the door with a hearty "Merry Christmas," on his lips.

Merry for whom, Luke wondered, sourly.

****

Jessie put on pantyhose and heels and the Christmas red dress her mother had brought from Chicago and then went downstairs to greet her family and her Mystic Hollow friends, Mabel Ruth, Millicent, and Maude.

After a hearty brunch of quiche, fresh fruit, sweet rolls, orange juice, bacon, and coffee, conversation about the excitement from the previous night, the group moved to the parlor for carol singing and a gift exchange. Kit took the role of Santa as he doled out unmarked gifts that included a shiny silver whisk for

256

Howard, a book about spells titled That Old Black Magic, for Monica, a men's shaving kit for Gillian and a Ouija Board for Kit himself. Jessie opened a box of cat food while Mabel Ruth got a size six cashmere sweater, Millicent received chandelier earrings, and Maude got the promise of a kitten.

Jessie answered the house phone. She told Crystal they were all thinking about Luke and her. It hurt to listen to the possessive tone in the other woman's voice. She told herself she could stand this for one more day. She told the others Luke was awake and Monica jumped up.

"Let's all take them breakfast!"

Jessie knew it was emotional suicide for her, but she couldn't resist. She helped her mom pack up the food and Great-Aunt Blanche's Wedgewood dishes, then they divided into two vehicles and set out for the hospital.

Her heart squeezed when she saw Luke's sunken eyes underlined with dark crescents. His face looked thin and stark with a day's growth of whiskers, and he had an IV needle taped to his hand.

Crystal, on the other hand, looked fresh and beautiful.

She updated them on Luke's surgery and his condition. Jessie half-listened while she set out the food. She knew all the facts. She longed to lay her cheek against his, ask how he felt, whisper comfort in his ear, but it wasn't her place.

"If all goes well," Crystal said, "he can leave the hospital in a couple of days then recuperate at home with supervision for about two weeks."

Supervision? Did that mean Crystal intended to

take care of him?

"We'll probably hire a day nurse," Crystal added, "but I'll be there at night." Her smile included everybody. Jessie waited for Luke to refute his ex-wife's words, but while his eyes never left Jessie, he said nothing until general talk broke out again. As she placed the food and juice on his tray he grabbed her wrist.

"I need to talk to you."

Her heart bounced around like a racquet ball. This was it. He was going to insist on the marriage, and she was going to have to say 'no.' She felt the tears gather in her throat and she swallowed hard.

While Luke and Crystal ate, more visitors arrived. Francine's arms were full of bagels and cream cheese, and Zach's arms were full of Francine. Neither of them could stop grinning.

Francie looked at the breakfast food. She threw a laughing glance at Jessie. "That's Mystic Hollow for you. Any kind of a crisis and we'll bury you in food."

Luke's eyes met those of his friend. "Looks like you might have an announcement to make."

"We're getting married," Zach said, simply. The huskiness in his voice revealed the extent of his emotions.

"I'm so happy for you," Jessie said to Francine under cover of the general rejoicing.

"We talked," the redhead said. Her face glowed. "Bobby had blindsided him with the news that Karl Reeves isn't his father. He and Karl talked. One of these days he's going to talk to Earl Russell, too. He gets it now that everyone loves him. Especially me." She exchanged a sizzling look with the ex-marine.

"Everything's going to be okay," she said, softly. "And those letters to Bobby Ray? It turns out they were really written by…"

Jessie realized, almost too late, what Francie was about to reveal. She burst into loud hacking coughs.

"Jessie," Maude said. "Are you all right?"

Kit grabbed a pitcher of ice water and poured some into a glass. Jessie waved it away. She had to keep the interruption going long enough for people to forget what they'd been talking about. She had to keep Francie from breaking Luke's heart by revealing Crystal's secret.

By the time Crystal entered the room, Jessie's face was red, and tears streaked down her cheeks. "What's going on?"

"Jessie is performance coughing," Luke said, dryly. "She's trying to keep Francie from blurting out the truth about you and Bobby Ray."

Shock cut off the coughing, but now her nose was running. She sneezed. Millicent handed her a tissue. She blew and then looked at Luke. "You knew?"

He nodded.

Crystal sent an apologetic look to Francine. "I am sorry about that. Bobby and I didn't mean to hurt anybody."

Zach's thick eyebrows wrinkled into a frown, but Francie slipped her arm around his waist and squeezed. "All's well that ends well," she said, softly.

"I feel that way, too," Crystal said. She moved next to Luke and knit her fingers through his. Jessie had to look away.

It was time to get out of there. "We'd better let Luke get some rest," she said to the others.

"I'll walk you all to the elevator," Crystal said, grabbing the shorter woman's arm, and propelling her out the door.

"I need to talk to Jessie. Just for a minute."

Luke's quiet words kept Jessie behind while the others headed for the elevator.

She sat on Crystal's cot. It was tidy and pristine just like the woman who'd slept there last night.

"First, I want to thank you for the warning. Eleanor Prendergast was shooting to kill." He frowned. "But this rescuing business has to stop. It's dangerous."

She suspected he hadn't heard about Eleanor's second shot and Bosco's heroic interference. She figured he didn't need to know.

"Do you hear me, Jessie? No more rescues."

She could safely promise that. Suddenly she felt unbearably sad, but she didn't want him to know.

"It was an adventure though, wasn't it?" She kept her tone bright. He didn't smile. "Why didn't you stay with me last night?" The question didn't make sense.

"It would've been a little crowded in here."

"You're my fiancée."

She didn't tell him Crystal had claimed a closer relationship. What was the point? This was the moment of truth and she had to find the courage to lie.

"Kit and I had things to talk about."

Luke's eyes never left her face. "You gonna tell me he proposed and you accepted?"

His flat tone irritated her. "You could at least pretend to be upset."

"I'm not upset," he said, slowly, "because I know it didn't happen. There's no way you'd agree to marry another man. You've promised yourself to me, and let me say right now, I intend to hold you to the promise."

There it was. That darned sense of honor.

"I made a mistake when I ran away from the wedding. I was a coward, and I let everybody down. I have to give it another chance, Luke.

Surely you can see that."

He shook his head. "You can't fool me, Jessie.

I know you. Right down to your yellow boots."

"We've known one another less than a week."

"It's eerie," he said, ignoring her comment. "Sometimes I feel like I've always known you. And it's more than that." The smile was gone now. "I trust you. I know you'd never leave me. Not you, Jessie."

His certainty irritated her. "How on earth do you know that?"

"Because you love me." The words were simple and, unfortunately, unarguable. Jessie couldn't think of anything to say. She just stared into those kryptonite eyes.

Crystal reappeared and sat on his bed. They were such a handsome couple, such perfect opposites of dark and light, male and female. She put her hand on his, and he didn't draw back.

Jessie tried to ignore the crack in her heart.

"I have to go," Jessie said.

"Thanks for coming," Crystal replied, all warmth and smiles. "And don't worry about this guy. I'll make sure he has a merry Christmas."

Jessie walked out the door and down the corridor toward the elevators. She half hoped she'd hear Luke's voice calling her back. The other half of her knew there was nothing to go back for.

****

As soon as Jessie disappeared around the corner, Crystal made an excuse to get out of the room. Luke wasn't having that.

"Come here." He kept his voice low and, he hoped, kind but firm. She came over to the bed, a wary look in her beautiful eyes. He patted it, and she perched on the edge. Her face was as smooth as ivory and right now it was equally as pale.

"What do you really want from me?"

She gave an elegant little shrug. "I want a fresh start. We had high hopes once. Why not again?"

"It's not going to happen."

"You said that before, but you don't mean it. You can't. You've always loved me. Everybody knows it."

He thought about Jessie's transparent excuses to break their engagement. Everybody certainly thought that he loved Crystal.

"You need to find a man who can love you for the person you are underneath the beauty."

"That's you."

He shook his head. "You made the right decision two years ago even if it was for the wrong reasons. I loved the beauty, Crystal. I think it was over before we ever got married."

"But everybody said we were the picture perfect couple."

He sighed and picked up her hand. "That's what I'm talking about. Life isn't a portrait. Marriage is give and take and arguments and problems and irritating relatives and an endless series of compromises, all of it made palatable by the friendship between two people."

"What about the passion?"

"And the passion," he agreed. "I imagine you felt

the passion with Bobby Ray." She hung her head. "This isn't about guilt. I just want you to see the difference. I got tangled up in the rush of having the most beautiful girl around choose me.

I don't even really know you."

"You could get to know me."

He shook his head. "I couldn't. It's too late for that. I've proposed to Jessie, and I'm going to marry her."

"But, don't you see? You don't have to. Didn't you see the ring on her finger? She's planning to marry Kit Carstairs. She doesn't need you."

"I need her," he answered her quietly. It was the simple truth. He needed Jessie with an intensity he'd never felt before. She warmed him, excited him, fed him, and accepted him. He wasn't going to explain all that to Crystal.

The look on his face must have convinced her because a rare look of defeat appeared in her lovely eyes.

"She's what you really want?"

"Yes."

She stood and he felt an instant's compassion. "Where are you going?"

"Home, eventually," she said, picking up her long white coat and her purse. "Tonight I'm going to a party with Roger. He's that hot intern."

Luke grinned. Wherever Crystal was, there was a man willing to take care of her. That man, however, would no longer be him.

****

Kit and Gillian were waiting in the Jeep. They jumped apart as Jessie opened the door. Gilly's mouth was as swollen as Jessie's eyes, and Kit was breathing as though the Shenandoah Valley was the top of Mount Everest.

In spite of her own heartache, Jessie was pleased.

Her cell phone rang while she was driving home. She ignored it.

"Want me to get that?" Gillian asked.

"They can leave a message."

"I'm guessing by the strained look on your face you left your own message back there at the hospital."

Jessie didn't reply.

"You're trying to run away, Jess," Kit said. "Again."

"It's different this time. The guy clearly wants someone else." An ironic laugh erupted in her throat. "No, wait. It isn't different."

"Except that this time you love the guy," Kit said, quietly.

She wasn't going to deny it. She wasn't going to talk about it either. "I'm tired of the whole thing," she said. "Really. I just want to go home."

They rode for a mile in silence, and then Gillian spoke again. "I'm not a big fan of psychic phenomena, but I can't help thinking you're here for a specific purpose. Great-Aunt Blanche wanted to bring you and Luke together."

Jessie nodded. "I think I was meant to help him break through his denial and deal with the past."

"And what about you?"

It was a fair question. "He helped me understand that I had to loosen the reins, stop trying to solve everybody else's problems."

"And then there was the passion," Gillian said, softly.

Her heart twisted. Yeah. There was the passion.

Jessie's cell rang again during dinner. She felt it vibrate in her pocket but didn't answer it. There just wasn't anything more to say.

She went upstairs after dinner and packed up her clothes. They wouldn't all fit in the yellow suitcase Luke had so grudgingly hauled up the stairs only five days ago.

Was Kit right? Was she running away again? Should she ignore the history between Luke and Crystal, ignore the way they looked at one another, the way they looked together? Should she take him up on his offer? How could she when she knew, all the way to her soul, what it felt like to really love someone. She knew she'd never feel like this about anyone else. How could she marry a man who felt that fierce, aching desire for someone else?

She couldn't.

But she'd miss him. For the rest of her life.

Dusk settled on the small town. The Maynard family and friends gathered once again around the fire in the parlor where they consumed wine and shared stories.

"This has been the best Christmas ever," Monica pronounced from her seat on the sofa next to her ex-husband. "So good, in fact, that Howard and I have decided to stay here for a few more days."

"We may even retire here," Jessie's dad said.

"That's wonderful," Mabel Ruth said.

"Excellent," Millicent said.

"Dear Blanche would have loved it," Maude added.

"You don't have to worry about the business, either," Kit put in. He spoke from the loveseat where he had his arm around Gillian. "Gilly and I will drive the Fusco's truck back, and I'll get back to the office."

That took care of everyone but Jessie. No one looked at her, but she knew they were waiting to hear her plans. Too bad she didn't have any.

"I'm going back home, too," she said, with a cheeriness she didn't feel. "I've loved spending Christmas down here in Aunt Blanche's house, meeting all of you." She smiled at the elderly ladies. "But I'm ready to go home. I took some library science classes in college. Maybe I'll look for something along that line."

"Libraries? I never knew you were interested in libraries," Kit said.

"The reverend shut down our library,"

Millicent pointed out.

"Maybe Jessie could start it back up again," Maude said.

"Hush, Maudie," Mabel Ruth intervened.

Jessie knew her cheeks were red. Mabel Ruth knew she couldn't stay in Mystic Hollow, and she knew why. The sense of loss slammed into her. She prayed no one would ask her about Luke and Crystal.

"Maybe you should stay, dear," Monica said. "You seem different down here in the country.

How astute of her mother to notice.

Jessie thought about the way she fit in the small town. She loved the quirky shopkeepers and the fact that you couldn't cross the Green without meeting a friend or acquaintance. She loved the lame festivals and the faux witches and Aunt Blanche's witch hat house. She didn't know Luke's immediate plans, but even if he and Crystal left Mystic Hollow, Jessie couldn't come back because what she loved far and away the most about the town was Luke Tanner.

Kit's cell phone rang. He left the room and came back minutes later and gestured to Gillian. Jessie didn't miss them until an hour later when Kit burst through the front door bringing with him the smells of the outdoors, the holiday and the night.

"Special delivery for Miss Jessie Maynard," he caroled. She'd been sitting by Pyewacket's family, saying goodbye. She looked up to see her sister, blue eyes glistening, standing before her.

"Guess Santa thought you deserved more than Fancy Feast," Gillian said. "Put your coat on. We're going outside."

It was easier not to argue. Besides, she could use the fresh air. Fusco's truck was parked in front of the house. Kit went to the back of it and opened the big doors. "Come on, Jess," he said. "I'll give you a boost," he said.

He wanted her to get in the refrigerated truck? She moved closer. Gone were the ice sculpture, the cake, and the finger foods from her aborted wedding. The space had been turned into a hospital room, and at its center, lying on a gurney and still hooked up to an IV, was a narrow-eyed Luke Tanner.

She thought he looked angry, and then she moved closer. Jessie watched his jaw clench and his knuckles turn white as his fingers curled around the metal sides of the gurney. Not angry. Hurting. She could only imagine what he'd done to his newly wounded body and his stitches.

She snapped at him. "Are you out of your mind? You shouldn't be here."

"I wouldn't be here," he said, evenly, "if you

would answer your phone."

She heard a gasp as he tried to control the pain.

"Dammit, Luke!" She glared at Kit. "How could the hospital release you in this condition? Where's your morphine drip?"

"They didn't release him," Gillian explained. "We conspired with one of the nurses, Mrs. Russell, to get him out. Oh, and the drip's still attached. He just insisted on turning it off."

"What?" Jessie knew she sounded like the worst kind of shrew but she didn't care.

"I need a clear head to talk to you."

She could see the white tracings around his lips, and his face was pale. Her heart turned over.

"I'll talk to you as long as you want if you turn that thing on and head back to the hospital."

"You do it," he told her. She had to get really close and examine the gizmo. She inhaled the scent of antiseptics and the odor of a man who hadn't taken a shower in two days. But the overwhelming scent was that musk that was solely Luke's. She wanted to lie down on the gurney and crawl inside his skin.

Jessie realized there was something missing. "Where's Crystal?"

"At some intern's Christmas party." The green eyes suddenly looked unsure. It was an expression she'd never seen in that rugged face. "She and I are finished. I told her yesterday and again this afternoon."

Jessie felt her heart cracking all over again.

He'd made this magnificent—insane—gesture, and it was all about his honor.

He seemed to read her mind. "This has nothing to do with Blanche," he said. "Why don't you try listening? Really listening."

She stared at him. She was so worried he'd reopened the stitches.

"Sit down," he said. "Please." She sat.

"I don't want to marry you because I have to. I'll admit it started out that way, or I told myself it did. But somewhere along the line things changed. I want you, Elf. I want you to be my wife."

A tiny bud of hope blossomed deep in Jessie's heart. "Seriously?"

"Yeah."

She thought about that. "What was the turning point?"

"I think it was when you shut me in the coffin." He picked up her hand and smoothed his thumb over the delicate blue veins. "Maybe even before that. I don't know. I'm not going to hold you to the engagement if you really want out, but I needed for you to understand."

She wanted to understand, but she had doubts. "I saw you with Crystal, Luke. I saw the easy familiarity of a couple that's been together a long time. I saw the way you touched her hair when she went to you in the church."

"I'd just been shot."

Jessie said nothing. It was an excuse. Wasn't it?

"Don't you understand? I'm free of Crystal because of you. I've never had anyone rescue me before. Knowing you taught me what I'd missed. It allowed me to unearth my feelings for Crystal and drag them out into the light. They were skimpy, puny little things. And when she turned up here, I acknowledged what I'd known for a long time: I was in love with the

269

fantasy Crystal, not the real person."

"And you don't love her anymore?"

"I'm not sure I ever loved her."

Jessie remembered the worshipful look on his face in the wedding photo. "I don't know if I can believe you."

A tremor ran through Luke's prone body. This time it was anger.

"You know you've called me a 'hero' more than once, but you think I'd lie about something this important or worse, that I don't know my own mind?"

He had a point. "I'm sorry, Luke. It's just that I know you're trying to do the right thing."

The anger seemed to go out of him. He went back to fondling her hand. "I am trying to do the right thing here, Elf. I'm trying like hell, but I need your help. The right thing for me is to spend the rest of my life with you. But, like I said, I won't force the issue if that isn't what you want."

"It is what I want." She hoped she wasn't making a mistake, but there were only so many times she could force herself to turn him down.

"You're my heart," he whispered. Suddenly, she knew he meant it. Her own heart leapt.

"I love you, Luke Tanner." The words jumped right out of her mouth.

"I love you more. Does this mean you'll marry me?"

She couldn't prevent the tears from gathering behind her eyes, and she couldn't keep them from falling. For a long minute she couldn't find any words, so she just nodded. He used his thumbs to brush the tears away. Their eyes met and held. "What're you thinking, sweet?"

"I'm wondering whether our children will have those sorcerer's eyes." Taking care not to dislodge the tubes she slid her body against his and felt the hard muscles and the even harder flesh.

He groaned. "Don't get too excited. There's nothing we can do now."

She placed her hand on his crotch and grinned at him. "If that's what you think, you've completely underestimated me."

Fifteen minutes later Kit and Gillian returned to find Luke and Jessie intertwined among the tubes.

"Look at them sleeping together," Kit said, "like a couple of lazy cats."

Jessie buried her face in Luke's chest. They hadn't been lazy five minutes earlier.

"I think we can leave the hospital," Gillian said. "Looks like they're both happy with their presents."

"I'm not looking for an exchange," Jessie said.

Luke's arm tightened around her. "No exchanges, no returns, no refunds, Miss Jessie Maynard," he said, his eyes full of love. "No more runaway bride. You belong to me, and I am never going to let you go."

That sounded good to Jessie. Real good. She waved away her sister and Kit as she arched up to kiss the man she loved. It had turned into the best Christmas ever.

A word from the author...

I was born in the Midwest, and until the age of five, I believed my hometown of Ann Arbor, Michigan, was named after me. My dad was a journalist and humor writer, and I followed in his footsteps. Since that seemed to be working, I went ahead and married another journalist. I've written tongue-in-cheek about lots of things like marriage, children, substitute teaching, and Little League. In my books I like to examine human nature with a light approach (though there are usually corpses involved), and I love to see characters find love in the most unlikely places. I've written seven novels, one of them a finalist in the RWA's Golden Heart contest, and I'm so pleased to become a Wild Rose author.

Visit Ann at www.annyost.blogspot.com and www.annyost.com

Thank you for purchasing
this publication of The Wild Rose Press, Inc.

If you enjoyed the story, we would appreciate your
letting others know by leaving a review.

For other wonderful stories,
please visit our on-line bookstore at
www.thewildrosepress.com.

For questions or more information
contact us at
info@thewildrosepress.com.

The Wild Rose Press, Inc.
www.thewildrosepress.com

Stay current with The Wild Rose Press, Inc.

Like us on Facebook

https://www.facebook.com/TheWildRosePress

And Follow us on Twitter
https://twitter.com/WildRosePress

www.ingramcontent.com/pod-product-compliance
Lightning Source LLC
Chambersburg PA
CBHW060527260626
47161CB00003B/799